Janeology

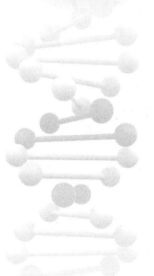

REVIEWS

College professor Tom Nelson has it bad in the wake of a devastating tragedy: the death of his son at the hands of his own wife, Jane, who evaded punishment by being declared insane. Tom, on the other hand, might not get off so easy. The prosecutors, believing that Tom should have known his wife's tendencies and shielded his children, are charging him with "failure to protect." As Tom wallows in his misery, his mother hires him an attorney, Dave Frontella, who adopts some unusual defense strategies, arguing that Jane's genealogy is to blame for her problems and that no husband could have predicted her actions. He even goes so far as to hire for his defense team a woman with "retrocognition," that is, the ability to use a person's belongings to re-create their past. Although the psychic-powers element might turn skeptical readers off, Harrington begins with a fascinating premise and develops it fully. In addition, Tom and his wife emerge as compelling, complexly developed individuals. This debut novel is as much a character study as a legal thriller.

—Mary Frances Wilkens, *Booklist*

This affecting story, with its brilliant array of genial, selfish, troubled, and plucky characters, accomplishes a wonderful feat by revealing specific and universal truths within all families.

—Donald Phillips, bestselling author

Janeology

A NOVEL

Karen Harrington

LARGO, USA

J A N E O L O G Y

Copyright © 2008 by Karen Harrington.

For information, contact Kunati Inc., Book Publishers in both USA and Canada.
In USA: 6901 Bryan Dairy Road, Suite 150, Largo, FL 33777 USA
In Canada: 75 First Street, Suite 128, Orangeville, ON L9W 5B6 CANADA,
or e-mail to info@kunati.com.

F I R S T   E D I T I O N

Designed by Kam Wai Yu
Persona Corp. | www.personaco.com

ISBN-13: 978-1-60164-020-8 | EAN 9781601640208 | FIC000000 FICTION/General

Published by Kunati Inc. (USA) and Kunati Inc. (Canada).
Provocative. Bold. Controversial.™

http://www.kunati.com

TM—Kunati and Kunati Trailer are trademarks
owned by Kunati Inc. Persona is a trademark owned by Persona Corp.
All other trademarks are the property of their respective owners.

Library of Congress Cataloging-in-Publication Data

Harrington, Karen, 1967-
  Janeology : a novel / Karen Harrington. -- 1st ed.
     p. cm.
  ISBN 978-1-60164-020-8 (hardcover : alk. paper)
  1. Filicide--Fiction. 2. Trials (Murder)--Fiction. I. Title.
  PS3608.A7818J36 2008
  813'.6--dc22
                              2008001054

D e d i c a t i o n

For my mother and father.

Acknowledgements

My immense thanks to the honest critiques, generous support and positive presence in my life from Lindley Arthur, Mylene Clark, Kathy Harrington, Eric Hazell, Catherine Heape, and Sandra Youngblood—all your words made a difference too large to count. The friend who pushes me to make everything better, Amy Hazell. Thanks to Don Phillips—everyone should have a friend like him in her corner. For her amazing belief and faith in me, Pat Chapman. Thanks to the sharpest editors, Mary Linn Roby and James McKinnon, whose polishing took a piece of coal and made it shine. Thanks to the extraordinarily supportive Kunati team, especially Derek Armstrong and Kam Wai Yu.

My girls—I just thought I knew what love was before you were born.

And Matt—your support and love have made me a better writer and a better person. I love you.

In almost every generation, nevertheless, there happened to be some one descendant of the family gifted with a portion of the hard, keen sense, and practical energy, that had so remarkably distinguished the original founder. His character, indeed, might be traced all the way down, as distinctly as if the Colonel himself, a little diluted, had been gifted with a sort of intermittent immortality on earth.

Nathaniel Hawthorne
The House of Seven Gables

PROLOGUE

I stared at my attorney as he began his defense that I did not share the blame in the murder of my son. That I was not neglectful in leaving my two children in the care of my wife Jane, who drowned my two-and-a-half-year-old boy.

Dave strode his six-foot-three frame across the room as he launched into his opening statement.

I had read that you are supposed to make yourself appear larger when threatened by an animal in the wild. Apparently, Dave believed this posture was helpful in the courtroom too because he stretched the expanse of his arms as he began speaking in a low voice, the kind of voice that beckons its listeners to lean forward, lest they miss something. His tone ramped up as he declared my innocence and stared at the prosecution's table, allowing time for the pregnant pause. He walked a few steps toward me. The jurors' faces were pinned to him and even the courtroom sketch artist looked up from her pad.

When the silence had passed, I knew he was about to make the suggestion that gave me unease, and with any luck, would give the jurors reasonable doubt. That Jane's genetic hard wiring might have been the chief culprit in her murderous actions.

"But, fellow taxpayers," he said, "the prosecution wants you to believe that my client bears partial responsibility for the commission of a crime at which he was not even present. That he should have been paranoid because his wife was depressed after a miscarriage. That he should have assumed her depression would lead to violence. Well, if that is a crime, then this whole courtroom is at risk of being tried. Millions of American parents take antidepressants. Millions seek counseling for any number of reasons. Should we call child protective services right now and rip the children away from those parents?"

Here Dave paused long for the effect, and I found myself waiting to breathe. I noticed a young female juror glance at Dave and smile. It probably didn't hurt my defense that he was so good-looking. It's not that I am unattractive. I'm tall, fit, green-eyed and still have all my hair. But cast us together in a movie and Dave Frontella is James Bond and I'm *Man in elevator #2.*

"There's not one of us here today who hasn't replayed events from the past and wondered how they might have turned out differently," he continued. "Who doesn't wish he possessed a psychic ability to foresee danger? To prevent a tragedy? Tom Nelson has."

Dave stopped in front of the jury box and rested his hand on the polished wood. "Don't you think Tom Nelson wishes he had perfect understanding of his wife? That he has spent countless hours reviewing all he knew about the wife he loved in search of some telltale sign? Don't you think he would trade his own life to have his son's restored? For himself and the sake of his son's twin sister, now left without a brother and for all intents and purposes, a mother?"

So he was going to use the rhetorical question as a persuasive technique. It would only work, I knew, if the majority of the jurors possessed a sense of irony. And from their stony faces, I could not be sure whether they sized me up as a whiny victim or simple cad.

"The real tragedy here," Dave said, "is that Jane grew up in an abusive situation, raised by a parent who grew up in an abusive situation. Her children were in greater jeopardy because of her genetic inheritance than from her husband's lack of psychic powers. Yet, would you blame her ancestors for the death of Simon Nelson? If it sounds bizarre, that's because it is.

"Albert Einstein had two sons, surely destined to be gifted with the inheritance of their father's mind. A lineage anyone would be blessed to claim, wouldn't you agree? Sadly, at age twenty, the elder son, Hans Albert, was diagnosed with schizophrenia. Prior to that, he had shown great potential in mathematics. Even toyed with the idea of psychiatry.

"Why present the genetics of Einstein? Because it's merely one startling example of the genes we pass on, sometimes for greatness, sometimes for madness. In fact, I will present to you emerging research that suggests that for killers, the part of the brain that creates a sense of conscience is less active. It's a biological dysfunction. And I will show you that it is probable that Jane Nelson drowned her son because she has this kind of biological disposition, coupled with a severe lack of parental nurturing."

Now, Dave glanced down, as if composing his next sentence. I knew he wasn't composing. He was waiting for the jurors to absorb his last words.

"Why should we charge anyone with a crime unless they perpetrated it or conspired to bring it about?" he concluded. "Tom Nelson is innocent. Innocent and eager to care for his surviving daughter, Sarah."

He sat down next to me, resting a friendly hand on my shoulder as he did.

Though his theories had their allure, the prosecution had their own theory, one that relied heavily on the public's inability to stomach the growing number of babies killed by their mothers. Wasn't that how one hot-shot reporter had characterized it in a newspaper editorial? That the public was wounded by the knowledge that more than 200 children are killed by their mothers each year in the U.S. alone. That eleven women are currently on death row for killing their kids. That the event is not as rare as we'd all like to believe. Then, his article compared Jane, Susan Smith, Darlie Routier and Andrea Yates with nice little bullet points on the differences and commonalities among mothers who stab, drown, stone and dismember their children. Apparently, the crime knows no age, race or income. The article proclaimed *"prevention is the key"* and suggested that parents need more education about how to care for children properly.

Perhaps it was my bitter mood when I read it, but it seemed that the article implied that because these statistics were public and infanticide was on the rise, I should have been acutely aware that Jane's drowning Simon was not only possible, but probable. I was guilty of ignorance. This, the reporter opined, is my legal *Titanic*, and I got the sense that he would have concluded, "putting Tom Nelson in jail will atone for all infanticide" if he could have.

And here was the prosecutor, a middle-aged woman with black hair pulled back in a bun, who just happened to let it slip that she was also a mother. No doubt her way of expanding her own presence in this particular legal jungle. She summed all of the murderous mother statistics from the editorial. She stated that I had ignored Jane's emerging illness to the detriment of my children and came just short of accusing me of turning on the water myself.

"People want it stopped," she said calmly, brushing her fingertips lightly across the thin wood divide between herself and the jury box. "I don't know about you, but I can no longer tolerate seeing little coffins on the news. The genetic theory posed by the defense is a popular one," she continued, "but it's a theory. Give little Simon Nelson justice."

Like Dave, she also paused at the end of a dramatic note, which I had learned is part of the art of a legal argument. And what more could she say about Simon anyway? She was desperate to describe his personality or even hint at his favorite flavor of ice cream, which happened to be chocolate chip. But mercifully, there was no one in the family who would provide any details about him for her case.

"His father should have protected him," she said. "He knew about his wife's frailties. He knew she was having difficulty dealing with the miscarriage. He knew she was taking antidepressants. Do you not know the weaknesses of those you live with?"

With this, she turned and looked directly at me and I felt twelve sets of eyes shift and follow her gaze, landing on me.

"Jane Nelson was a woman without support," she continued. "It does not excuse her crime, no, but her husband knew her better than anyone. He knew if she was capable of caring for small children the way any intelligent person can discern a quality child-care worker. By observation."

Dave squeezed my shoulder. It was intended to be a comfort, but it failed and he knew it. He would never stop trying, though. He would die before being intimidated in his own arena and would use anything he could to produce the right effect. I knew what was coming next. He slid an open photo album from his side of the defendant's table to mine. Before me were the pictures of his aforementioned theory on Jane's genetic inheritance and lack of nurturing. The evidence. Her mother and grandmother. Her father and his mother. Family heirlooms including a stuffed monkey, a picture frame made of seashells and a leather-bound journal.

His emotional staging complete, I took a drink of water and looked thoughtfully at the jury box, focused on no one in particular. It was enough though. It rendered me able to endure the remainder of the prosecutor's nonchalant disclosure of what I had come to call the "other" Jane.

The hospitalizations, she said, the post-partum depression, the bipolar diagnosis, the miscarriage, the various drugs, the increasing reclusiveness. And, saving her most dramatic stinger for the end, she carelessly tossed off a sentence about how I had witnessed Jane about to put Zoloft in the twins' juice, and "that this alone should have been enough to warn me that she might be psychotic." She said this in one excited breath, the way I imagined she might sound imparting a hefty piece of gossip to a girlfriend.

I looked down and found I could no longer look at the photographs. I pushed them away, looking down at my scuffed shoes, thinking, oddly enough, that I should buy a new pair, but that I liked this pair. The pair my daughter has stood on when we danced together.

Did I wear the sober face, the expression Dave wanted the jury to see? One that asked them to be reasonable, fair and open-minded? That begged them for the freedom to dance with Sarah, my miracle girl who survived?

PART ONE

CHAPTER ONE

Here's what I remember about that day. What I can't forget about that day. It was hot and humid. My sweat-soaked shirt clung to my skin under the oppressive June heat. There are dozens of photos showing me like that. Dozens more of me as I was led away by an officer, my tie flapping up as I stumbled over the plastic toys in our front yard.

And then they led me to the jail where I found myself with Jane. We were alone in a cold room and I kept plucking the shirt material from my chest, still overcome by heat and shock.

There were no attorneys then. Funny, it's hard now to remember my life before attorneys. That day, we were just two people sitting in a room waiting to have a conversation. You would never know that hours before Jane had turned on the kitchen faucet, filled the sink with water and killed our son Simon. And then she attempted the same with little Sarah, who God knows must have been terrified as she watched her mother do this to her brother before being chased through the house until she, too, was caught and submerged. But I learned that later.

If I had known those details when I went to the jail, maybe I would have been raging, maybe violent. Who knows the appropriate response to having a wife who kills? That day, I felt stuck, nervous and hesitant at meeting my own wife. I was forty-one years old and should have been in control of my emotions as I entered the holding room, but as I felt the thick door click closed against my back, I had the urge to turn and run.

Jane looked normal. Or perhaps normal for Jane. She wore no

reaction of any kind to seeing me. Her body was relaxed, her legs crossed. She greeted me with a light, dry voice, saying my name in her usual fashion by drawing out the vowel.

Toooom.

The intimacy of it made me ill.

"Tom, are you okay? I wondered when you would get here," she said, standing.

"Jane, sit down."

She backed away and slipped back into the plastic chair. We looked at each other for a long moment. I searched her blue eyes for traces of murder, believing I should see something black that belied her beauty. Some flipped switch. Something red or black. I thought perhaps I saw less white in her eyes, but that might have been a trick of the room's flickering fluorescent light. The only visible difference was what she had on: a county-issue orange jumpsuit. The orange reflected off her face, giving her a sun-kissed glow, like she might have spent a day at the beach instead of within the cement-grey walls of a jail. Even her hair was still in its trademark perky ponytail with wisps of dark blonde highlights framing her face.

"Are we going home?"

My mouth was dry. I licked my lips. I heard ringing in my ears.

"We're not going home. You're not going home."

"I guess I know that. They said you would say that."

"Why, Jane? Tell me. What's going on because I can't figure this out? Tell me what happened."

She was devastatingly casual.

"I had too much. I was done being a mother, you know?"

"No. I don't know. Why couldn't you tell me? Ask for help?" I said, clawing for air. "Sarah is still alive. Did you know that? She is holding on."

Sarah had a thin pulse when paramedics arrived and was critical now, and I was desperate to be with her.

"Jane? Do you know what you did?"

I stood and looked away from her, bracing myself against the wall. Anger welled up inside me and I was glad because it was finally an emotion I could recognize. My hands wanted to encircle her throat, but I forced them into my pockets. This couldn't be my wife. The woman I loved. Love.

The ringing in my ears got louder. I heard the sound of something breaking, like a piece of cold chalk snapping in two, a bone giving way. My heart dividing, part of it tearing away at a fault line, a tear which began when the dean had appeared in my classroom doorway.

"Don't argue, Tom," he had said. "There's been an accident."

"An accident?"

"Please go to your home with this officer."

The man in blue stood at my door and would not meet my gaze, shuffling his feet and staring at his shoes. Finally he took me by the elbow while the dean entered my classroom.

Jane was tapping the floor with her foot now. I looked at the black and white clock on the jail-room wall. Ten after nine. My life seemed about to dissolve into something unrecognizable. Her voice, her careless words. *I was done being a mother.*

"Are we going home now, Tom?"

"No, Jane."

"Because I didn't take my pills yesterday. There was a doctor in here earlier and he wanted me to get them. Will you bring them to me?"

"When was the last time you took them, Jane?"

"I don't know. Maybe last week. The day the ice-cream maker came, I think."

My mind tumbled. How could she think of an ice-cream maker when she had destroyed both our lives? And then, because I couldn't think of another thing to say, I got up and left.

"Toooom?"

After I left the jail, someone, I don't know who, drove me to the morgue to identify Simon. Someone among the nameless bystanders helped me fog-walk through the details. I was told I could identify him via a photograph taken after death, but I refused, perhaps because I knew that I would never really accept the fact that he was dead until I saw his body. Until I saw his chest was no longer rising and falling with every innocent breath.

There were several forms beneath white sheets before me in the bitterly cold room into which I was taken. It looked deceptively peaceful. A woman in a white lab coat slowly pulled the white sheet away. It was Simon, blonde and blue and wet and still beautifully innocent in the animal-print pajamas I had put him in the night before.

I wanted to hug him, throw a blanket over his body to warm him, carry him home where he would be safe. Instead, I ran out of the room like a coward. I had to get air, to look at something else and replace the vision of all that was left of my son, stretched out on a metal table. What I couldn't know then was that that image would never go away.

I sat outside on the morgue steps, trying to breathe, until someone brought me a bag to breathe into and told me that my church pastor, Jeff, was there. Not that he's really *my* pastor since I haven't been to church in months. I can't claim him, but he claimed me. I pushed the bag away from my face and, still finding it hard to inhale, wished both to be at peace with Simon and alive for Sarah.

"There aren't words," Jeff said, sitting down next to me. "There aren't words."

"What good are you then?" I asked him. He looked down and rubbed his palms together. Probably a practiced gesture, I mused, that they teach in the seminary.

"God is here," Jeff said.

"Where the hell was he twelve hours ago?"

I got up and started towards Jeff's car. I knew I couldn't drive and I needed to get to the hospital. To see my Sarah. God's man could be my chauffeur. That was the least the good Lord could do for me today.

In the car, I took the paper bag and put it over my mouth again, deciding I had to pull myself together long enough to see Sarah. This was the moment when a hungry camera's flashbulb consumed and captured my agony. Me. My pastor. A shaky paper bag. I have never forgiven this intrusion on my grief.

At the hospital, Jeff and I sat next to Simon's twin, angelic Sarah with tiny curls framing her face. Curls created by the ceaseless twisting of strands through her tiny fingers. Her face so like her mother's, pale and heart-shaped, a crimson mouth. Tubes flowed from her nose. Her normally spirited eyes were closed, sunken and circled with blue. The next twelve hours are critical, they told me. Her young brain had been oxygen-deprived yet, in classic hospitalese, they tried to comfort me by saying she was fortunate to have had such a quick response from the paramedics. They couldn't know that the effect on me was the opposite of comfort because their words just added to my confusion about why she needed a paramedic's quick response in the first place.

I laid my head against her arm and patted the soft curls of her hair. I wanted to sing that song that soothed her as a baby, but somehow couldn't remember the words.

"It's going to be okay, Sarah," I said, wanting it to be true for her, but knowing I was lying. It wasn't going to be okay. "Just come back to me. Don't leave me, sweetie-pie."

It is at this point, I thought, that people start bargaining with God. *Save my daughter, God, and I'll devote my life to You. I'll give money. Build a church. Help the poor. Just save my daughter.* But I never had the capacity to be that person and instead my thoughts were dark. I was angry and wasn't prepared to negotiate. My son was gone, so now, I reasoned, it was His turn to give me something back if He ever wanted to hear from me again. And then I thought of Jane and tried again to make sense of what she had done, knowing that to reason with horror was as fruitless as forcing a square peg into a round hole. Still, I tried.

Jeff appeared to be lost in silent prayer, but as I stared at him, incredulous that he should seem at peace in the midst of so much confusion, he opened his eyes and said, "God works in mysterious ways, Tom."

"Go away," I said. I knew that I was being a son of a bitch and I wanted him to think of me as one. I wanted him to leave and take his acceptance with him.

"It's all right, Tom," he said. "Let it out. You can tell me anything."

Was he prepared, I wondered, to hear what Jane had said? *I was done being a mother.* Or the part about her not taking her pills for who knew how long?

As it turned out, I didn't have to say anything because the next day, Jane talked. She told her interviewers how she methodically went about the previous day's events. She told them she had been watching Charles Stanley sermons on tapes the night before and that something in his message told her the time was right for her children to go to heaven. Then she told them I wasn't there a lot and that she was overwhelmed. She told them I was a good husband but lousy father. She told them an embellished story about putting the Zoloft in the twins' juice.

These facts made their way from police reports to news editors' desks. The reporters started firing up with theories and descriptions of Jane that belied the ways in which I knew her. My tragedy became their latest topical storm. As a professor of literature, being so academically immersed in stories, I began to feel a kinship with Ted Hughes and his poet wife Sylvia Plath. How he must have felt, seeing his wife's suicide as a headline in the papers while he was still numb to it. Worse yet, how to later explain to his two children that their mother had loved them. How helpful it would be if I could somehow channel his grief-etched wisdom. He would be my mentor and I his student, and he would teach me the ways of surviving an insurmountable agony while keeping a stiff upper lip for the children.

Every news outlet and investigator wanted to know what had gone on between us during those last days, particularly concerning the drugs and her mood. I didn't talk to any of them much. I was still trying to answer those questions for myself. Of course, there was Jane's jail room confession. *I was done being a mother.* Jane didn't tell this to anyone else, and I kept it to myself, convinced it was the right thing to do for Sarah. Later, I would wonder if it might have helped me to mention it.

Somehow in the midst of all this reporting and digging, there was a funeral with a small coffin where, to his credit, Jeff did not preach, but offered a simple psalm. This was followed by sleepless nights, the company of the TV and the constant red blinking on my answering machine with messages from my parents or Jeff or the odd reporter. My only routine was trekking to and from the hospital where I kept a careful watch on Sarah as she recovered in small, slow steps.

When I wasn't with Sarah, I was very productive. I whiled away the time drinking Jim Beam and watching sand flow through an hour glass knick-knack Jane bought when we had been traveling in Georgia, before the children had been born. I turned it over and over, watching the sea-blue grains drain from one glass compartment to the other. Time passing. Nothing changing.

So went the hours which blurred into a month of days. I didn't eat. I got drunk. I didn't shave. I decided to sell the house. This would be a therapeutic change, my mother insisted. A house, she said, was just a building, a structure with four walls and a roof. But mine was also a crime scene. A crime scene with lush and blooming bougainvilleas, azaleas and roses that I wanted to hack away for mocking me with their steadfast cheer. And I would have. One day I searched out the garage for the hedge trimmer, revved it up and lopped a whole cluster of pink roses to the grass before my realtor yanked the power chord then deftly distracted me by asking about Sarah and what kind of music she liked.

"Anything that involves a purple dinosaur or a princess."

"Mine too. My Beth is four going on fifteen. Now, let's talk selling price."

I quickly felt pathetic, standing there holding my instrument of rage clogged with petals.

She was careful to remind me that selling the house now, given its "crime status," would amount to taking a hit on its value. I insisted we were going and she promised to do her best. She added that I should be on guard for reporters posing as buyers.

Her advice would prove right on the mark.

They invaded everything. They hounded me at the hospital. Then they followed Sarah and me to her doctor's appointments. To McDonald's. To our front yard when Sarah came home. They left messages in my mailbox. They badgered my neighbors and colleagues.

Why is he selling? What is he hiding? What really happened in that house?

I turned the hour glass over again on a cardboard moving box and bargained with myself.

After this hour empties, you will get up and eat. After this house sells, you will get up and be a father.

And it all did pass. Jeff helped Jane get a lawyer and they entered a plea of temporary mental incapacitation. I visited her frequently in jail, but she never really talked. It was mostly me reciting facts about the news and the weather and sometimes a mention of Sarah. Once or twice she asked me to bring her a paperback romance, which I did. I would have brought her anything if it made her talk to me.

It took months to seat her jury, and then I had to numb myself to her trial, to the daily reading of painful facts, to the sunny, poster-sized photo of Simon on the prosecutor's display easel, to watching Jane, someone I simultaneously knew and didn't know, across the space of the courtroom, to hearing the lawyers argue whether Jane had met Texas' definition of insane, which, I learned, presumed she could not distinguish between right and wrong.

Some of the information seeped into my consciousness, but most did not, and I was relieved when it was over. Ultimately, Jane was found not guilty by reason of insanity. She was sentenced to a mental institution for an undetermined length of time. I resumed teaching as soon as it was done, eager to surround myself with young students interested in fiction, and even more eager to get a semblance of routine in my life.

A full year after Jane's sentence was read, I heard the newspaper thud on the porch of our new house, and, thinking that perhaps today the headlines would exploit someone else's life or at least vilify a politician, hurried to pick it up. So I was a loser who found brotherhood in the misfortune of others, as if we were all members of some big, miserable club. As I read the print, I found my membership in the club was acutely current. Seeing a headline suggesting an epidemic of infanticidal mothers, comparing my Jane with the likes of Susan Smith, I gave the finger to the universe, or any photographers possibly still lurking about. The resulting picture, published as it was the next day, did not go over well with my mother. Not that it mattered. Not that anything seemed to matter anymore.

PROSECUTORS WEIGH HUSBAND'S CULPABILITY IN TODDLER DROWNING
September 1, 2003

Prosecutors in the case against Jane Nelson, the mother accused of murdering her son last summer, say they may pursue child endangerment and neglect charges against husband, Thomas Nelson.

The Harris County District Attorney's office has assigned a prosecutor to the case after receiving numerous calls and emails suggesting Tom Nelson's negligence at leaving his children unsupervised with his wife.

At the time of the murder, Jane Nelson was receiving treatment in the form of drugs and counseling for post-partum depression following a recent miscarriage. She had been hospitalized once for attempted suicide.

It has been widely reported that a neighbor told police he once heard Nelson state that he preferred not to leave his wife alone.

Jane Nelson was committed to a state mental hospital earlier this year.

CHAPTER TWO

I have to admit, my mental state was also in question after Jane's trial. I was a functioning alcoholic until I met Dave. Then, I became an alcoholic in denial. Not a big leap, but a small improvement nonetheless. After I was charged with failure to protect Simon, I had even floated the idea of finding a drug dealer on campus. Me. A buttoned-down, briefcase-carrying academic, seeking out an elixir to temporarily end my pain.

Drinking was no friend to me, of course. The more I consumed, the more depressed I grew. Sarah, who by this time had stopped asking if mommy was coming home, told our neighbor that I had started a bottle collection. I immediately let the garage door open and the light reflected off tens of empty bottles, lined up neatly along one wall, encroaching upon my parked car. My habit tapered off considerably then, thanks to the innocent *j'accuse* of a four-and-a-half-year-old.

This was about the time my mother hired Dave to defend me since it seemed doubtful, she told me straight out, that I was in any condition to help myself. My bird-to-the-world photograph in the newspaper had proved her point well enough, and she used that example at every turn to remind me of how I had embarrassed the family.

She was right.

So when Dave met me, I was barely employed and enjoying my sloppy, semi-sober state, in need of a shave and a shower and grading my students' papers by reading only the first and the last page. When he barreled into my house, he introduced himself with a handshake, pumping my hand enthusiastically and entering at full speed before I could stop him. He was the kind of big, broad man you don't find in the teaching profession, the polar opposite of a Woody Allen type, so I didn't protest. I sized him up quickly. He must have been a football player or some form of confident jock in his past life. And he still had the kind of thick, product-laden hair that women love and young men assume will always be theirs. Exactly the kind of charmer my mother would have chosen, I thought.

"Where's your daughter?" he asked.

"Staying at a friend's house. Why?"

He taped his business card to my refrigerator and told me to call him anytime, day or night. Then he planted himself on my sofa, opened his briefcase and, instead of pulling out a legal pad, he set out a steel thermos of strong black coffee and two mugs.

"Who the hell do you think you are?" I asked, mostly for effect since I had been saying that to a lot of people lately. I found it was the best response to anyone asking me questions and it shut them down at warp speed. But I got the feeling Dave would have an instant answer to this question, and it made me like him instantly. That and the fact I knew my mother had picked him. She had sent over thick attorney profiles of three suitable candidates, and I had reluctantly browsed through them all. She told me only one was interested in my case.

"I'm the guy who is going to shake things up," he replied. "Have a seat and give me your complete biography. Leave nothing out."

I didn't relish returning to grading papers, so as I filled him in on the details of my recent life, he filled me with caffeine.

His reaction to the prosecution's charges was equal to mine. He was incredulous.

"Well, hell. Let's just try her pharmacist, too," he said. "And the doctors who treated her, because really, it's not her fault. For the love of Mary, don't they know you and Sarah have suffered enough? The Texas legal system is more kinked than last summer's garden hose."

Then, with measured words, Dave proposed a bold theory. It sounded both practiced and powerful. Jane snapped because generations of cold-blooded, impulse-driven genes were ready to erupt within her. Her predilection for sudden violence was inherited like diabetes or a gift for music. This down-flow of bad DNA struck each branch of the family tree as it tumbled down, rendering me innocent of blame, at least as far as legal reasonable doubt was concerned. Dave could offer the jury his genetically predisposed theory as an explanation to build my defense. It was an explanation of her actions, but not an excuse, he would be careful to note, owing to his hatred of the overuse of the insanity defense. With that breathless idea unleashed, he then uttered a simple, "What do you think, Tom?" His tone was equal to that of someone soliciting an opinion on which color of tie he should don. *Navy or Red, Tom?*

"How would you *possibly* present this? I mean, how do you even know about her DNA or family tree when *I* never even met her parents?"

"You might be interested to know, Jane recently shared some of her family history with her doctors," he said decisively. "That's what got me and my horse on this trail."

Now, not to say Dave Frontella is a loose cannon, but the articles my mother sent over suggested he had a reputation for being abrasive, so I figured he must have obtained this new information about Jane by dubious means. He was described in one newspaper as a "bulldog with an extensive vocabulary." His bio stated he has built a career on defending cases that seek to find blame in medicine and psychology instead of good old-fashioned personal responsibility. His specialty has been defending schools and teachers from overzealous parents who want their kids to receive special treatment based on an attention deficit hyperactivity disorder diagnosis. So his introduction of this theory was going to turn some heads, but he did it for good reason. To offer the data and then pull the proverbial rug from beneath the jury, citing the ridiculosity—yes, that is his word, *ridiculosity*—of blaming anyone other than the person who committed the crime.

His argument would be simple, he continued. Jane committed the crime. I would have prevented it if I could. It could be demonstrated that I had been a dutiful and faithful husband, encouraging Jane to make doctor's appointments, attending church with her, filling her prescriptions. But did all of this constitute a good defense? An argument even? Do I have enough documentation that I was an attentive spouse to prevent going to jail? In the end, all I could reason was that it didn't matter if it was nature, nurture, or my neglect. My son was still dead. My daughter still had no one to mother her. And I had a wife only in the legal sense.

I know what happened. I know the truth. And not even the facts as they came out in Jane's trial sufficiently captured the repulsion I felt. How could they? Was the jury on the scene, as I had been, twelve hours before she held the twins under water? Did they see that morning how she poured Cheerios into small white bowls, sliced bananas onto their placemats and kissed their mussed heads? Should I have somehow predicted infanticide would follow? My mind drifts away and I'm married with two children again.

"So, Tom, will you be late today?" she had asked.

"I don't think so," I answered from behind my morning newspaper. "I don't have any student conferences after my classes."

Simon and Sarah sat playing with their cereal, tossing pieces onto the floor. While I ate, she pulled up a stool at the kitchen counter and began reading from a Bible devotional. Her attachment to scripture, she said, helped her deal with the miscarriage she had experienced many months before. And, she said, it was supposed to keep me from being insensitive. She'd made this comment the time I'd asked her when she was going to stop crying, a remark I regretted instantly.

Dave would excavate many memories like this one, which was about as much fun as having double-root canals. Still, he did help.

"Now, Tom. I'm not going to kid you. There are a couple of precedents for these kinds of charges. And their sentences have stuck. But in those cases, the prosecution proved that both spouses were aware that abuse was taking place, which led to the death of a child. From what you've told me, at most you're guilty of being an insensitive ass. And if there's a law against that, my exes would have me convicted yesterday."

"I don't want to be separated from my daughter," I said. "So I'll let you know what I decide. Thanks for coming."

With that he cocked his head at me like a confused dog. "What do you mean what *you* decide?"

"I mean when I decide if you are hired."

"I'm already hired, Tom."

"My mother? She's paying you, then?"

"Yes. Why?"

"Her motives aren't always pure. You might be interested to know that she wants to raise Sarah on her own. So if any of this defense strategy gets me acquitted but leaves me without my daughter …"

"Let's get more than a few things straight," he interrupted, adjusting his starched shirt collar. "One, I *am* your attorney and I *am* defending you. Two, the idea is that we will go and defend you against these charges. The defense will result in an acquittal, and if I can wrangle it from the media, an apology."

The thought of an apology was nice, though it would never happen. Still, it was a nice bargaining chip.

"This defense you have concocted," I added. "I'm not sure if I'm going to buy it, and I'm pretty open minded. So tell me, there's nothing I can do to prevent a trial? Plea bargain? Community service? Fines?"

"Hell, no. You've got to pull yourself together. Act the part. Look the part. Grieving father. Remorseful husband. Would take the place of your son if you could and damn straight would have swept Jane into a circle of care before she did this if you had known the severity of her illness."

Dave moved closer to me then. More accurately, he got in my face.

"Your mama told me you were in sad shape, but this isn't the time to give up. There's the principle to fight for here, not to mention Sarah. There'll be no admission of wrongdoing. You weren't there. You didn't do anything wrong. Any plea compromise suggests otherwise."

"Just between you and me, I don't want to go to jail, but if it weren't for Sarah, some days I feel I should go there."

"I don't work for clients who have already convicted themselves," he said, standing, arms akimbo, his brow tense with exasperation.

"Okay," I said. "You pass the test. Now I know whose side you're on. Sarah's side."

"Damn straight."

"The only reason I'm willing to go to trial is for Sarah. If you think the result is going to be the same, that I'll get the five years, well, I'd rather just go and get it over with. Some days I think that would make more sense anyway."

And there it was. The first time I had told anyone but the hourglass that, were I on my own jury, I would be in doubt as to my innocence.

"I appreciate what you are saying," Dave said. "I really do. But those are emotions talking and emotions won't win you an acquittal. If the jury gets it into their heads that you feel you ought to be convicted—that it's what you want—they'll do it for you. They will convict you if so much as your eyebrows tell them you want them to convict you."

I reached under the chair cushion and pulled a flask to my lips. Dave ripped it from my hand and tossed it across the room.

"No drinking," he said. "It doesn't earn you any sympathy from me or ease the pain, so you're throwing your good money away."

"You're not paid to tell me how to live my life." I stood up, facing him with all the gusto I could muster on my wobbly legs.

"Since your mama is paying me, I guess I am." He pushed me back into the chair without effort.

"Tom, I am on your side. *You* be on your side, too, and we'll get along just fine. I'll call you in the morning."

I let Dave out and stumbled back into the living room to get drunk again. I kicked my ungraded school papers aside. I'd give them all a B in the morning. Then I picked up the newspaper, reading the previous day's headlines, searching for a new member of the misery club. I searched for a headline that spoke to me like a message from God, wringing out any detail of how a reporter might have editorialized his way into someone else's life. And like a grumpy old man, I argued with the paper for failing to ask all the right questions. I had begun to notice how the media thin-slices a story to capture one dimension of a person. The negative dimension. The sensational dimension. That was what had happened to Jane on the printed page. The media had distilled and reduced her until she bore no resemblance to the Jane I knew.

They labeled her and refused to look back, and I was left to debate with only myself. When they said she was reclusive and anti-social, I saw her shyness. When they said she paused too long between questions, I saw the person who chose her words carefully.

But should I do the same as the media had done? Should I look at those qualities in her and draw simple conclusions? It would make it so much easier if I could hate her.

I drank some more and willed the alcohol to allow me to hate her, but it had the reverse effect. I missed her. I craved her. My mind and heart filled with her beautiful pale face, with memories of her.

Jane hadn't always been ill.

A familiar phrase came back to me and urged me on. She had told me once that the mask of self-control is a powerful antidote to the chaos that rages within us all. Those were, in fact, her very words. I had understood exactly what she had meant because that was my kind of philosophy, too, my kind of world view. She believed that everyone we encountered, no matter how self-possessed they may seem, was covered with hidden scars. She was so sure of this. And, of course, as an emergency room nurse, she had seen the worst of humanity in many bloody forms. The end result was that she had developed an inner calm, a peace that attracted me completely. I fell asleep dreaming of that peace and how she looked the first time I met her. The first time I kissed her. The first time we touched.

I awoke the next morning, crumpled on the sofa, the empty bottle on my chest and the ringing of giant church bells in my head threatening to shatter my eardrums. Turns out it was only Dave's office calling to set up an appointment with his newest client.

CHAPTER THREE

Sitting in a giant brown leather chair, his feet propped up on the polished mahogany desk no doubt high-paying clients had paid for, Dave flipped through notes and talked to me as if I didn't really have a blinding hangover.

"We need to prep you on how you will describe Jane," he said. "Make people see that she was not always sick. I think I know all the basic facts. You have been married, to date, ten years. Two children. What I need to know is what drew you two together and so forth. Start from the beginning. What was she like when you first met?"

Where was Dave last night when I was swimming in all these glorious memories? Now, I had to recall them through the fog of Jim Beam.

"Do you need more coffee?"

"No, the double-shot espresso your assistant gave me is winding me up nicely," I said.

It was easier than I had thought to go back ten years. Jane was an emergency room nurse when I met her, and everything about her conspired to make my Florence Nightingale fantasy come true—her glowing, fair skin, her smile and sunny blonde hair, the way she walked in her white hospital scrubs. I had rarely been in the hospital my whole life, but there I was one day after part of the apartment complex I lived in had a huge fire. It had swept across several buildings in the early morning, catching most people unaware.

There were serious cases. Melting skin. Red, angry burns. Several of the injured were kids who wailed with a ferocity that my mind can still call up today, along with the reek of charred hair. Along with other confused tenants, I had tried my best to help the young and old out of the buildings. Then in a sort of weary caravan, we followed a line of ambulances to the hospital.

The burned kids were sorted out in triage and that was when I first saw her, framed against the backdrop of the green tile walls of the hospital. Her focus was on the orderlies who brought in each of the kids. I noticed this because there was a certain chaos to the scene with adults and parents clamoring for attention. She slipped away for a moment to the nurses' station where I saw her clip a small, fuzzy brown bear to her shirt, the kind that kids attach to backpacks. As she got closer to where I was standing, I saw her attention flow to the children exclusively. Along with a couple of doctors, she zigged and zagged through the hospital hallway where the kids were lined up on gurneys or in the arms of other frightened tenants like me. When I looked at the burns, I shivered. Jane breezed through them, past them. She looked in each child's eyes. Later she would tell me that's how she could assess the seriousness of their pain, through their ability to look straight at her. The harder the stare, she had said, the greater the pain. And the thing was, the kids sensed her calm and responded in kind.

"We're going to treat you in four minutes," she said to a four-year-old girl. "Can you be strong and wait that long?" The girl nodded, and I watched Jane brush her cheek, unclip her brown bear and kiss the girl's cheek with it. Then she went down the hallway, caring for each child and adult with the same tenderness and respect. By the time she had reached them all, the sobbing was at a lower pitch.

And then there was Roger.

Looking back, I can trace the first seeds of my love for Jane to him, the central force that brought us together. He lived with his mother in the one-bedroom unit above me and we often talked about baseball. I carried him into an exam room where Jane and a doctor took him from my arms. From what I could see, he had at least one severe burn on his leg, and he had not stopped shaking since I found him with a paramedic in the complex parking lot, his mother having been taken by ambulance earlier.

By now, the nurse/doctor relationship had become apparent to me. Jane was good cop, nurturing and gently distracting the patient. The doctor was bad cop, prodding and testing, barely saying a word. Jane held Roger's hand. I tried to stay focused on Roger, watching their movements in silence as they examined his burned leg, but her pale beauty caught me off guard, and I think I stared at her in my awkward dumbness.

"You've got a bad patch there too," she said. "Roger, here, is going to be fine. Aren't you, Roger?"

She was touching me then, only I didn't realize until she delicately tugged at a piece of my shirt sleeve that refused to pull from my skin. I would not remember until later that I had helped an elderly man climb through his window when a flame shot up and grazed each of us. I had tamped it out on the grass and thought nothing more of it.

"Roger, sweetie, I'm going to cut your shirt now," she said. "You may feel a chill at first when the air hits it. That's normal."

"It stings! It stings!" he cried.

"It's going to be okay," Jane said. I patted Roger's shoulder and he looked at me with teary eyes.

"You're doing great, champ," I said. "Just great."

"Do you know what happened to Froggy, Tom?" Roger asked. "Did you see him?"

His eyes clung to me with hope.

"I don't know, Roger."

Jane looked from me to Roger and back as though I had given the wrong answer.

"Who is Froggy?" she asked. "Your friend?"

Roger nodded. "I take care of him for our science class."

"Then you probably know that they hate fire. Froggy would have been one of the first to hop right out of there, the minute he smelled the smoke."

"Froggy can smell?" Roger asked.

"Of course he can smell," she said as she applied the last of the bandage to his leg. "Isn't that right Mr. ...?"

"Uh, Tom," I said. "I mean Nelson. Tom Nelson."

"That's correct about frogs, isn't it, Mr. Nelson?"

"Yes. Yes, I'm sure of it. Froggy would have gotten out the minute he smelled the smoke."

"And now Froggy has probably found some trees and water to rest in. And I'll bet that later on Mr. Nelson will help you look around for him."

They both looked at me. She, accusing and serious, one eyebrow arched in questioning perfection. *You must go look for Froggy.* He, hopeful and earnest, prepared to chalk up this horrible day as a blip if only the frog might still be there. *You must go look for Froggy.*

"Roger, as soon as I'm out of here, I'll go look for him."

"And if Mr. Nelson doesn't find him, Roger, it just means that Froggy waited for you until he needed to hop away to safety."

I waited in the hallway with Roger until his aunt carried him to his mother's room. After they left, I continued to watch Jane tend to the needs of the children. It was a ballet of questions and answers and she never lost her step.

"That's good. So how would you describe the way she made you feel?" Dave asked, jolting me back to reality.

"In awe. The way you watch someone who is fully in their element, doing exactly what they were put on this earth to do, and you wonder if you ever had a day in your life with that much directed purpose." I broke off. It was one thing to remember privately and quite another to put the effect she had on me into words. I thought on it again and decided against telling Dave that the gentleness she extended to Roger inspired me to do what I previously thought only happened on TV—purchase a replacement Froggy and pawn it off as the original to a trusting child.

"And those were the qualities you wanted in a wife and mother?"

"Of course." I could see where Dave was heading, this game of tell and show. He wanted to acquire more quick descriptions of Jane that could be reduced into summaries of her character. I wanted to resist him. Just when I was feeling the balm of remembering the true Jane, he would turn this into evidence for my defense. What Jane and I had in the beginning was at risk of being scrutinized, and what might lie there? If there were signposts of her future that had been obscured by my attraction to her, I did not want to see them. Not then.

"And how did you come to ask her out?"

"She asked me," I said. "In a manner of speaking. We were in the hospital cafeteria getting coffee, and she suggested we sit together."

"Good conversation or just about Roger?"

"I asked her how she dealt with her job without letting it bring her down at the end of the day. Did she remember all the sad faces and the hurt? And that was when she said it. 'The mask of self-control is a powerful antidote to the chaos that rages within us all.'"

"Wow. Who wrote that?" I had asked.

"Jane Downing, of course." And she smiled and extended her hand, which I took nervously in mine and shook it longer than necessary. "It's not so hard," she said. "Children are the innocents. They are easy to care for because they don't blame."

Before long, I started remembering more and more about her, not realizing I was remembering out loud.

"I felt her love and compassion radiate right into my bones, so I asked her out right then. Our first date was the next day and that turned into the beginning. Maybe it sounds a cliché, but I knew I never wanted to be more than two feet from her warmth. She was a beauty. Smart. Funny. Thoughtful. I mean, I felt I was overreaching, like I didn't deserve all of her."

"That's great," Dave said, grinning, satisfied, as though I had passed a test. "Can you say it exactly like that again? And look in the mirror. Memorize the expression on your face. And add that you thought, here is the mother of my children."

"I *did* think that, Dave."

"Then it shouldn't be a problem."

"I want to tell the truth about her, not this rehearsed stuff."

"It's not rehearsal. It's preparation. I need to know how you will answer. I need to know you aren't going to step on your own defense. Trust me."

What I thought was that I had no choice. Dave was arguably the best attorney I could have for this case, strategy or no.

"Here's the thing," Dave said, rising from his chair. "They are going to come at you. *You must have known. You had to know. How could you live with her, love her and not know?* The reporters, the suggestive articles, the one-hour news magazine shows, they've all profiled the case. They think this case is black and white. You have to show them the gray. A spouse does *not* know every fiber of his mate. Gray."

"I'm done for the day," I said, but he pushed on.

"Why didn't you get more help for her after the Zoloft incident? Why didn't you hire a maid or a nanny? Why didn't you let her continue her brilliant career as a nurse? Why did you neglect that side of her? If you hadn't, you could have magically prevented this tragedy. You, Tom Nelson, should have known every motivation, every thought of the person you lived with."

I stood up and faced him. "The woman who did this isn't the woman I married," I said, measuring my words carefully, unwilling to let him bully me into the tears I had already decided to save for later. "We made those choices together. This is what we wanted. She chose not to work. She refused more help at home. It was offered and refused. I did know her!"

Dave smiled again. He didn't have to say it. Memorize that response too.

He was right, of course. The accusations he had shouted haunted my waking hours too.

We can tell. Why can't you, Tom Nelson?

You would think after all those months, after Jane's trial and all the medical testimony that put her in an institution, I would be on the road to coming to terms with my role in her actions. But I wasn't. I still could not believe my Jane had done this and I admitted as much to Dave.

"It's unfair, but our defense has to be emotional, Tom."

"You can stop telling me that. You don't know Jane."

"No, I don't."

"Before," I said, steeling myself, "before this she was much like any suburban mother."

"And you should remember that part of her, but your job is not to defend her character."

"Then whose is it?" I demanded.

"Tom, we're getting off the path."

"No, I want to know. When do we get to defend who she truly is? Are people just one thing? No second chances? Just defined by one day?"

"No, that's why we are talking about her character and her other qualities. But it's important to keep in mind what we're up against and deal with reality."

"Reality," I said tersely, "or perception?" On some level, I felt angry towards Jane for not being here. That feeling wasn't new. But this day, if she were present here and now, Dave could see for himself those soft, intangible qualities I was helpless to describe.

I could only do so much in my love-swept descriptions of her. Finally, I shot a look at Dave. "I want them to see her as I did. If even for the briefest moment."

"Seeing her the way you do, Tom, that's only for you now. Asking anyone else to is like asking a New Yorker to see planes headed toward buildings without suspicion. The innocence of flight is gone. A plane cannot go back to being a plane once it has become a weapon."

"It seems so unfair. That's the hardest part, you know. Seeing her name mentioned alongside infamous child murderers. And now, with your 9/11 comparison."

"I was only trying to ..."

"I know," I interrupted. "But I'm the only one left to defend the other sides of her and sometimes, I hate to admit, I wonder why I still do."

"This would normally be the time I offer my clients a drink," Dave said, grinning.

"It's okay," I said. "You're doing your job. But just for the record, I don't think I'll always like how you do it."

The truth was that I craved a drink desperately, and if I had known where he kept his liquor, I might have fought him for it. In his own insensitive way, he was right about Jane's reputation. He could just as well have added, "A woman cannot go back to being a nurturer once she has killed." I knew it to be true, but somehow if I could convince just one other person on the planet that she was not a monster, that I was not completely insane to have loved her, then maybe I could sleep peacefully for just one night.

"Sometimes I wish her parents were here," I said to Dave. "They would have stories like mine, wouldn't they? About a different woman."

He nodded before rearranging papers on his desk, turning his back to me so I could grieve alone. I had to let the tears come, remembering her as vividly as I had.

The examination of Jane's motives was ongoing. It was like a second job, and I felt at risk of becoming so addled with the details that my head might explode bits of testimony in front of my class. Or worse, that while reading Sarah a bedtime story, my mind would trail off into some twisted place.

There was an old woman who lived in a shoe. She had so many children; she didn't know what to do. So she was done being a mother.

Next was the review of her trial. Fortunately, most of this was done by Dave alone.

The legal team that had defended Jane had given a lot of weight to her medication—or lack of medication—as a defense. The theory, as I recalled it, was to present a poor combination of drugs that, taken together, had proved volatile. The records of prescriptions had been contradictory because she went to more than one doctor, something I was surprised to learn. She had allergies, chronic pain in one of her knees, and for each a bottle of pills. And she was taking Zoloft for depression following the miscarriage. Her attorney argued that the pharmacies should have better verified her prescriptions with her doctors, that the insurance companies should have done their job and noticed certain drugs were being "overused." In the end, the blame defense was unsuccessful. The prosecution had countered with many doctors who testified that Jane's combination of drugs had never produced psychotic effects.

I had expected to feel some relief at the end of her legal battle. But none of it sat right in my gut. Reviewed under the light of my own legal predicament, it left me with the gnawing thought that maybe I hadn't seen Jane as ill because I didn't want to see. Maybe you only see the person as you first knew her. Maybe my future prosecutor saw this doubt in me at Jane's trial and first made a note in the margin of her legal pad.

Husband knew.

"Let's talk about the miscarriage situation today," Dave said on my next visit to his office. "When was that again?"

"It was a year before."

"Before?" he asked.

"Before. Before the incident," I answered, still grappling with the right words to reference that day. Since Dave had suggested that Jane's reputation invited comparison to terrorists' planes gunning for buildings, I guess I could have marked it as my own 9/11, referred to it as 6/21. Most of the time, I settled on the description the papers often used. *The incident involving Jane Nelson.*

She was, I think, about five months along when she miscarried. When she started bleeding at home, she recognized the signs. She didn't rush to the hospital or call her doctor right away. Instead, she talked to her belly, begging the life to stay with her. She cried to herself, she told me later, sitting on the cold bathroom floor. The twins knocked, tried to shove stuffed animals to her beneath the closed door. That's how I found her, hugging her knees, wet with tears. She let me hold her and I stroked her hair as she let out the last heavy sobs. I loved her deeply then, perhaps because I saw the vulnerable side of her she rarely had on view. I remember everything about what must have been no more than twenty minutes of grieving intimacy—the scent of her skin, the cool tile floor, the pink stuffed bunny near the door. It was as if the part of Jane that was weak let me inch closer than I had ever been.

But all too soon she became her old, logical self and pushed me away, giving me instructions on what to do next.

"I'll call my doctor tomorrow," she said. "They'll do a D&C. Something must have been wrong with the baby."

"I'm so sorry, Jane. I love you."

Her doctor prescribed antidepressants and suggested counseling. She quit taking the pills after discovering she didn't like the sexual side effects. Then she started taking them again with no explanation. I was glad because it signaled to me that she was taking care of herself, that she understood her own grief. In fact, because her emergency-room-nurse confidence surfaced each time she made a medical choice, I decided she knew absolutely what was best. I only wanted to support her.

"And what about the counselor?" I had urged. "Should you see him again?"

"I know I need more time, but these doctors want to delve into my childhood," she complained. "What's the use of that? It's over. And the pills take the edge off. I'm fine, Tom. Don't worry."

Then there was the now famous suicide attempt. How can a suicide attempt be famous? It happens when your spouse privately confides to her doctors that she tried to do herself in. It happens when the prosecution accesses those records and springs it on you in your deposition.

"So, Mr. Nelson. Your wife told Dr. X that she attempted suicide six months after the birth of your twins."

I felt as though someone had struck me in the stomach. "What? How?"

"Are you saying you are unaware that she tried to kill herself?"

I glanced at Dave for help.

"Would you elaborate on your question?" Dave replied.

"Gladly," the deposing counsel said. "Mr. Nelson was out of town at a conference, leaving her alone to care for the infant twins. His wife called a neighbor to sit with the twins, ostensibly so she could go to the grocery store. But, as we now know, thanks to Mrs. Nelson's defense, overwhelmed and depressed, she purposely ran her car into an embankment."

The assistant district attorney looked up accusingly over the rim of his glasses. It was clear that there was no doubt in his mind that I had failed her.

I was incredulous at the implied charge. Naturally, this was a moment I wanted to question Jane, to have one of those heated spousal discussions where you challenge her version of the story as laughable. Because she hadn't been left completely alone. My mother and father checked into a nearby hotel and were available to her day or night. And as I recalled it, Jane described the accident to me as, in fact, an *accident*. I believe her precise words were, *a son of a bitch was talking on his cell phone and swerved into my lane.* As for her injuries, she had scrapes on her face from the airbag and a bruised knee. And didn't the police report call it a minor accident? But in the context of a deposition where my every action was being scrutinized, the prosecution suggested the minor accident was a cry for help, and with it showed me as an unfeeling cad, oblivious to his wife's acute depression.

I desperately wanted to say something, but Dave's look cautioned against the sarcasm I wanted to unleash. *Suicide? You've got to be kidding me! Her favorite mini-drama was on that night and she would not have missed it.* Later he would tell me her declaration would be easy to refute in court with the police report. The district attorney wanted to bait me into saying something that might help them slant it their way. Still, I pressed him for more of an explanation.

"I mean, why would she make that up?" I whispered to him at a break in the deposition. "It's almost as if she is working against me. Like she wants to give them the support they need."

"She's surrounded by mental health professionals twenty-four seven. What else is she going to use to bond with them?"

I looked at him sharply, but then nodded in agreement as it sank in that he was probably right.

"Let's get lunch," Dave suggested. "Next, they are going to depose a couple of your former neighbors. One says he saw Jane crying at the mailbox pretty often. One said he tried to talk to her, but she ran inside. Was this about the miscarriage?"

"You can't assume the crying was over the miscarriage," I said sarcastically. "Around that period, it was often because a package hadn't arrived. I assumed it was her hormones still out of check."

"Don't say that on the stand. It will just give weight to the argument that you weren't carefully seeing a downturn in Jane."

"You don't have to keep reminding me that sometimes I was an ass as a husband."

"That's just the thing, Tom. I do. Anything that leads to a failure in protecting your children is fuel for the prosecution."

The wagons were always going to circle back. Anything I had ever done or not done was going to have an accusation attached, an extra meaning. By then, I should have been accustomed to this reality, but it would merely lead to a path of my own unanswered questions.

"So, the packages," he said. "Let's stay on track. What was this all about and does it have any relevance?"

Relevance, I wondered. To most, probably not. But again, everything with Jane was now about looking back.

The shopping phase. The increase in the number of purchases from the Home Shopping Network. The number of shouting matches she and I had over the rising quantities of nameless stuff taking over our garage.

"I don't really want to talk about this, Dave. On its own, an increase in shopping is just an increase in shopping. Retail therapy. What's next on your list of questions?"

I could tell Dave was surprised I was trying to give him the brush-off. For the first time in my life, I could understand why many celebrities go through multiple attorneys. When they have jerks like me for clients who don't care if they get convicted, the attorneys must want to quit first.

"Okay," he said. "Offset the prosecution's portrait of you as a distant husband. Focus on those kinder things only you would know about Jane."

Here was an easier turn for me, an easier path to travel down. A path I welcomed if only to remember who it was that I had first loved. There was the lust too. Did Dave want to know about that as well? Of course, why wouldn't he want to make people see Jane's sensual dimension? And here I stopped myself, wondering how it was that I was beginning to understand this preparation through an attorney's eyes. What memory would suit this goal? Our first love-making? The first exchange of "I love you?" Our spontaneous engagement?

It was on a trip to New Orleans. I like to think of myself as the type of person who thinks all future paths through to their many possible ends, but I found myself borrowing against two credit cards for an overpriced ruby ring and asking her to marry me in the rain-soaked streets of the Crescent City.

It's funny how I remember the smells of the weekend so vividly— the soft lilac scent of her shampoo that I drank in as I buried my face in it. The musky vanilla of her lotion that I consumed in little kisses all along her arms. The nuances of the wet streets and the aromas that wafted out from the various cafes: coffee and liquor, seafood and freshly baked bread. When the rain got too heavy, we retreated to our hotel suite and opened all the windows.

Weather is a matchmaker, she had said while we drank tea and mixed it with the tiny bottles of brandy and whiskey we bought at a corner shop. I remember watching the profile of her face as she sat next to the window, a steaming mug in her hands, the rainfall framing her image. I didn't have a camera and I remember chiding myself for it as her pose so needed to be captured and painted by an artist at a later date. I had to settle for staring at her, and when she caught me, she blew me a kiss and asked me if I wanted to play Scrabble. Her favorite way to play was to make all her words drip with innuendo. It wasn't uncommon for us then to have *nibble, lick and touch* spelled across the small travel board.

"Tom, did you hear me?" I heard Dave say. "Did you think of a Jane memory?"

Dave's voice intruded on my brief escape.

"Yes. The day I proposed."

"Great. Spill it."

"Are you sure this will help?"

"Can't hurt."

I began telling Dave about the day in New Orleans when I proposed to Jane.

I remember nervously waiting for the Scrabble game to end, fumbling with the ring in my pocket.

"We're like two magnets," she had said. "The flat ones because they are irresistibly attracted to one another."

Then she kissed me and I thought this was the moment, that we would stay in this embrace and she would pull away while I deftly slid the ring onto her finger. And it might have remained magical like that had not real life intruded in the form of a housekeeper knocking at our door. Jane loved room service and fresh sheets, and would interrupt almost anything to have them.

"Marry me," I had begged, my voice shaky with nerves. "Please, marry this silly man."

Our embrace gave way long enough for me to hold the ring up

between us and read her recognition of the antique ruby gem she had coveted through the glass of a store window just hours before.

"Well, of course, Tom," she said casually. "I would love to marry you." And taking the ring from me, she slipped it on the third finger of her left hand. "Now, will you get the door before she goes away?"

The proposal left me feeling strangely unsatisfied, as though I'd eaten a gourmet dessert that looked rich and decadent but ultimately failed to deliver. The practical side of me crept back in as I opened the door and received the white sheets she had ordered, and I wondered what I had just done. But then she received me warmly, wrapping her legs around my waist and shouting, "I am the future Mrs. Thomas Nelson!"

Afterwards, she would write me love notes and tuck them inside my wallet. She'd leave messages between the pages of my textbooks, underneath my pillow. Sometimes she'd include a photo of herself, or a sticky note sprayed with her vanilla perfume. Always the scent of vanilla in those mementos. Or so I imagined it was there.

"And your engagement ring," Dave was taking notes now. "It was the antique ruby they found in the kitchen sink, right?"

"And I'd like to get it back." I was still entertaining a fantasy that I would present Jane the ring again one day, in what circumstances I did not know. Just that it was hers and the man in me wanted to see it on her finger.

"You will. In fact, I'm going to get a replica made, now that I see what a romantic fool you were about it. When they show it to you on the stand, and they will, you're going to react. We should work on the reaction."

"I'm taking a break." My mind was tired of traveling. The sudden descent to reality, when I would be alone later that night, thinking about New Orleans, would be crushing. To give myself something to look forward to, I intended to call Dave on his cell phone around three a.m. and give him a restless night too, in the form of a revelation that couldn't wait until morning. *Did I mention she was a great lay, Dave? Would knowing that make the jury more or less sympathetic?*

I got up and went outside for a walk. Dave's office was downtown and that day I was glad for the hustle and bustle. It was wonderful to get lost in the midst of so much life going past, the lives of other people, all of them busy with their own affairs instead of calculatingly selecting the details of their past in preparation for some sort of apocalypse.

I observed a man sitting with a young brunette on a park bench. The pair were eating lunch and laughing. He leaned in and kissed her. It would never occur to him, I mused, that he might ever have to recall this happy, fresh-made memory as innocent proof of normal attraction. That he was right to kiss her, and any man in the same situation would have done as much. There were more people like them in the park that day. I scanned their faces, wondering who among them would commit a future evil and who among them would be left in its wake. Then I eyed the heavens for who was playing chess with my life. I had not, until then, asked the question "why me?" But I had asked "why Jane?" so many times.

Later that afternoon, Dave drew many more "normal" Jane and family stories out of me—the move to Galveston for my new teaching job; the small blue house with the great garden; the long walks on the beach; the job she took as a hospice care nurse, which she held until she had the twins. After an hour or so, my recitation of these things was reduced to a list of facts on a timeline.

"And how did Jane get on with your colleagues? Did she make friends after you moved to Galveston?" Dave asked.

"She seemed to get on with the wives very well. But most of her time was with the twins," I said.

The women, I recalled, talked about the beach and books they'd read, and they shared recipes. From what I overheard at these faculty functions, it seemed to me that Jane was enjoying an intellectual charge as a result of discussing something other than teething toddlers and PBS shows. But I soon learned I was wrong.

"Tooooom," Jane had said. "Why do we have to stay at this stuffy party? I'd rather read a tabloid about people I don't know than hear about someone's great purchase of a vintage book with its spine intact."

"Come on," I responded. "The wine is flowing and at least it will give us something to gossip about in bed."

"I don't want to gossip in bed. That's not what I'm made for."

That sort of remark was always enough to make me down my wine and do exactly what she wanted.

"As my teaching hours got longer," I told Dave, "she began dropping by the college unannounced. She'd say she was there to bring me lunch, or it was because Simon and Sarah had begged her to come. I knew she was bored so I tried to indulge her, but it became a problem."

"A problem?" Dave probed.

"It was a distraction from my preparation for class. Or it absorbed my grading time, which then had to be made up at home. We fought about it."

I remember once she'd wanted me to go and get a drink right before a class started. I suspected there was something wrong and she wanted to talk. I told her as much, explaining how irrational it was for her to expect me to ditch my class, and couldn't we talk later. One time I relented and canceled my appointments only to find she wanted to talk about something in the paper that struck her fancy. Like a sale on patio furniture or a piece of wood found in the Himalayas thought to be part of the ark. It didn't go over well.

"Toooom, are you really paying attention? Because I'd just like to get some of the same attention you give your students."

"I'd just like to know what will get us to the end of this conversation right now," I said with all the sarcasm I could muster. It instantly became one of those moments when men know that their mouths have defeated them. But my pride was equal to my stupidity, and I didn't apologize even though her eyes begged me to. She stood up, holding her chin high and then ran her finger along the beads of her necklace, a gesture that eerily reminded me of my mother.

"I'm making pot roast tonight," she had said on her way out. "Don't be late."

"We had long arguments about these interruptions," I told Dave. "She said she just spaced out sometimes and wanted to see me and was that such a bad thing?"

"So you thought nothing of this," Dave asked. "You felt she just needed a break?"

"At the time, yes. Of course, you have to remember that I was bombarded daily by my freshman composition students with their notions of changing the world. It seemed so juvenile for Jane and me to have the same kind of conversation that I had with students with Ipods attached to their heads."

"This is the stuff the authorities like to make a big deal of, Tom. That perhaps you didn't notice because you were consumed with your work. Because if my time-line is right, this was after the miscarriage."

"The authorities. I'm sick of what they think."

"You may very well feel that way, but remember that *they* play a key role here."

I hated *they*.

They believe they are the authority on what happens in other people's homes. *They* believe they know how other people should act in the face of tragedy, particularly when it comes to styles of grieving. As if there was some one-size-fits-all guidebook which *they* used to compare one man to another.

"They don't know my Jane," I told him. "But they claim to."

"We've covered this territory and I'm sure you don't want your mother to be billed for it twice."

"You're a funny guy. Do you hire yourself out for parties?"

"You'd be wise to stay focused now."

Dave continued peppering me with questions, but I wasn't focusing. My mind was on Sarah. Her birthday was coming up and I was fidgeting over what I could do for her. Another birthday without Simon. She told me the only thing she wanted was to spend it with Mommy and I was trying to figure out if it was a good idea. In truth, she had seen Jane intermittently since the trial. We both had as we were allowed twice-monthly visits, but they were never productive and left Sarah more confused. As for me, I had only seen Jane once or twice in the last year without the buffer of an attorney. Our conversations, or what made up for them, were strained and never resembled anything we had shared in the past. We hadn't even touched. The married inmates had to request conjugal visits, and as far as I knew, Jane had never done this.

"Okay, Tom, let's go over the results from Jane's doctors again," Dave said. "I want to get your response to some of this analysis. The prosecution is going to use it."

During Jane's evaluation phase, I remember feeling hopeful. A handful of doctors put together their expertise to help us get a new perspective on her mental breakdown. My sense of hope increased then, as I felt this would be the path to my own understanding as the medical community unraveled the mystery for me. But if anything, my understanding grew more tangled under the weight of definitions like psychosis and schizoaffective disorder. In the end, everyone on both sides agreed Jane was mentally ill. But the verdict hung on her knowledge of right and wrong and whether she knew the difference at the time of the drowning.

"A Dr. Milic, forensic psychiatrist, recommended her continued treatment at the hospital," Dave said, shuffling through papers. "Do you remember his report?"

"Dr. Milic evaluated Jane from a distance, as I recall."

He was a high-paid expert, called in for his analysis, which consisted of reading transcripts of conversations between Jane, the 911 operator, police and other experts.

He never actually met with Jane himself, hence my skepticism about his so-called evaluation. His was ultimately the deciding report. It was eagerly awaited by both sides of the case since her sanity the day of the drowning was being challenged from every angle. Key to this particular point was the fact that she told the UPS delivery guy to call 911, signaling to prosecutors that she clearly knew she'd done wrong, and was anything but insane.

Dr. Milic had noted that some of Jane's responses may have indicated that she was trying to act insane by alternating silence with chatter. And he also included the Zoloft incident.

"Jane recalls preparing juice for the children," he wrote, "and crushing Zoloft to mix in. Says the children were wild and Tom wasn't home although he came in just before she gave the twins the drink."

"You want to go over this later?" Dave asked.

"No. I don't want to go over this later." If I had my way, I would never have set eyes on Dr. Milic or his expensive analysis again.

"Fair enough," Dave responded. "But tomorrow we'll start on our talking points about how well Sarah has been doing in your care. Get a good night's sleep. We have a little more than a week to go."

"Dave, you are …" I wanted to rant, let loose a scorching tirade that had been forming at the back of my mind about how sick of him and his questions I had become. Something along the lines of his needing to get a life and stop messing in mine. But I kept it under wraps for the moment. "Good night."

I picked up Sarah from pre-school and took her to McDonald's. Watching her tentatively play with other kids in the PlayPlace saddened me. As another young girl asked her if she wanted to go down the slide, Sarah looked back at me with a heartbreaking half-smile that I often interpreted as, "Is it okay to play with someone other than Simon?" I smiled and waved and was glad I was wearing dark sunglasses. She didn't need to see her father's sadness too. Soon, I would have to pack her off to my mother's house where she would stay while I was on trial. I wondered how much she really knew about what was about to happen, if she knew there was a chance that she might be under her grandmother's care indefinitely.

Later that night, I would have my answer as I tucked her in and found she had hidden that day's newspaper under her pillow.

"What's this?" I asked.

"I wanted to look at it again."

I unfolded the paper and saw the article she was hiding. The reporter had done an expert job compacting two years of hell into two deftly worded paragraphs.

Thomas Nelson, 43, will stand trial next week on child endangerment charges, stemming from the 2001 drowning death of his son at the hands of his wife, Jane Nelson, 38. Prosecutors argue he endangered his children by leaving them in her sole care when he was aware of an escalating mental illness.

Late last year, a Texas jury found Mrs. Nelson not guilty by reason of insanity. She was committed to Cypress Creek Mental Hospital in Houston where she will continue treatment for an undetermined period of time.

The couple is still married.

"There's a picture of you and Mommy."

"Yes, honey, there is."

"Is it about Mommy being in the hospital?"

"Yes. And about Daddy, too. Remember I told you, I have to go and explain a few things about Mommy. But you'll be with Grandma and Pop-Pop, and when it's over, I'll tell you what happened."

"Can I keep the article?" she asked timidly.

"You want the picture of Mommy?"

"Yes," she said, and I kissed her on the head. "I thought I could keep them for her."

"Okay," I said, suspecting this wasn't the first such picture of her mother Sarah had collected. There was likely a box hidden somewhere in her room that contained little things about Jane. Pieces of her mother in black and white.

Later, I cut the article from the paper. It struck me as a good idea to have it laminated and shrunk to wallet-size so I could simply hand it to people when they asked me what was new.

I hugged Sarah and offered her ice cream, but she said she wanted to read alone so I kissed her and said goodnight.

Downstairs, I wandered from room to room. Our new house is

a rental. If you crane your neck just so, you get a view of the water. I rented it for the attic. It is floored and dark and has a locked door where I packed away all of Jane's belongings. I occasionally hide an empty bottle there too, the ones I consume right there while I imagine Jane among her possessions. Where I fool myself into believing I can still smell a faint whiff of vanilla lotion.

Deciding against jumping back on the wagon, I finally turned on the TV and got stuck on a talk show about teens rebelling against their parents through their fashion choices. I wanted to have *that* problem. I didn't want God to work in mysterious ways with my life.

Despite Dave's warning, I still owned a gnawing sense that I needed to go through this trial and let the jury decide my fate. Was it so someone else could tell me if I was to blame, or to provide me with some sort of absolution? I would have turned to God—should have turned to God then— but I hated emergency room Christians, and it occurred to me that being a courtroom Christian would be an even higher form of hypocrisy.

I tried to focus on the television program with its screaming parents and teens, but instead the horrible June day and its events played out in my mind again and again as if it had just happened. I replayed the small choices I made in the days and hours before it happened. What had I done wrong? Had it been the way I kissed her? Should I have done an extra load of laundry? Should I have accompanied her to that garage sale the weekend before? Should we have shared another cup of coffee that morning? And, God, if I had done everything differently that morning, would Simon be upstairs sleeping now?

As if for more clues, I had gone over my own police statement and her attorney's time-line from the day of the murder possibly a hundred times.

That morning, I picked up my briefcase, kissed her on the cheek and let the screen door bounce as I passed through. Our dog Ricky ran out the door with me. I heard the sound of a neighbor's early morning sprinkler across the street. The day was already warm and bright. I think I waved at my kids, but I don't remember. I know I didn't kiss them. So what else had I missed?

Three hours later, a policeman appeared in my classroom doorway to tell me I was wanted at home, and because he refused to elaborate, I pulled into my driveway knowing only that there was a problem with the children. Soon, the officers on the scene filled in the blanks. A UPS delivery man had arrived at our door to find Jane soaking wet and shivering. She told him to call 911. The police found my twins lying together in the kitchen, wet and unconscious, under a thin sheet.

As for Ricky, well, he did not fare so well either. I had called around for him nightly, thinking he had run away with all the commotion. Finally a neighbor could not bear the ruse any longer and tearfully told me Ricky had been found dead in the children's backyard play pool the day of the murders. So what did I miss?

A weakness, I know, but I cannot answer the question: did I share Jane's guilt? Previous defendants facing "failure to protect" charges have been given up to five years in prison. Would the jury see in me a man who daily replayed the lists of things he could have done different?

"No, Jane, you sit down and let me give you buttered toast."

"I won't be late. In fact, I'll be home early to take you to dinner."

"Let me sweep up these Cheerios before I go, Jane."

"Oh, and one more thing, honey, are you capable of murder?"

With all I have lost, I knew I could not lose five years with my daughter.

So Dave's bad gene theory marched forth. But the journey to creating this defense, well, it didn't include merely my own memories of Jane. To find those errant genes, I would soon learn, we had to climb up and down her family tree, a feat that was sometimes as bizarre as Jane's crime itself.

CHAPTER FOUR

8:45 pm

Dave was preparing the dark-biology defense in ways I could not have guessed.

Naturally, I was behind in my work, so when my mother offered to come for Sarah the next day, I agreed. There was, thankfully, still work. Final term papers were in and I intended to barrel through them at one sitting. I had to if I wanted to keep my job, which only continued to exist because of the dean's fragmented memory of my past performance.

Still, I relished the idea of distracting myself with reams of student essays full of quasi-philosophical paragraphs about life and love and, this semester, the interpretations of *Alice in Wonderland*.

I had amused myself by reading them over a dinner of corn chips and a tall glass of Jim Beam and Coke. The corn chips were part of a trick I'd learned when I began teaching, one that had quickly become a tradition. The crunching sound in my head could give even the dullest sentences a cadence that forced me to keep reading.

This night, the corn chips didn't do the trick. I barely got through fifteen of the essays before slumping over with Anna Dempsey's paper in my hand. I could not remember the last time I had slept through the night. Cat-napping had become a poor habit. Students roused me in class by nudging me with a text book. Angry drivers honked their horns when I nodded off at a long light. A spilled drink often awakened me in front of late night TV. The naps were only ever naps, not the long slumber I needed to function.

During these restless episodes, I always dreamt of Jane. A recurring scene had us playing Scrabble, laughing as she came up with one sensuous word after another. I dreamed she ran her fingers through my hair and kissed me. Then we would lie close in bed, my hands reaching for her. But she would roll away and the bed would suddenly grow wider and wider as I clawed at the sheets, trying to pull myself toward her.

And then the Coke would spill or a horn would sound off and I, finding myself aroused, would stumble back into consciousness with an appetite for Jane I could not satisfy. When fully awakened, the pain of all that had happened would pierce my mind and I would chastise myself for wanting to make love to the wife who had killed my son.

Thankfully, this time the doorbell woke me up before the dream bed had started to widen. I sat up abruptly, spilling soda over Anna Dempsey's paper, which was, perhaps, all the grade it deserved. Before I could get up, Dave let himself in.

"You missed our appointment," he hissed.

"I wouldn't say I *missed* it," I said, drinking down the remainder of my booze before he could take it away.

He sniffed my cup for the scent of liquor. "Jesus Christ, Tom. The trial is one week away!"

"Haven't you read the papers? I have a very capable attorney."

"How many?" But before I could construct an answer, he lifted the near-empty bottle of Jim Beam from the chair.

"Tom, you are one sad sack."

I began to restack the essays. "I was working. What do you want from me?"

"You know what I've been telling you. Your countenance is key. Your attitude."

"Save it. I know the drill, remember? The jury will take note of every expression on my face when I testify. I get it."

"I told you when I took this case that I wanted to do everything possible to gain your freedom," he said, throwing himself onto the sofa. "And it appears you are going to do everything to work against that goal."

"I'll be sober at the trial."

"It's not how you take care of your liver that bothers me. It's your self-defeatist attitude."

I could see he was at his boiling point and I rather enjoyed seeing him twist.

Now he stood up and threw me a serious look.

"You better get some coffee in you. This is going to be a long night."

"Forget it," I said. "I have to finish my work. We can talk in the morning."

"I'm not asking."

"Are you threatening me?"

"No attorney worth his salt asks a question he doesn't already know the answer to, and no good attorney goes into court with a fool."

He pulled his cell phone from his pocket and dialed a number. "Remember when I told you my research team was going to work on Jane's genealogy? Go clean yourself up. You have a visitor coming."

"Dave," I said, but he held his hand to my face before I could utter a defense.

"Fine. But if we have a visitor, you're buying the pizza. Number's on the fridge."

With no desire or energy to argue further, I hauled myself upstairs and into the shower. As the warm water hit me, I leaned into the tiles and thought, *Good one, Tom. Your best counter when cornered is demanding someone buy a pizza. You are so dead if you go to jail.*

When I returned downstairs, I did, in fact, have a visitor who looked more relaxed and at home on my couch than I had ever been. Dave was engrossed in his PalmPilot and the visitor sat cross-legged, smoking a cigarette. For an instant, I felt that I was the intruder in their house.

She must have heard my steps on the stairs because she turned then, and I saw her in full. A lithe, attractive, amber-skinned woman, bejeweled in every way a woman can be jeweled. Bangles and earrings glittered against her skin and I was briefly transfixed by the sparkling stone that shone from a side piercing in her nose. Her eyes were the lightest yellow-green I had ever seen and looked even lighter framed by her tan complexion.

Then, shaking back into reality, I ran a hand through my hair and shot a look at Dave, who neither turned nor responded to my presence in any way. "There's no smoking in here," I said to her.

"Oh yes," she said in a velvety, Lauren Bacall voice. "You look like the kind of man Jane would have chosen. The male mirror of her. Good bone structure. Prominent jaw. Thoughtful eyes. Better hair than her, though." She punctuated her sentence with a long drag on her cigarette, no doubt the instrument of her dulcet tones.

"Dave?" I asked. "Who is this?"

"No wonder the universe gave you one boy and one girl. The photos in the paper don't do you justice. Let me have a better look at you."

"I'm not following." I looked at Dave again, who was unusually silent. "Is she supposed to style me for court? Is that what this is? You got me a stylist to appear better for the jury?"

She and Dave laughed simultaneously, and I wondered if this was just a grand joke, so I manufactured a nervous laugh, picturing myself as the subject of one of those hidden-camera shows and not wanting to appear impossibly slow.

"My dear Tom," she said with familiarity, "this is about a journey. Jane's inheritance. Helping you, love."

"Jane's inheritance?"

"The sins of the fathers and the mothers," she said, her smile vanishing behind a serious composure. "The stigmata of generations of blood. The good and the bad passed down. Now, where are Jane's things, dear? Upstairs I presume. Behind a locked door, yes?" And with this, she ran a ringed hand through my hair, a gesture that should have alarmed me, but left me strangely still.

Dave and this woman stood looking at me expectantly, as if I was supposed to be on the same page. Yes, of course, I thought. Sins and Jane's things. That makes it all very clear.

"Is this a joke, Dave? Because I'm not in the mood."

"Mariah has information that may help our case, Tom. She's a relative of Jane's. Mariah Hernandez. She's part of our team now."

And with that, she took my hand in hers and smiled at me warmly.

"You have a Bible here?" she asked.

"Uh, yes. Upstairs."

"While I make myself comfortable, will you and Dave kindly retrieve Jane's things," she said. "I believe she has a family trunk. Let's start with that. Bring it down here along with your Bible. Where is your kitchen?"

"That way," said Dave. Then he took me by the elbow and headed up the stairs. "Come with me."

"This is crazy," I said, wresting my arm from his clutch. "Who the hell is in my kitchen? And how does she know I have a trunk?"

"Are you opening your mind?" He fixed me with a humorless look.

"You tell me what is happening and I'll let you know if I want to open it."

"The short explanation is that I'm not going to let you screw up your own defense. You are innocent, but your attitude and your behavior are going to convict you. That said, Mariah, the woman in your kitchen, is a clairvoyant."

"A clairvoyant is part of our team? Superb. Cut to the chase. How does my trial end?"

It seemed that since Jane had snapped, events and people in my life were conspiring to up the crazy ante. A clairvoyant as part of my team fit the bill.

"There is a theory that biology is destiny," Dave offered. "Mariah has information about Jane's forbears."

"And how about tonight's lotto numbers?" I said. "Look, I'm sorry I missed the appointment, but I have work to do."

Dave turned and gave me a wry smile. "You know, it always strikes me as funny when parents do this."

He baited me with silence until I asked, "What?"

"They say they will do anything for their kids, but when they come against a wall, it's 'anything except *that.*' Ever noticed how many parents make those kinds of exceptions? Don't be one of those, Tom. It's beneath you."

Dave looked down at me, looming with the advantage of being on a higher step on the stairs. He stood tall and got into his quiet posture. The one I would later recognize as his courtroom stance.

"A distracted, career-focused husband who is out of touch with his wife. Always bringing his work home. Maybe flirting with coeds. Meanwhile, the wife is at home, caring for young toddlers, isolated from intellectual stimulation, surrounded by chores she can never fully check off the to-do list. No family support. She may even feel you were attracted to other women. That you didn't understand her. That she cried out for help and you didn't listen. That she attempted a suicide you weren't even aware of. She goes to doctors for help, but you don't see it as a sign. She suddenly snaps under the pressure, maybe even thinks of killing herself too. And now, as a result of impulses she could not control, she may be forced to spend her life in a mental ward while your innocent son lies dead and buried. And all of this could have been prevented by a more attentive husband with an open mind."

When Dave ramped up, he was powerful. Mesmerizing. I could not look away even though I felt like a young boy getting a lashing from his father.

"You get it now, Tom? That is exactly how the prosecution is going to characterize the relationship between you and Jane. So unless I can introduce as evidence the receipts for all the rose bouquets and romantic weekend trips you bought, you'd better just listen to my advice and see what this woman has to say."

I tried to hold my focus on him, to absorb all that he had said about my less than attentive skills as a husband, things I already knew, but this current theory still did not compute. "I can't believe that you think this path is a good one. I thought you were going to rely on what Jane told her doctors."

"We'd be foolish not to at least explore it," he said. "This path might have psychological benefits for you beyond this trial."

"So now you're concerned about me psychologically?"

He charged upstairs and all I could do was blindly follow, wondering what psychological benefits Dave believed a clairvoyant could provide.

My father was often one to say that if you felt outwitted in conversation, don't remain silent. Silence, he said, implies unease. So over a giant pizza, I allowed myself to appear filled with unease, saying nothing and craving another Jim Beam.

I said nothing as we arranged Jane's trunk near the sofa. I said nothing as we ate pizza, or as Mariah poured strong, black tea into three mugs and smiled at me in a way I read as condescending. As

Dave flipped the pages of his yellow legal pad, glanced at me, and made notes. I could only watch two people who looked as if they had all the answers and were waiting for me to catch up.

Finally, Dave asked, "Tom, are you ready?"

"I'm listening," I said, hearing the doubt in my own voice.

"Let's start from the beginning. Mariah contacted me a few months back with the suggestion that Jane's flash of violence was not unpredictable if only we looked at her family history. Incidentally, she contacted Jane's attorneys last year, but as you might imagine, they declined her help."

"Go figure."

"Her theories, if you will, will help me link Jane's behavior to family traits. I found a study showing how the biological children of criminal parents are more likely to break the law. But we don't know much about her parents. Or her parents' parents. So she is going to help us meet them."

"Meet them," I repeated.

"By examining objects owned by or picturing the deceased, she can tell us where Jane came from. What her parents were like. Their choices, ways of thinking, perhaps madness and violence. What she does is called retro-cognition."

"There was madness in her family?" I asked. A million other questions danced in the air, most pointedly, how objects from the deceased could tell us anything and if I opened my mind any wider, would it crack.

"Mariah is going to give us a bigger picture to consider," Dave said. "That you, or anyone close to Jane, could not have prevented her violence because she may have inherited her impulses. She may even have inherited her ideas of how to raise a child. Mariah can shed light on the combination of environment and heredity that made Jane who she is."

"So, she's going to tell us what exactly?" I asked, aware we were talking about Mariah as if she was not in the room with us. I looked at her, and she was still collected and peaceful, her hands folded in her lap, her legs crossed Indian-style.

"She's going to enlighten us on generations past in Jane's family," Dave offered. "On both her mother's and father's side. We'll follow the genealogy to see what was passed down to Jane. Call it personal archeology."

"Tom," Mariah said softly. "I can see you are skeptical. That is good. Most of my clients feel the same way. It's perfectly normal."

"Perfectly normal is the last way I would describe how I feel," I said as I paced toward the window and wondered if I should get the hell out of my house. "I mean, you appear to know Jane, yet I have never heard of you. Not even a mention and believe me, if there was a psychic in the family, Jane would have mentioned it."

"Oh, you wouldn't have," she said casually. "I move a lot. You know how extended families can be. Tom, I want to help you. I really do."

And Dave added, "You know I do too. All we are saying is just allow us to explore the path of genetics and family history. If at the end of our talk you still dismiss the idea, we'll let it go altogether."

I looked at their faces. They were earnest and sincere as far as I could see.

"Okay, why do you assume there is a link between Jane's family and her actions," I asked. "That is a pretty big leap. Just like the prosecution wanting to hold me partially responsible. It sounds, I don't know, out there."

"Unless there is a force more powerful to change the course of a person's life, he is destined to unwillingly take on the traits of his progenitors," Mariah said with complete confidence, as if this idea was as well proved as gravity.

"Like?"

"Something biblical. Something spiritual."

She handed me the photo of Simon I kept on the refrigerator. It showed him with his best toothy grin, head propped up on his hands, his elbows dug into the sand of the beach near our old house.

"There are genetics. And there are biblical curses passed down from all the generations," she said. "Curses that follow one generation to another unless they are broken off."

"Curses?"

"Let me show you. Did you find your Bible?"

I handed it to her and sat down. She flipped through its filmy pages and read aloud.

"'I, God, show this steadfast love to many thousands by forgiving their sins; or else I refuse to clear the guilty, and require that a father's sins be punished in the sons and grandsons, and even later generations.' Exodus 34:7."

She looked up and stared at me, through me even. Something familiar danced behind her light eyes.

"You still have many of Jane's things. The trunk. I wonder why you kept it."

"We always used it as a coffee table. She kept baby things in it. I assumed she would want it again when …" My voice failed me as I grappled with the truth. It was doubtful Jane would ever have use for the trunk again.

"Everything is connected," Mariah said softly. "Blood. Experience. Who we love. I like that Jane chose you."

She turned her attention to the trunk and for the first time, I noticed things about it I never had before. It was a rich black with bands of wood encircling it, the grainy knots of the wood interesting in their own right. The top of its lid was slightly bowed up. The handles on its side were old and frayed, likely made of braided rope.

"How did you know about the trunk," I asked, all traces of

defiance drained from me now.

"It has been in the family, of course," she replied assuredly. "When I read about Jane in the paper and saw her picture, the image of the trunk kept coming back to me."

She then opened the aged lid and it creaked slightly. She searched through its contents and finally removed a large photo album. The edges were worn and it was bound with leather ties.

"Here it is," she said, resuming her comfortable place on the sofa. "The picture. You might say it is because of him that this whole business started."

It was a faded black and white snapshot of a man in a wrinkled shirt. I could not recall seeing the picture before, and if I had, it would not have had any meaning unless I had asked Jane who he was, which of course I had not.

"I am thinking about desperation and theft," she spoke calmly. "Even our great-grandparents' surname does not belong to them. Scollay. Who knows what it should have been. A precarious though original start in the world, for a family to be headed by a man with a stolen name, don't you agree?"

"Are we ready to start," Dave asked.

Mariah nodded and closed her eyes.

Another question began forming in my head, but I tamped it down, not wanting to play the role of dense follower, the part of the clueless skeptic as regularly depicted in movies. That poor, bumbling doofus who forces the hero to stop and wearily explain in slow, exasperated huffs, the background information for the benefit of the audience. That guy is as necessary as he is pathetic, and since I was quickly becoming him, I forced myself to try and suspend disbelief, if not in thought, in appearance. After all, everything had already been taken from me. My son. My wife. Possibly my reputation. Why not let my better judgment go, too?

"Yes, by all means, let's start," I said with mock enthusiasm.

Mariah explained simply how she would see things and people in the past through retrocognition, the opposite of precognition. Being her special gift, she would examine the photos or objects around her and see what "they wanted to tell her." So she began by moving her hands through the photo album's pages. Her hand finally came to rest.

"Jane, of course. About age ten." She handed me a photo of a young girl in denim overalls, one hand perched on her hip, a silver bracelet dangling from her slender wrist, offering the photographer a get-this-over-with smirk. It was Jane, of that I was certain.

"Do you remember seeing Jane with that silver bracelet?" Mariah asked.

"You know, I think I do," I said, staring into the faded picture. "Sarah often plays with it."

In a way I feel I'll never forget, Mariah's composure suddenly transformed. Eyes closed, mouth open, she rested the photograph against her chest and drew a deep breath. Her back hunched and a smile spread across her face. I watched, bemused, as she pulled her knees to her chest, in the innocent carriage of a young girl. And then her mouth turned up at the corners in an uncanny mockery of Jane's smile.

"A car," she said, her voice now in a girlish pitch with the faintest trace of fear. "Men and pockets. A cat. Time for laundry. A lady keeps asking me questions and I keep wondering when my mother will come."

PART TWO

CHAPTER FIVE

Texas — 1976

The blue Buick had come to a stop five miles from the Texas-Mexico border. There were two survivors, both sitting in the front. Apparently they had picked up a hitchhiker. That was the one in the backseat, the one they said hurt my mother. The others didn't even have to go to the hospital. Not a scratch. But the man in back lay there bloody and swollen, his weathered face slack against the blue vinyl seat. Folds of skin filled with dried blood. The murder weapon and a necklace were found under the seat. At least, this is how I imagined it all happened from what I've heard about the car accident.

I sit in a jail room and try to overhear more while the lady cop makes phone calls. The other officers drink coffee and talk about me. I guess they think I can't hear them, but I can.

"The kid must be upset," I hear one of them say. "We're waiting for her father to come and get her. A Samuel Downing of Del Rio. He didn't sound too happy about having to get her."

I hear another officer say that some of the blue vinyl had stuck to the dead man's face and peeled off when they got him out. He was headed to Mexico after killing two women.

"He was done for, plain and simple," someone said. "An eye for an eye and all that jazz. Justice on earth or on a piece of toast."

I wish I had a piece of paper to write down what he said. I want to remember "justice on a piece of toast."

The officers keep talking and I'm glad they do because I'm bored and tired. They keep talking about the dead man and what had happened to "the women." That's what they call them. But that was "a whole 'nother story" as they say in Texas where this all happened on a hot night that turned into a bitchin' morning. That is what I would have written if I had a piece of paper. Where I live, a lot of things are bitchin'. That's what my mother always says anyway.

They send a lady cop into the room to talk to me. I guess she's a lady cop, but then she says something about family services and I don't know what that is. She wants to know more about the women and how the day all started. The women are my mother, Vicky, and her friend, Carol. Carol has a daughter too who is ten like me. Her name is Sally and we all live together in an apartment with bad curtains.

The lady copy wants descriptions of them—names, and a bunch of other things. I can't think of what to tell her even though she is trying to be nice.

"Your mother is a pretty lady. And she has a pretty daughter too," the lady cop says.

I don't like that the lady cop is trying to be that nice. I already know my mother is pretty. Pretty enough to attract drunk men. That's what I overheard Carol say one night. They never thought they were pretty enough, but I still thought they were, in the magazine sense.

They could have been sisters, the way they looked the same. Dark brown hair they home-permed. My mother said she read somewhere that, "curls around the face get you a date." They plucked their eyebrows so high that I thought they looked like they were waiting for an answer to a question. They looked especially this way when they wore blue eye shadow.

They had big breasts like magazine women too, but my mother had to buy the kind of woman's chest you can put under clothes. She bought them from a magazine that advertised how to increase your bust size. It was easy to slip them in and out, rinse and leave them by your sink at night. One time, she did that and a man discovered them the next morning and put one of his cigarettes out on it. But that's a whole 'nother story.

Both Carol and my mother have long legs and pretty pink-painted toes. Perky Pink I think was the color on the bottle. I always told my mother she was pretty, but she didn't listen. She said she attracted plenty of fists to the face. She got those fists from the "game."

The lady cop asks me more questions about the game, and I tell her it's a way to stretch things out between pay. That's because paychecks from working at the local A&W and the Lucky Lady gas station didn't add up to much, even if you did stuff stolen cheeseburgers or lottery tickets into your purse. Which they did all the time.

"How have things been at home," the lady cop asks, so I describe home for her as best I can.

Home for us wasn't much of a place. I mean, it had curtains, which they both thought made it look more permanent and nice. But it really gave the place a sad look like the inside of one of my friends' trailer. I shared a room with my mother. That is until these men spent the night. Then my room was the closet. I slept in there most nights anyway and I'd started hanging little pictures on the walls to look at when I couldn't sleep.

Some of the furniture in the apartment was stuff from slow drives down neighborhood alleys, the kind of neighborhoods where people get tired of perfectly good flowered couches and faded green plastic patio chairs. We even found a TV that didn't have any sound, but showed the picture well enough. And it was fun to sit and wonder what the people were really saying, or make up stories to go along with the action. That's how I started my talent for imagining things.

So I would sit on one of those old flowered couches, and they would watch TV with a drunk man until he got drunker. When he passed out, it was time for the daughters' part of the game. We were to search the men's pockets. Most of the time all we found were those little minty toothpicks or an off-brand condom. Then my mother would say "Yeah, right. In your dreams, bucko," or something like that. Of course, sometimes the condoms did get used. I knew this because there was a perfect round circle on the nightstand in one of the bedrooms where one of the condoms leaked and ate through the finish on the table and is now always covered up with a coaster or a picture frame.

Sometimes we would strike gold in the form of five-dollar bills. Twenty-dollar bills were a real treat. That meant that even us girls could buy something like an ice-cream sandwich or a package of colored ponytail holders. It was those times I guess I didn't mind so much what we were doing. But being one of the pocket-searching ten-year-olds made me know more about the world than most people under twenty, which my mother said was a good thing. My mother said I was lucky and smart to already be aware of the world. She said I should always be aware of men and what they will try and do.

I don't tell the lady cop all of this, but I tell her about searching the pockets because that was what had happened the night before with the man who ended up in the Buick.

I know the lady cop probably thinks these are terrible mothers, these women who don't have any more sense than to have little girls search men's pockets. I don't know. I'm not a mother. Maybe I'm making my mother and Carol sound completely rotten, which is not that they weren't at times. I mean, they could think of really creative ways for us to "get it" as they warned us all the time. You're going to "get it" Jane! Don't look at me like that Jane, or you'll "get it." Sometimes "getting it" would include shoving our faces in the toilet.

The lady cop says that my mother doesn't sound like she was always good to me. She wants to know if she hurt me and I tell her most of the time they acted like us ten-year-old girls, like they didn't get that they were moms who were supposed to know better than their kids. They flipped through the TV or magazines and told us what boys they thought were cute and which famous people we should date, like Shaun Cassidy. They told us they wanted to buy more pink things for our room and spent too much money on some fancy-label clothes. They wanted us to fit in at school. And at school, I guess you could say we didn't really look like girls living in an apartment with sad curtains and drunk men on weekends. We were always neat and clean. We had the latest-character lunchboxes, matching Scooby-Doo metal squares with our white bread sandwiches inside. We had this even though there wasn't much to eat on the weekends. So I don't agree with the lady cop.

We weren't allowed to smoke or have our ears pierced even though we begged to have them done. And we wanted perms like them, but the moms refused. They also dropped us off at the library, not the mall like other kids, which would have been bitchin'. No, we had to hang at the library and giggle about getting into all the books we shouldn't have been reading, like romance novels. We would read the lines out loud and imagine what it would be like to be one of those people. But that is really, really a whole 'nother story because the truth is, we didn't really have to act out the romance novels or imagine them at all. We could hear them being acted out behind the thin walls of our apartment. And then we'd really giggle because we'd say, "Hey, that sounds like Marisa and Rip."

See, we didn't have the worst mothers on earth. I didn't think so anyway.

The lady cop gives me a Coke and asks me more questions about what happened that day. She asks what made it unusual.

What happened took place on one of those days when the beds are still unmade at noon and the sink is full of dirty dishes. There was a stack of dirty clothes by the bedroom door that smelled like something wet and sour had been there a while. But the smell could have been the trash with all the cat litter stuff. The cat, Gene, seemed to make as much smell as us. The only thing he was good for, according to my mom, was fending off bad people who searched the trash. She's got this thing about putting old bank statements and the men's stolen stuff in the same trash bag with Gene's dirty litter. This, she says, will be the penalty for anyone trying to get into something they shouldn't. And I guess this is an okay thing to do, although I think there are more uses for Gene than just that.

So I was supposed to haul the laundry over to the laundry room. There would be at least three baskets of it, that is, if we had baskets, but we didn't so we usually hauled it in what my mom calls bus traveler luggage—old white pillowcases that you can easily drag across the pavement along with your box of soap. I wanted one of those little red wagons to make this work easier, but my mom said no. I kept hoping we'd find one on one of our drives down the alleyways of the neighborhoods, but I suppose they're too useful to throw out. Not like our flowery couch, I guess.

The lady cop repeats what I said.

"The laundry. That's what you were supposed to do this morning."

Instead, since it was Saturday, we watched morning cartoons. My mom got ready for her shift by putting on her A&W Root Beer uniform with a large plastic name tag that says VICKY in big black letters. She's worked there a while, but is saving to finish her education at beauty college because she had to stop getting educated when she married my father. Some of the best times we have are playing beauty parlor at home where we all sit around and give each other manicures.

Before she left that morning, she barked out some chores toward my back. I pretended to acknowledge what she said but was really fast-forwarding my mind to a half hour later when she would be gone and I could be lazy until a half hour before she got home.

Sally was sitting next to me, doing the exact same thing. Carol was still sleeping with last night's "Rip." Sally had a sad face over that because Carol had promised to take her to get a haircut. Her bangs are beyond bangs now, as they say, and she might as well grow them out.

During a commercial, I went into my mom's room to gather up my clothes. I stopped at her dresser and pulled out her silver charm bracelet. Sometimes she would let me wear it around the house, so I slipped it on and let all the charms dangle around my wrist. I was in no mood, as my mother says, to do the laundry. But then I saw a new romance book under her bed, and I suddenly wanted to get to the laundry room and read. This story, according to the back jacket, featured Cassandra Langdon and Bolt Kensington, "two star-crossed lovers who rendezvous on the great stony moors of an English country estate, only to find a dead body. If they report it, their passions will be discovered. What should they do?"

I couldn't wait to get into it because I wondered what I'd do if I ever came across a dead body. Of course, there was sure to be a lot of hot sex and all that stuff, most of which I skimmed since every book had a lot of it and there was nothing new after the first few. Plus, I figured I knew how it felt. Once, I asked my mom what the big deal was and why people want to do it all the time. She told me to think about how, when you get out of the shower and you grab a Q-Tip and run it around in your ear, it feels so good. She's known that I loved the whole Q-Tip part of baths since I was a lot smaller, so I immediately think of how a few times I've taken a shower or washed my hair in the sink just to be able to clean out my ears. So she goes on about how sex is like that feeling times ten and suddenly I get the big deal about it. I felt very lucky to know this information.

So I went ahead and got the laundry bundled in our laundry pillowcases. I didn't really feel like being there watching cartoons when that new Rip guy stumbled out of Sally's mom's room anyway. I'd had that experience before and I prefer these men when they're drunk and it is okay to search their pockets.

I begged Sally to come with me, at least to get it started, but she wasn't having any of it. So I stuffed the box of soap into the pillowcase. I knew it would get dented and smushed as I dragged it down the stairs and I would "get it" later from my mother, but I thought "What the hell? I'm doing the work, aren't I?" That's the kind of logic that didn't go over real well with my mom, but sometimes it felt good to talk like someone else. And, it turned out, that was going to be the least of our problems, what with the whole blue Buick thing ready to happen about fifteen hours later.

The lady cop looks to me like she has a perm and I ask her if she gets many dates because I want to see if my mother is right.

"Honey, let's talk about that later. I just want to hear about your day. Do you want something to eat?" I say that I do and she leaves and comes back with a cheeseburger and fries.

"Whenever you are ready, finish telling me the story, honey," she tells me when I start to eat.

So I tell her about how I got to the laundry room and how it smelled like soap and underarms. I put quarters in the washing machine and looked at the new book. One of the first words is "rendezvous" and I make a mental note to look it up in the dictionary. It sounds like a word I would like to use when Sally and I playact.

I began reading while leaning against one of the warm dryers, so warm I wanted to crawl inside and lie down like I'd done before. But instead, I settled in and read the first page, which started on page ten, so I'd already made progress. Because I decided I might want to write these kinds of novels some day, I turned down the corners of pages that said things in a new way. By the time the first laundry buzzer went off, I had turned down three pages. I unloaded the clothes, put another load in and settled in for more reading. About this time Sally came racing in and told me to get home right away. She said my mom was home early because she'd finally gotten herself fired.

"She's throwing things," Sally told me, all upset. "I think she hurt Gene. She threw him against the wall."

"And Gene is your cat?" the lady cop asks and I ask her if they've found him and if he's hurt.

"I'll check in a little while, honey," she tells me. "What happened when you and Sally got back to the apartment?"

I tell her how we ran back home. Sure enough, my mom was still tossing things around, chain smoking and trying on new outfits. Gene was under Sally's bed and we couldn't get him to come out. Mom screamed at me because one of her tank tops was still in the laundry room. It didn't seem to count that I'd been washing it.

After a while, she settled down in front of her make-up table and started applying blush. She said she'd been fired for taking money from the cash register, even though she'd sworn she wouldn't do it again. Then she was putting on her "get 'em in the net" outfit, which is a purple sweater with a scoop neckline and this great gold and pink necklace with specks of gold that sat just right around her neck. It's a beautiful necklace that she told me she got from her grandmother and is going to be mine some day. That is, if she doesn't hock it again. It was supposed to be a necklace that had been in the family for decades, maybe centuries, and the only thing she had that she knew her own mother had once worn.

So I took it as a good sign when she put it on and we both smiled at each other in the mirror. She always told me that, even if you're feeling low or look like crap, a necklace will make you look pulled together. She said she felt much better. I told her she looked pretty and not to worry about her job.

I'd seen my mom like this before. Even though I was ten, I knew the meaning of the "calm before the storm" because I had read it in many books. Getting out that necklace meant the storm was coming. When things didn't exactly go my mother's way, she usually blamed it on "her two favorite louses," my grandfather and my father.

"If it's a big love, Jane, you'll get a big mess. Remember that," she said. "Men make babies and wars and then leave the scene of the crime for someone else to clean up."

I can tell the lady cop is impressed that I could say this because she nods her head and puts her hand up to her mouth. She might be entertained, but I'm getting bored. No one has told me what I want to know about my mom and Gene. And I wish I still had my paperback because Rip and Cassandra had just stumbled upon the dead body of a man dressed in horseback riding clothes with a silver flask in his pocket, which Cassandra thought was a clue.

"Do you know what shoplifting is, honey?" the lady cop asks.

"It was really my fault," I say. "We usually only get things we really need. But I got the can of cat food, and that's not my mother's fault. How hurt is she anyway?"

"Keep telling me about the cat food. It was for Gene, right?"

My mother had told me she just needed some smokes and once-a-month products at the grocery store. We'd done this trick before. I'd go in, get a few things. I'd get them to give me the cigarettes after I'd made sure they'd seen the box of female products in my basket. Then I'd pretend I forgot to get something from another aisle. My mother waits in the car right by the curb outside the store like she always does, and as soon as the electronic doors swing open, I run to her car. She drives away fast. We always laughed when we got to a place where she could stop. Then she would kiss my head and brush my hair back and tell me how proud she was of me. We've only done it a few times, ten maybe, when she was between paychecks.

Anyway, when she came home today, dressing to go out, ranting about her lost job, about my jerk father who doesn't send much money, and about how she's down to her last cigarette, I knew a storm was coming. And before I could believe it, it was me who suggested the grocery store thing.

Before I knew it, we were in her hatchback, driving up to the front of the store. I went inside and put the stuff in a shopping basket. Then I saw the red and blue cans of cat food, which were only forty-nine cents, so who would care. Besides, Gene needed a treat that might make him come out from under the bed. But when I got to the door, someone grabbed my arm with such a jerk that the stuff in my basket went flying, and I saw my mother's eyes narrow at me and heard her rev the car's engine.

"Momma, wait!" I called as she sped away. I pulled free for a moment from the arm holding me back and I tried to run toward the red taillights of her car. "Momma, wait!" But she was gone.

Next thing, I am sitting in this room that's too bright and this lady cop is asking me new questions, like do I know a man named Brian Garza and has he been at my apartment before.

"When is my mother coming for me?" I ask for what feels like the fiftieth time. I'm so tired and I really am starting to worry about Gene. Plus, all our laundry is still in the laundry room and sometimes people steal it and my mother is so mad already I don't want to get in trouble for that too.

The lady cop tells me I'll be staying here for a while longer and that I'm doing a good job and do I want something else to eat. She takes me to a different room, a place that seems like a jail cell, although she tells me it isn't. There's a cot, a sink and a small table in the center. They bring me some fried chicken and I eat it pretty fast because who knows if mom will give me dinner after what happened.

The lady cop comes back in with a Scrabble game and lays it all out on the table. The letter tiles. The timer. I ask her again about my mom and if it's true that she is hurt because I heard an officer say something like that. She just asks me if I know how to play this game.

And I guess we play a long time because the next thing I know, I'm waking up under a thick blue blanket that smells like rust, and it hits me that I'm not home. I close my eyes and see the red taillights of the hatchback smear into a blur and I know something has gone really wrong.

Later the lady cop tells me more about what happened. She says they took my mother to the hospital because she was hurt, but that she died while they were bringing her into the emergency room. She didn't get to the hospital in time, and they believe this bad man named Brian Garza killed her. She says he is the one who died in the back of a blue Buick that was apparently headed for the Texas-Mexico border.

The lady cop pauses and tells me she will tell me the rest later.

"No," I say. "I want to know everything now."

I found out that my mom had gone to her favorite bar after speeding off from the grocery store. She brought home Brian Garza. I guess they were going to do the whole pocket-searching thing with Sally. And I guess that's what started to happen, except that it took a bitchin' turn. Those were my thoughts, not the lady cop's. Brian Garza had some drugs, a piece of round peppermint candy and about a hundred dollars. But maybe he wasn't drunk enough to be searched because Sally got hurt, too.

And of course my mom and Carol didn't like this so they must have done something, maybe attacked him with a hot curling iron. Anyway the lady cop says there were fresh red burns on his arms, so I fill that part in for myself. There was a lot of screaming. That's what neighbors said. And my mother's jaw was broken because she put up a fight. And drugs spilled all around, white powder everywhere. The neighbors heard a gun go off. Three times it did that and no, it couldn't have been the TV because it has no sound. And when the police came, the man was gone. And Sally, well she was shot through the chest. And Brian Garza, the man, thought he could lift the gold and pink necklace, because they found it in his pocket later. The lady cop told me some of this and I imagined some parts. Either way, my mother was gone.

I'm so hot and thirsty when the lady cop finishes telling me this story, which is like something I would read on the back jacket of a book.

"So then, will I stay here," I ask the lady cop.

"Oh, honey," she says and gives me a big hug.

"What is your name?" I ask her and she looks at me funny, like I said part of a joke. "Why, it's Rose, honey."

"That's a nice name for a cop," I say. "So will I stay with you, Rose?"

"I'm not a cop, honey. I'm from what they call family services," she says and hugs me again. "This is my card. You can call me any time. And I'm going to make sure someone from family services gives you a call when you get to your new home, okay?"

She said they've contacted my father and that he'll be here in a few hours "to collect me." *To collect me*. I'd never heard that before. It didn't seem like the thing you do when you pick up your daughter who you haven't seen in five years.

Rose gives me a plastic bag with my mother's necklace in it and tells me my father can help me get my stuff from the apartment. Then she gives me another hug and takes me to another room that has a bathroom and shower. After she leaves, I take a long shower and cry under the water. I stand like that so long that I stop crying, but you couldn't tell because the water is still on my face. Then I wrap myself in a scratchy towel that smells like bleach, and a few more tears come. I keep wondering why my mom was alive until they got her to the hospital. That seems like just the opposite of what it should be to me.

And I wish I knew what happened to Gene, if he's still hiding under the bed. I know he thinks all of this is his fault and can't understand why no one has come for so many hours. No one has come to collect him either.

CHAPTER SIX

Midnight

Dave and I watched Mariah as she took several deep breaths. She muttered indecipherably as though she were speaking in tongues. After a while, she relaxed, rolling her neck around and stretching her arms upward. I had been so caught up in the story that she told in a little girl's voice that it was startling to see her again with the composure of a middle-aged woman, years falling back into her features. For a moment I doubted what my eyes had seen, what my ears had heard.

I whispered to Dave, "Do you really think that story about Jane was true? I mean, it sounds more like something my fiction students write."

Dave reached for a slice of cold pizza. "It isn't like this is biblical history. Some of these facts can be uncovered."

"Ask Jane if you don't believe," Mariah said, putting the charm bracelet on the coffee table. My eyes followed it and I stared at the shiny trinket as if it were a holy relic. "Poor young Jane," she said.

Poor young Jane?

On its face, the story could have been calculated to arouse my pity. How could it not? Still, that was my Jane in the picture. Was it the same Jane who looked at life in a free-spirited way? The playful, creative Jane that I recall enjoyed filling in details about people she watched across a room or a restaurant.

Dave had opened his laptop and was now busy pecking away at it, clearly on the hunt for something.

"Here is something, Tom," he said as he read from his computer screen. "A police report on Brian Garza."

"Seriously?"

"If it happened in Texas, I can access it, yes," Dave said and then began reading. "In 1976, Brian Garza was implicated in the murder of Victoria Langley who was survived by one child. J. Downing, age ten."

The cursor blinked intently beneath the initial J, but I still didn't believe it. A bad habit of not trusting the written word had been drilled into me by countless reporters using poetic license with my life. Just because Dave pulled it up on an Internet search didn't mean anything certain.

"I'd want to get an official report on this, notarized by the district in which this was filed," Dave said, almost echoing my thoughts. "Running off in a car to leave a child to face the law," he said. "I thought I had heard of a lot of bad scams, but that one ranks right up there at the top. Who would do that to their child?"

I flinched at Dave's question. That was the most frequent comment made about Jane.

Who would do that to their child? Who would drown them?

Besides, if what Mariah had done had any validity, if even a crumb of it were true, why hadn't Jane told me about it? But then Jane had told me very little about her childhood. Just that she had been raised mostly by her father. That she had a small transistor radio and loved listening to Glen Campbell. That she had wanted to be an emergency room nurse for as long as she could remember.

I tried to put myself in the seat of a juror, listening to how Dave might explain Jane's relationship with her mother: that it lent credibility to her inability to nurture and protect like a mother if, in fact, the last time she saw her own mother she was purposely leaving Jane at the scene of a crime.

My mind insisted on playing the role of the prosecutor, too, and dismissed the notion that neglect and abandonment by her mother exempted Jane from being a responsible adult.

Again, I was left between the two arguments, desperate to find an easy answer to the incomprehensible 'why' of it all. Why do some people snap and others, given the same childhood experience, do not? I didn't want to fall into a trap of rationalizing her actions, but the image of the young girl in denim overalls with the half-smile haunted me, and I wondered when the picture was taken—was it before or after she was left by her mother?

True or not, this left me with an unwelcome sadness for the young, ten-year-old Jane and Gene, the forgotten cat. I told myself to shake it off. These were the same emotions generated by watching a hard-luck story play out on a made-for-TV movie. Just because I felt sympathy didn't make it true, and surely a jury would feel the same way.

Dave stood up and rubbed his temples. It was a practiced move I had observed watching him cross-examine a witness in our depositions. He would appear to feign confusion over a simple matter, making him seem more like a bread and potatoes everyman who needed only the basic ingredients of the case, a man who put adjectives and imagery on hold. I was sure the emotional trauma of the story appealed to him. In fact, he was probably giving himself a mental high-five because Jane's original defense team didn't have this information.

"So, Mariah, you met Jane after her father came for her?" Dave asked. "When she was ten, you told me."

"I only saw her once or twice with her father," Mariah told him.

Now that she had completed what I could only think of as her performance, she looked tired and worn.

"Only once or twice," Dave repeated.

"Her father and my mother worked at the same café," Mariah said. "Sometimes our paths would cross there. She was usually by herself, reading or writing in a notebook."

"And did she tell you this story herself?"

Mariah fixed him with a stern look.

"Little girls tell stories of how they wish things were, not how things really are," said Mariah. "My own mother told me that Jane's mother had remarried and sent Jane to live with her father. So I never asked more about it."

The wind kicked up outside and caught on a chime on our porch, making it beat in tap-taps against the house. It made me think of Sarah. She always begged me to lift her so she could set the chimes in motion and watch them sway in the air. Now I was up and looking outside, noticing how the wind was shifting the leaves around the yard. A spray of lightning streaked across the sky and lit up the night. It must have been after midnight. If a storm was coming, it would be a nice accompaniment for sleep, but I knew it was likely I would be awake now even if there hadn't been a clairvoyant on my couch.

Dave paced back and forth in front of the fireplace, his hands twitching. I expected that he must be missing a dry-erase board and marker to make notes on as he thought through his questions.

"Okay, so this establishes some important facts about her childhood," he said. "I wonder what would change if I got the police reports on this and showed them to her doctors. Get them to testify on the effects of losing a mother at that tender age. Make the jury see she had no maternal model. It establishes part of a motive. It could be a thread."

"So you think somewhere in that pile of manure is a pony," I said.

"If that's how her mother treated children, it points to what she thinks is acceptable behavior," Dave said calmly. "All her mothering was preadolescent, before she had more facts about the world. It could have left Jane set to unravel before you ever came into her life. A deeply buried resentment against her mother combined with acute abuse and a youthful propensity for fantasy fiction rendered her unable to develop a normal picture of motherhood."

"Oh, thank you, Dr. Freud," I said sarcastically.

"Careful or I'll bill you for psychological counsel too," he said with an easy smile. I returned an admittedly juvenile roll of the eyes, a look often mirrored back to me by young students displeased at a weekend assignment that threatened their freedom to consume hours of television.

"Here's my proof, Tom. When her own mother was up against normal pressures of life, she resorted to illegal activity. So much so that her own daughter thought shoplifting would ease her mother's pain."

He is just doing his job, I reminded myself, wishing there was a way for him to do it without me. I felt the tug of believability in Dave's theories and realized I would have been fully convinced by them hours ago if we were analyzing anyone other than my wife.

Outside, the chimes played their sunny tune again, and my mind ran to thoughts of my children. I looked across the room at another picture of Simon and Sarah on the mantel. It was a black and white photo taken two years earlier, both of them smiling, beaming and hopeful. They wore matching blue overalls. Sarah had a straw hat. Simon had almost a whole mouthful of teeth. It had been taken on a sunny Labor Day, at a picnic with neighbors, and I remembered Simon had corn on the cob for the first time. It was an altogether different life then. I felt I had achieved the American dream with Jane, the kind of existence where people discuss their broken-down washing machines or the state of the economy. That night back at home, Jane had snuggled with me and talked about having more children.

"Today was perfect," she had said. "I want to put it inside a snow globe and watch it forever. We should try for another baby, you know."

"I like the trying part."

"Come here, you dirty old man."

"I love you, Janie."

"Just don't ever go to get cigarettes and not come back."

"I don't even smoke."

"Well, cigarettes always get the bad rap. What would a husband go for nowadays?"

"Hmmm. Maybe dental floss."

"Good one, Tom. You wouldn't want tooth decay on top of a bad conscience, would you?"

I could not, for the moment, bring myself to admit that Dave had a point about Victoria, Jane's mother. No, the Doubting Tom was my role. But still, I knew I needed to raise my daughter. Having her taken away would be more than I could bear. The waters were rising, yes, but I had one huge reason to search for a lifeboat. My daughter. And to achieve this, apparently we had to go down this dark, meandering path.

Sarah. Sweet Sarah Rose, who did not deserve any of this pain. *Rose.* The sappy, old lady–sounding middle name Jane had loved with a passion equal to my dislike. But now, of course, I realized why she had fought so hard for the name. A woman named Rose had once been her only comfort on a decidedly bleak day.

"Tom, you ready to move on now?" Dave asked.

"What?"

"Earth to Tom. What were you just thinking?"

"About Sarah," I said, not knowing if I should say anything lest I lose my composure all at once. "Yes, we're moving on."

The stealth with which Mariah moved in and out of the room unnerved me. Somehow she was there again, sitting before the trunk, picking through it with the care of an archeologist. But now, each piece she pulled from it stirred in me great curiosity. I wondered why I had not looked in it before.

Mariah removed a gray box and opened its top. Inside was a dark leather, loose-leaf notebook. Papers and photos peaked out from all sides. A few of these loose documents fell to my living room floor as Mariah opened the old book. She sorted through them slowly, separating a faded yellow piece of paper with a photo taped to it.

"Here she is," she said. "Victoria with her baby. Jane looks about a year old there, wouldn't you say?" she said, handing me the photo of a slender, dark-haired woman in a tailored grey suit. Her face appeared to be looking past the photographer to something off to the side. The child at her side looked expressionless and straight ahead. On the back of the photo in tight black script read, *Me in Texas, smiling at Sam.*

Mariah turned her attention to the folded yellow paper. "It's an article from 1971," she said. "Its title is 'How to Fix a Black Woman's Hair.'"

"So this is Victoria, huh," Dave said, grinning. "She's a looker. Wonder what made her change her look from elegant suit to scooped-neck sweater."

"Clearly, you've never been to a faculty holiday party," I said, recalling the number of my female colleagues who donned corporate attire by day and man-catching outfits by night.

"She dreamed of working as a beauty operator," Mariah offered. "I sense it seemed as important for her as traveling the world is for some. And I'm getting a vision that she was a contradiction. A huge dreamer, but impossibly practical," Mariah said, turning her gaze once again to the picture.

"Children aren't born practical," she said. "Life makes them that way when they are forced to constantly make the best of every situation."

"Is that your opinion or a spirit talking?" I asked.

Mariah shot me a look. I had an obligation, I told myself, not to let my critical thinking skills vanish. I stared at Mariah until her eyes fell shut.

"Victoria Langley, mother of Jane," she whispered. "What will you tell us? How did you come to be so practical and yet so reckless?"

I was certain I saw a shadow cross her face as she spoke.

"I'm seeing the color yellow," Mariah said. "Smoke. Someone is smoking. And I see several men. It's someone's birthday. She wants us to know, what? The day she found a husband."

Her voice trailed off to a different place and then, as if she'd lived in my house for years, she swung her legs onto the sofa and stretched out in a relaxed pose. The photos came to rest against her chest. Her right hand moved to her lips and then away again as she exhaled deeply.

"These men. They have no idea one of them will soon become a husband. But who?"

CHAPTER SEVEN

Fort Worth, Texas — 1963

It's late and she is trying to find a husband. Thought she would have been married by this birthday. That was the goal, wasn't it? The magazine said it was possible.

Tell yourself you will be married by your next birthday and you will be surprised at how quickly your goal is realized. Follow these easy steps.

So she has stayed up tonight with the rest of them, smoking Benson & Hedges and drinking coffee. She has it narrowed down to three candidates now. The men drink beer, which is good for now, although she won't allow it after they are married. But tonight, beer helps them reveal their true selves. What is that expression? *Enter the wine, exit the secrets.* She drinks from her pea-green mug and looks at them, but pretends not to. By her third cup of coffee, the conversation turns to politics, to Kennedy, his views on the war and why he is coming to Texas.

"Does anyone want another beer," she asks in her practiced, wifey voice. Then she blows a puff of smoke into the men's faces, her mouth closing into the perfect round circle.

Victoria Langley is an alluring woman. That she knows it makes her think she is more attractive to the men. Her hair isn't teased like most women's. Instead, she has grown it to her shoulders and brushes it with long strokes each night.

Keeping it long and loose makes you appear obviously attractive. Combine this style with cat-eye glasses to give you a smart, bookish look.

"So you are staying?" one man asks. He is good-looking and works at Carswell Air Force Base, which has made him a good prospect. But he is on, what, his fifth beer? And now he is letting his eyes take a walk across her body. A slow walk.

"For the time being I am staying," she says. "Mrs. Parsley and I have come to an agreement." Mrs. Parsley owns and runs this ramshackle boarding house. The agreement is that she will give her a manicure and do up her hair once a week. All the boarders are men, except one. Except her. She slipped into the male group mostly due to Mrs. Parsley's feelings about cash, which happen to be that she likes it. She likes it in neat envelopes at the beginning of the month. And since most of the men don't have cash, Mrs. Parsley relented and allowed a woman to board, though she worries about Victoria's safety, about the propriety of the arrangement. But what Mrs. Parsley doesn't know is that it is the men who should worry.

In the three months she has been a boarder, she has let different layers of her availability appear. But the process is taking too long, longer than the magazines say it should take. They say she should let each part of her charm and allure peel away ever so slightly. A modern woman should watch movies to learn the techniques of poise and grace.

Tap your cigarette into an ashtray, allowing a red polished fingernail to be displayed. Do not be afraid to express ideas on the state of the world.

She runs a polished finger under the pink and gold choker necklace resting on her slender throat.

A woman can discern a man's level of compassion by reading his response to a story. For example, some article in a newspaper may be helpful.

"Has anyone heard anything in the news lately?" she asks.

"It's all bad," a man named Steve says. "All about the war." Steve is kind, but he is older. Maybe too old. Still, he is a possibility.

"All of it?" she asks. "Isn't there something at least close to home? Something in town?"

"They found a family that was so poor they were sharing one bar of soap," another man offers. His name is Cleveland, and he wears a patch on his shirt that says Cleve. She hasn't decided if she wants to be the wife of a patch-wearing worker. Could she imagine herself ironing over the letters C-L-E-V-E for the rest of her life?

"The family had something like twenty animals living in the house," Cleveland says.

Now she is focusing on how to make smoke rings with each puff of her cigarette, but it is not working. The rings don't look anything like the way Lauren Bacall makes them.

The too-happy lemony color of the kitchen counter and vinyl flooring make her head ache. She leans forward and taps her cigarette into the ashtray. She removes her glasses and sits back, recrossing her legs.

Unlike your mother's generation, today's woman can occasionally say something shrewd and colorful about her past.

"I heard a story at the beauty college," she says. "But it would bore you men."

"No, it wouldn't."

"Tell it. Tell it."

"Yeah, what do you women talk about there anyway?"

"You are making fun of me now," she says, smiling sweetly.

"If you tell the story, you get the last piece of cake," he says. His name is Sam and he has been quiet all evening, nursing one beer for what, an hour? He is in the final three. He keeps to himself and has a strong, tall back and a lantern jaw. Stop-and-stare good looks. She hopes he will be the one. That he doesn't yet know her desire amuses her.

Victoria rises and moves to the counter where she lifts the glass dome from the cake plate. She dips a finger in the lush white icing and licks it off. This is her favorite man trick. Lock. Load. Fire. Leave them slack-jawed.

"This cake?" she asks.

"Yeah, that cake."

"Come on. Sit down."

"Have a beer, Vicky."

"It's a very troubling story, really," she says, sitting back down. "And it really would help to tell someone else. See, it's about my friend. She was crying in the ladies' room today. She told me it was her birthday and about what happened to her on her tenth birthday. She was hurt by this man. And do you know what the family said? They said, why ruin a good man's reputation when the girl will just forget anyway." Victoria puts her hand to her mouth. "I've said too much."

"That's awful."

"There are some real sons of bitches out there. Sorry."

"Incredible."

Maybe if he hadn't come to the house. Uncle Joe, isn't that what they called him? Uncle Joe. But he wasn't really an uncle. He just came out to their house ever summer like the rest of them. Every summer people came like a migration of birds. You could count on it. But they didn't come to see her or her father. They came for the view and the beach and what they could eat.

The day had started well, hadn't it? It was her birthday and she got a new fishing pole from her father. She had been fishing out by the jetty. Uncle Joe had greeted her and complimented her skills.

"I used to fish quite a bit. Never as good as you," Uncle Joe had said. "But you know what's a really hard fish to catch? A tickle fish."

That was when he began to chase and tickle her. He had done it the year before, maybe the year before that, too. She had tossed and turned that night on top of her quilt, an old, worn design with pieced fabric laid out to form fans in mostly greens and purples.

She had her eyes closed but felt uncomfortable and restless.

When a crack of light sprayed into her room, she played opossum, keeping herself still with eyes shut tight. Her father coming to kiss her goodnight? But then the slit of light vanished and she felt the weight of a body lying next to her, smelled the scent of stale beer on his breath.

"Play dead lion with your Uncle Joe," she heard him say before it began.

She tearfully told her father, of course, but he dismissed her account of the rape as a story, a fantasy. So she begged and pleaded and spoke facts a young girl should not know until she could see in his face that he believed her. But then, her father, what a louse, talked to his sister and parents. They all agreed silence would make things clean. She overheard that exact phrase. Silence would make things clean. Clean!

"What did you tell your friend at the beauty college," Cleveland asks.

"What could I say?" she says. "Happy Birthday?"

The kind of man her father was, what a louse, wasn't he? Ruled by fear. Fear of the world. Fear of taking a stand. Fear of venturing more than a mile from his house. Barely eking out a living building the odd bookcase, repairing the clapboards on houses, designing picnic tables. You would have thought this would make him strong, but no, it was just the opposite.

And he was odd. He embarrassed her around her friends. Or, if she had friends who came around, she would have been embarrassed because he kept a damned stuffed monkey in the house. A stuffed dead monkey! It sat right by the front door. Its beady eyes were black and deep, like it still had some life left in it. Like it was looking at you and wanted to speak. And the way it was posed, like a soldier called to attention. Its name was Marzipan, that's what she was told to call it like it was a pet or something. Marzipan! A name she heard spoken by her entire family as if he was a relative.

To hear him talk, the monkey was smarter than half of the people her father knew. Even her mother, because didn't he complain to the dead stuffed monkey that her mother caused her own death.

"Where was the mother when this happened?" Sam asks.

"The mother," Victoria says. "She died when my friend was one. A car accident in winter. She lost a toe and her mother died or something. But it's no big deal, though. She said it saves on nail polish. Isn't that funny?"

All she knows was that the car slid off the road into an icy embankment and was discovered three days later with the mother and one-year-old child huddled together. Her mother was dead and stiff, the infant alive and shivering. Frostbite claimed a toe on her left foot. In her imagination, her mother's frozen arms encircled her, keeping her alive.

She likes to imagine that her mother told her stories, poured all the advice into her little ear that she would have doled out across an entire lifetime. Wouldn't that have been nice, having a mother's advice instead of a magazine's?

Her father, what a louse, he never said anything about the missing toe. Never a kind word. And not even a single picture of her mother in the house. Not one. And then there was the time she had spied her aunt kissing her father on the lips. The lips! And not long after, the aunt went and killed herself. And it was about this time her father started calling her names. *Victidiot* was his favorite. He thought he was so clever, didn't he? What a louse.

The men stare at the floor like scolded boys. They haven't touched their beers. It is only Sam who looks at her in quick glances as he peels the beer label from his now empty bottle.

Victoria feels the men's tension, but she can't be sure if the silence shows compassion or not. Probably not. Her father, what a louse, was always silent and what did that reveal about him? She once made a list.

Lacks courage
Thoughtless and crude
Unsuitable for love

Thank God he is still in Cape Cod where she left him. Far away, but not really far enough. How many years ago? She was seventeen and never looked back. Stole money for the bus, tossed Marzipan in the trash and took off.

"I guess this is my cake," she says sweetly, rising to take her reward. "Thanks gentlemen."

"Thanks."

"Don't go now."

"What are we going to talk about tomorrow? Jesus!"

Victoria puts the cake on a plate and excuses herself from the men to go to her small room with its aged twin bed where she lies down, still in her waitress uniform. She looks at the clock. Just a few more hours until she must wake, go to the beauty college and then to her long shift at the diner.

Victoria slides off her shoes, looks at her damaged foot and thinks what she's always thought. The space where a toe should be is the only real reminder of her mother. And is something that's missing a reminder? She will write that question down later. Maybe ask the men at breakfast. See what their sober response is before she chooses a final candidate.

After the business with Uncle Joe, she had been at the breakfast table the next morning with her father, what a louse. She silently shuffled her eggs into the ugly fruit border of her plate, his voice haunting her thoughts.

Play dead lion with your Uncle Joe.

She had a hard time getting it out. She asked her father if she could speak to him privately outside. He said she could say anything. Anything at all in front of those uninvited guests. Yes, all of them! So she finally gets it out in small bursts of words.

Uncle Joe … my room … touched me and I don't know …

He shouted a look that she was a liar. A liar! His looks said as much. Then he had the nerve to say she invented this story like many others. That everyone else should stay and enjoy their breakfast. That she should get out of his sight and stop bringing shame onto the family. So out she went and walked along the beach letting the warm water flow across her toes. Her nine toes. And by the time she returned, Uncle Joe was getting into his car with his one packed bag. He winked at her just before he climbed behind the wheel. Winked at her!

Victoria undresses down to her bra and underwear, slides on a soft pink robe and climbs into bed, the cake plate by her side. She pulls a magazine from her bedside table and skims through it as she eats the sugary icing in small, quick nibbles.

Happy Birthday to me.

There is a knock at her door. She hopes it is him. She knows it is him.

"Victoria?"

"Come in."

He opens the door. "Is it okay?"

She pats the space beside her on the bed.

"You have kind eyes," she says. "I'll bet you wouldn't let anything bad happen to someone you love."

"Don't think too much of me."

"Well, what is the worst thing you have done? Tell me now so that everything else will pale."

She hopes he is in her net. There are holes big enough for him to escape, to swim through easily, but he doesn't move. He sits there and gives her a slight smile.

"Okay," he says. "I have a hard time keeping a job."

"Why?"

"I get angry when people don't follow directions."

Victoria thinks on this admission and she reads it as compassion and vulnerability, the two qualities that make for the best husband.

"So what about you, Vicky?"

"What you don't know about me could fill up a book," she says.

"I'm pretty sure I know enough."

Then Sam looks down the length of the bed. Toward her legs. Her feet. Her toes.

"Don't feel sorry for me."

"I feel things for you, but sorry isn't one of them."

She runs her fingertips over his ear, brushing a bit of blonde hair away from his face. At the beauty school, they will be learning to cut men's hair in the coming weeks. She'll cut Sam's shorter after they are married.

Yes, she thinks, he is the one.

CHAPTER EIGHT

2:30 a.m.

I could see now that the force of a deceased presence took a toll on Mariah's own spirit. She excused herself and went outside. Dave made notes while I tried to remember times Jane had spoken to me about her mother. Two occasions came to mind: at our wedding and after her miscarriage. Never around the birth of the twins. Of course, she told me she had died and I didn't inquire further. Now, I wondered why I hadn't at least asked how she had died. Perhaps it would have led to more revelations. Perhaps I had started to ask Jane and she had distracted me with sexual innuendo in the playful way she always did when she wanted to change the topic. In retrospect, the rarified time during our courtship when we discussed our parents was interview-like. They were the details we said just to get them out of the way, checked off the list and on to deeper things, or as I now realized, to get her into bed.

"So, where did you grow up?" I had asked.

"Texas. You?"

"Me, too. My parents live in Houston."

"Mine are dead. My mother when I was young."

"I'm sorry. Do you have any siblings?"

"No. There was just me and the occasional pet."

"Have you always wanted to be a nurse?"

"Always. How about you? Always a teacher?"

"One of the advantages to this occupation is that I get to tell others what I think. So, yes."

"I like to travel, don't you?"

"I'd like to say yes, but the truth is the only time I don't want to go home is when I'm already there."

"Where do you see yourself living in five years?"

"I'm licensed in Texas so, why don't we stay here?"

"We? I like where your mind is going."

After the miscarriage, she mentioned her mother in such a low voice that I had to ask her to repeat it.

"My mother would have wondered why I was so attached to an unborn child," she had said one night while making dinner.

"Who?"

"My mother. She would have told me to just get over it."

"Gee, that's pretty insensitive."

"You had to know her. She was good at letting go of things. And I should get over it. I should just move on. We have Sarah and Simon."

"We'll try again." I hugged her close.

"I don't want to try again, Tom. I'm just telling you now. I don't think I could."

"We don't have to decide anything now."

"You're not listening. No trying again." And she shook loose of my hug and turned back to the kitchen sink.

"You talked to that therapist, right?"

"He just said we should get a shared hobby."

"A shared hobby? Is that all he said?"

"A little bit of nonsense about how I shouldn't take the loss personally and that it happens to many people and I am not alone. A bunch of stuff I already know."

"I know."

"But a shared hobby. I've been thinking about it and it sounds like a good idea," she said finally.

I thought maybe it would be something like cooking or sailing or fishing, jogging even. Garage-sale hunting as a hobby never crossed my mind. But over months of spousal bonding via shopping, I found there was much to learn about my spouse. For example, garage sale aficionados like Jane are a talented mix of hunters and gatherers. The truly good ones are about as devoted as Marines, knowing they will reap success if they are the first to land and the last to leave.

Jane's instructions were clear. Show up before the sale opens. Don't be afraid to bargain or get physical if you really want something. A conversational knowledge of Spanish is imperative. Wear comfortable shoes.

We did find bargains that were useful—the double Adirondack lawn chair, an old light fixture I rewired and hung in the kitchen, clothes for the twins, a gas grill. Jane loved anything that had been used by others. It gave her the opportunity to imagine the lives they had lived. She made up stories about the people who sat at yard sales, watching their possessions, clothing, dishes, old appliances, being examined by strangers. She pulled me into the story-telling game too, making it the part of the experience that most closely resembled a "shared hobby."

"Who sells a clown head? And where's the rest of it?" Jane had asked.

"But that lady bought it. Did you see her? You would have thought she'd found a first edition Hemingway," I gossiped back.

"I've seen her at other sales," Jane had said, while admiring the new teacup set she had just bought. "Maybe she has the rest of the body at home and is now going to piece it together."

"Wasn't that an old *Twilight Zone* episode?"

And so it went. Her garage sale phase. It seemed to pull her back into orbit. I was a compliant companion, but after a while, as the junk from other people's lives piled up in our garage, it became a point of contention. After our last big argument, she stopped shopping. I came home one Friday to find that a sale was going on in our garage. She had smiled at me and said the Zoloft was cheaper. We laughed.

Only next the Home Shopping Channel became a part of our lives. Old junk was replaced by new junk until there was no corner of the house not filled with it. Because it was nearing the due date of the miscarried baby, I let it pass. I had given up trying to argue with her about it, believing it was a phase that would go away on its own. And it did, of course. I sold all of it after Simon's death and let the proceeds dent the huge credit card debt she had amassed. In the newspapers, no one mentioned the financial typhoon that follows tragedy. But wouldn't that be what young Jane called a whole 'nother story?

I smiled at the vision of her again, ten years old, overall-clad, pining away for time to read forbidden books. With Victoria for a mother, Jane could not have helped but be precocious, perhaps calculating, setting a time-line for finding a husband, seeking out and discarding male candidates without their knowledge, all the while having such a dim view of the opposite sex.

Impossibly, I was forming a connection between Victoria and Jane, allowing myself to see the pair of them in concert as mother and daughter tried to make it through the world, trekking down alleys in search of furniture or painting each other's toes. I wanted a drink in the worst way. If I was going to bend my mind to these fantasies, at least, I thought, I could blame it on the booze.

I started toward the kitchen hoping I could find a forgotten bottle of Vodka in the back of the freezer. I stopped when I saw Mariah at the bay window that fronted our house. Her appearance surprised me as I hadn't heard the screen door squeak open. In the pale light, her features were softened and I thought I detected something familiar about the curve of her jaw. Was there some small resemblance in the shape of it?

"Shhh. Do you hear that?" she asked softly.

"What?"

"The water? I can hear the water."

I had never heard the water from this house, and I didn't really think it was possible. Then again, most of the hours I had spent there involved alcohol and TV. If the house next door had caught fire, I would likely have missed it. Perhaps ocean waves could be heard from this distance.

"It was a cold day when he died," she whispered. "He was thinking about her, mourning her, really. Shaming himself for calling her a liar."

"Who are we talking about?" Dave asked, looking up from his notes.

"Horace Langley. Victoria's father. I'm getting an image of water. I can hear it. Close enough as if it's on his feet."

It was then I noticed she was holding something that resembled a child's toy. It was a monkey, stuffed, its fur matted with age. She started to breathe so heavily that I put my hand to her.

"Wait," Dave warned. "She's traveling."

She began her next story in choppy, short breaths. "I feel air. Lack of air. Images of water. Something metal. Death and cold."

CHAPTER NINE

Cape Cod — 1975

The cold feeling washes over Horace that today will be the last day of his life.

He is right.

It isn't just the infirmities of old age, though they are circling the wagon. The bladder is no longer reliable. The teeth are chalk. The lungs are living on canned air. He knows it because the devil whispers dark memories in his ears all day, making him unable to enjoy the approach of the reaper in ways he imagines most do.

"Why did I listen to my father?" he asks to no one. He feels the futility of no one hearing his questions, of no one listening, but pushes on anyway. Some things must be said, if only to himself. "No one will mourn me for any reason. It is as if I didn't exist."

Whispers continue and Horace shakes his head. He doesn't like to remember that day, yet he can still hear his father's voice with the intensity of a thunderbolt. The day when he leaned on his father's unwise wisdom.

She is a child. She will forget it. Why ruin the reputation of a fine doctor?

He has spent the day sitting in front of the bay window in his old cape house, watching the ships round the lighthouse. At least, he thinks they are ships, as his eyes no longer have the power they once did. Alone, he tries without success to shrug off the past images and voices that seem to be more memorable now than yesterday's breakfast. The ones that center on the women he has loved and hated.

Horace has been confined to a wheelchair for two years, held down against his will by failing lungs, sentenced to a life that is not quite death, but nearly so. Part of the tether is the oxygen tank by his side, connected to him through the tubes flowing from his nose, taped against that fleshy part of his face where the robust mustache of his youth once was. The tank is his only companion. He wanted a dog to pet, but his wife said no. To spite her, he had made a friend of his air tank, which he called Frank. Frank the tank. His one joy is that he has insisted she address it as Frank as well.

He knows his last breath is out there, stalking toward him, but he continues to struggle through the time, telling Frank about the ships coming in, the white and red lighthouse and how he read in an article it is now so much like himself, slowly slipping into the sea, crumbling under its own weight, an inch nearer doom each year.

He remembers something happy. He had kissed a girl there, had dodged the round beam spraying its guiding light from shore to sea. He remembers brushing the golden blonde wisps of hair away from her chin and mouth and how near her face had been to his. The well of excitement spread from his stomach to his throat, catching him at the knees as their lips touched. When they merged, he could have sworn he tasted the color pink.

"Frank," he says in a tired, scratchy breath. "I can see her now. My first wife. My first love. I wonder if her eyes would look the same. You can't dim that color of blue. If you can, there is no God."

Frank sits in silence except for the great pants of oxygen he steadily gives over to Horace.

"To go there once more," Horace continues, "to feel the sand in my toes. Can't manage that, the wife says. The old biddy." Why, he wonders, when he is long past being able to force his will on his wife, has she become so much more concerned with the quality of his living death.

"She would think it too much a hassle to fetch my body from out there," he says. "To her, I'm just another chore. And of course, she is right. I am of no use, Frank. None at all."

He is certain she wants him dead for the house. She has said almost as much when he, pretending to be asleep, overheard her talking to her sister on the phone. But on that point he refuses to agree, mustering the last crumbs of passionate argument he can still rouse. Sunset-View should stay in the family. The old lady would surely sell it and the one good thing he could leave his daughter would vanish.

"I want my Vicky to have it, Frank," Horace says. "I know. You don't have to say it. These walls mean something different to her. Still, it should be her choice. Maybe use the money for the child."

As Horace dozes off, memories flood his mind. All of them came here for the summer, pretended to be a happy family, but it wasn't pretend for him. Not at the time anyway. His trunk, full of pressed clothes, was sent ahead by train. Hannah's things, his twin's things, were stuffed in a brown paper bag she was forced to carry. His mother stayed inside, alone, while his father led the race out to the water, teasing them to try and see France across the sea. Then, the family and friends joined in the long summer days of lobsters and beer.

Vicky, if she is coming, should be here by now, he thinks, even if the trip from Texas is long. It has been a week or more. The wife went on and on about his being on his deathbed. If that doesn't bring her quickly, or at all, what will? And then he remembers that, in this family, members either act impulsively or not at all.

"Examples? You want examples, Frank?" he says, finding his heartbeat racing ahead of his words. "I could give you many. Stories I wasn't even supposed to know. Things I should perhaps not have seen. But I was the worst. The worst. I cannot even speak of it. And then there was the wife. Being widowed, I wanted a new mother, any mother, for my daughter, who seemed beyond my understanding. After the Uncle Joe incident was swept tidily under the rug, it seemed right that she have a woman nearby."

Victoria lived in a constant state of impetuousness. How many times had she acted oddly, her habits strange? Her attachment to magazines was unusual—she'd shut herself in her closet to read them by flashlight. Sometimes she stole money from me to buy them. And then there was her lack of ambition of any sort, her fascination with Texas. But what was odd, really? The way she preferred being alone, or the way she could have tireless fits of screaming just as she would wake?

"Perhaps she was ill-off the day she was born, Frank. Maybe it was wrong to give her my mother's name. Still, that's no way for a young lady to behave."

He had, in fact, named her after his mother to please her. It hadn't worked. It had been Hannah's idea to do it, as she was always looking for that crack in her mother's hardness through which she might be able to crawl in.

"Name her Susannah Victoria," my sister Hannah had said. "It will honor mother."

The sound of a pot crashing against the kitchen floor jars him awake. Frank sighs. Horace moves his hand to pet the cool metal to see if he is still alive.

"Perhaps if Hannah and I had disappeared like those other unwanted babies … But what choice do any of us have in the matter of being born? Still, I heard mother and father arguing about babies, about us, as if there was still a choice, as if we were not yet born. She complained that two was too much. Father shouted about all the … what did he call them? … 'abbreviated pregnancies' she'd had before he made her keep us. Said it had gone on long enough, this disposing of her insides for convenience, and that she had to keep this one. But there was never another one. Not after us."

He runs the cuff of his shirt sleeve across his chin. It comes away damp from his own drool. He longs to talk to his daughter. He wants to tell her that time plus tragedy always equal comedy. He read that somewhere, maybe in a fortune cookie.

"I listened to my father," he says. "He said that children forget things. He said it was best. That it would ruin a reputation." Horace wipes his face. "But I should have known better. Children don't forget. Hannah didn't forget."

A steely chill washes over him as he calls up the day his mother had tried to rid herself of Hannah for good.

They were at a carnival, their mother weaving between tables lined with neat rows of jewelry. The whole place smelled of hay and defecation. They were there because his father had a stall where he demonstrated the talents of his trained monkeys. His other children, their mother called them. There were freaks and performers in every corner—the fat lady, the hermaphrodites, the man with three arms. And two five-year-olds walked through the maze with astonished delight then begged their mother to see the snake man up close until she relented.

"Someone needs to stay with me," she had declared in the same impatient voice she used when there was to be no argument. "So you must go one at a time. Race, you go first. Hannah will wait with me."

He watched the two shiny coins bounce in his palm. Without a backward glance, he darted inside the red velvet tent, losing himself in the excitement of it all.

"When I returned to mother, Frank," Horace says with uneasy breath, "Hannah was gone. So I said, 'where is Hannah?' and she just looked at me as if I had asked her how the earth was made. It was hateful the way she treated Hannah all the time. And because I was weak, and didn't want to lose the tender place she reserved for me, I stayed silent. Not even a whisper. Silent. And now I am dying and there is so much to say and no one to listen. But for you, Frank."

Horace cries until it turns into a sobbing cough and holds onto Frank with one hand for balance.

Later at home, a policeman had come to the door, Hannah's timid face peeking out from behind the leg of his dark blue uniform. The officer was angry, that much was clear. He talked to father in low whispers. My mother stood with no expression, neither sadness nor alarm.

"Father sent us upstairs, Frank, but I went to stand at the head of the stairs and listened as best I could, hoping the voices would grow louder when the officer had gone. But the door closed and my parents seemed to say nothing. So then I hoped Hannah would fill in the missing pieces later. But she never did, and I was left with not so much as a rumor of what mother had done with her that day.

"Much had changed, though. Mother displayed less affection to our father, she stopped calling me by my pet name, and Hannah was often put in too hot baths until her skin reddened, if she was bathed at all. She found hiding places away from our mother that even I didn't know existed. And this went on until mother seemed to forget she had a daughter at all. It soon became an understanding between twins that Hannah would have preferred to stay lost.

"When it was much too late to save Hannah, I learned bits of the truth from my dying father. Perhaps he, too, was staring down death and looking across the landscape of his life. He was typically a quite positive person, this much I know from having read his diaries. He loved my mother, but it hadn't been enough. Hannah was without blemish. Her heart-shaped face glowed, finely framed by her dark hair. Her eyes were pale and clear. Because she was the mirror image of mother, or what mother should have looked like without the deep scars and pocks across her face, she was hated."

Death is so near, Horace can feel the steadily approaching rattle. His coughs strain the tubes connected to Frank and he claws at each breath as his lungs fill.

"My first wife, God rest her soul, she would have been a wonderful mother to Victoria, Frank. Damn her for leaving us. She would take us to the lighthouse, Frank. She would have given me a dog," he says.

He sees a new ship out in the bay, coming toward the lighthouse, and wonders what she carries. The surface of the sea is stirring with whitecaps and he thinks it must accompany a cool wind blowing off the coast. The way it had when he was young and in love, when life stretched out before him.

"If nothing else, Frank," he says weakly, "do you suppose the wind never changes? If everything else does, don't you think it's possible wind is the one true thing now as it was then?"

"Horace, dear, are you awake? There is a telegram from Vicky."

She stands at the door, at his back. He can see her bony reflection in the window. The very shrill of her voice irritates him. He hates when she addresses him with a false endearment for they have never been "dear" to each other.

His wife pauses and gives him the letter.

He waits for her to shuffle off in her old, dingy green house shoes, glad she will not be witness to his tears. He doesn't have to read his daughter's message to know he won't see her again. It likely bears a similar response to other letters she sent to him. *Stop contacting me! Do you understand? Can I be any more clear? I want nothing from you. I won't give you the satisfaction of saying I hate you. Hate is just the other side of love and I won't give you even that. Ever.*

He crumples the sealed letter and drops it to the floor. If only he had not taken his father's advice it might read differently. *Dearest Father, I was so happy to hear from you and will be at your side as soon as I can. Love, Victoria.*

But he knows why. He had known better, despite his anger at

seeing her flirt with Dr. Joe. It seemed to him then she might have brought it on herself. That Hannah had endured much in silence. That young girls forget and Victoria would, too.

"But she didn't forget, Frank. And I have nothing left of her. I don't even remember what she looked like the last time I saw her. All my memory will allow is the image of her as she sat at the breakfast table, silently moving her scrambled eggs over the yellow plates with the fruit border, hunched over like a timid dog, trying to look invisible. The way Hannah would look when I tried to coax her from a hiding spot."

And now, death is coming fast. He feels it settling down about him like a thick fog. No amount of remembered regret will stall it further.

So he rolls his chair toward the traveling trunk which bears his initials on its side. Frank drags obediently behind him, letting out heavy hisses of air as Horace strains to open the lid. He finds his father's favorite monkey, Marzipan, rescued from the trash after Victoria left home, still with the same knowing expression he had in life.

It is difficult now, dragging Frank still more, clutching Marzipan, and heading toward the small desk. But he does so and pens Jane a letter, telling her to be kind to her mother, that her grandmother was a darling woman, that her aunt Hannah would have loved to know her, that her mother Victoria has the family necklace of pink and gold beads from England and that she is to make sure Jane receives it one day, that the trunk and all of its contents are hers to do with as she wishes, and that the house on the Cape is hers as well. He wants to write that he loves her, he wants it to be true, but he doesn't know her. He has never met her, not even a picture has been exchanged. So he cries and performs the final act of his life. He seals the letter with a dry kiss, hoping it will be enough.

CHAPTER TEN

3:30 a.m.

I stood over the old gas stove in the kitchen, waiting for the tea water to boil and my nerves to settle. The first time I heard the definition of "failure to protect" charges, I was at a loss. How could you fail to protect someone if you weren't present when they needed protection?

But then there was Horace. And Vicky. And Dr. Joe. And I finally understood a measure of the charge against me. It is so easy to see the wrong in others before we recognize it in ourselves.

Could it be that the prosecution needed look no further than Horace Langley for a precedent-setting example of failure to protect? Still worse, failure to acknowledge? Horace's denial of Dr. Joe's abuse could have been equivalent to my failure to protect my children from a mother's psychotic snap. Again, was there any guide for how to live, how to deal, after the fact?

I let the fantastical ideas unravel into a full-blown scene in my courtroom. My jury. My judge. The prosecution strolling right to the front with the evidence of that one time, that one moment, when I experienced denial and looked away, then, freeze-frame and pull in tight on Tom Nelson and his complacency. I shout to the judge, *Have mercy on me! I couldn't see Jane that way. You wouldn't have either!*

Retrocoging through time was not yet producing the so-called psychological benefits Dave had promised. Sure, I was beginning to embrace the notion that a meager few of Mariah's facts might have a grain of credibility. Through Mariah, both Victoria and Horace recounted how the same event had effectively blackened their relationship. But a part of me, the ever skeptical part, questioned whether the handling of the Uncle Joe incident had not been embellished by memory over the years. If nothing else, Victoria had shown herself to be as inventive as she was manipulative. And Horace's guilt over failing to protect his sister could have co-mingled with his inadequate handling of his daughter's abuse.

Fortunately, the steam from Mariah's mystery tea had a calming effect, and I decided for the moment to stall my mind. Glancing at the clock, I told myself the late hour was confusing me. For now, my ambivalence toward both Victoria and Horace, real or fictional, was justified. After all, he seemed to have lived a miserable life, vised between his mother and his daughter, weakened by parental models of inaction. How could he have seen the truth until the very end?

Mariah's visit to Horace on the last day of his life showed better than Dante what a pre-death purgatory may look like for the modern man, a place where you are forced to shore up the rationales for your behavior, a waiting room where you must sort out the misdeeds of your mother. I was at risk of getting too Freudian, maybe even too *Frontellian*. This was a philosophical concept I might have perused if, in the process of filling my mug, I had not dropped the boiling kettle.

Grabbing a clutch of kitchen towels, I mopped up the mess. I saw a small pink ball underneath the refrigerator. It was Sarah's. Picking it up, I was overcome by a further rush of psychological what-ifs. What if this chapter in her life impacted Sarah negatively when she became a mother? How could it not? What if I learned more oddities in Jane's family and subconsciously assigned those qualities to Sarah, pre-judging her personality, waiting for her to abandon or neglect someone important? Time to stuff the genie back in the bottle, send Mariah on her way.

Biology is destiny.

No, Tom, Sarah isn't all Jane. Her DNA owes half of itself to me and my family. Right then, hearing Sarah's voice would have been the only calming balm, if only to lay claim to her by hearing her call me Daddy.

I threw the dish towel down and laid my palm on the telephone. I dialed the number and let it ring once then hung up. It would have been selfish and desperate. She would still be asleep, of course, curled up in the bed that had once been mine, safe in my mother's house.

Perhaps if I could look into my own family, my own set of objects of the deceased, I might find a fair stack of interesting misery. What I would pay to see my mother's face if I suddenly showed up on her doorstep with Mariah and asked her to hand over Grandma's diamond brooch, so I could learn how she was treated as a child.

As I tossed the pink ball from hand to hand, I wondered if Sarah still had enough child in her to be resilient, yet enough maturity to comprehend. She knew Simon was dead. She had attended his funeral and the burial, run her hands over his name on his headstone. She understood mommy was in a hospital. She had never talked to me about the day of the drowning. The therapists agreed she would speak of it when she was ready. She had never asked about her dog Ricky. I could not be certain, however, I was capable of understanding the part of her who had lost her twin. Hearing Horace and Hannah's story, I accepted as much. It must be as though some part of you had gone ahead without leaving so much as a note. Only Simon could make her understand some things.

Mariah rounded the corner then, finding me slumped on the damp floor. She recovered the tea kettle, refilled it and placed it on the stove.

"That was the monkey, wasn't it?" I asked. "The one you were holding. That was the one he was holding when he died."

"Yes, I believe it was."

"You'd think having a stuffed monkey would have come up in a conversation with your wife. *By the way, dear, did you know this taxidermed little primate used to be my grandfather's friend, Marzipan."*

"Unless she read all the journals in the trunk, she wouldn't have known its significance," she said, smiling at me warmly. "I will make you something to eat. My mother used to say that we can understand things better on a full stomach."

"I'm sorry," I said. "I've been so self-absorbed, I haven't considered what a strain this is for you. Why don't you go home and rest?"

"I understand that getting information very quickly is important for your case," she said, pulling things from the refrigerator. "And there's something about the next generation of her family. I already have a powerful sense it will be useful to you."

"How can you tell?"

"It is the natural dance of generations, don't you think? That events will come full circle?"

Dave entered the kitchen before I could ask her what she meant. He was studying his legal pad, not showing the slightest trace of fatigue. Even his shirt still looked pressed and neat. "Are we cooking something?"

"Eggs," Mariah replied.

"How very symmetrical of you, Mariah," he said.

I shot him a quizzical look.

"Eggs for Victoria," he said. "Fruit bordered plates."

I ran my hand behind my neck thinking how single-minded Dave was at all times. It was either a gift or a curse and likely the cause of his having three ex-wives. If my future life did not include a jail cell, I intended to make a friend of Dave just to witness him in an encounter with a formidable woman. Somehow I knew the single-mindedness would still be to his advantage with the opposite sex.

"What do you make of Horace's story?" I asked. "Besides the egg factor?"

"Clearly, Horace's mother had a preference for one twin," he said. "It's possible if the jury hears that story, they will make the connection to Sarah's survival."

My face must have shown my displeasure at this particular point because Dave quickly interrupted.

"It's a conjecture, Tom, not a certainty," he said with a paternal authority. "As I understand it, we are to next delve into the story of Horace's parents. So the jury is out, so to speak, until we learn more about their lives."

We ate scrambled eggs in silence, the teakettle's whistle the only interruption. After we filled our mugs, we returned to the living room and surrounded the trunk once more. It was then I caught a glimpse of the faded stenciled initials on its side. H.L. *Horace Langley.*

"Here is our next piece," Mariah announced. "Jane's great grandfather's journal. There are entries, drawings, notes on scientific experiments. Somewhere in there is the story of his wife, Susannah."

She handed me the heavy leather journal. It was as thick as an encyclopedia and almost as weighty. I flipped through its yellowed pages and as I did so, they gave off the aged, buttery scent I loved about old books. The handwriting was neat, the letters uniform, and I would have liked to study it in a context other than searching for the reasonable doubt Dave said we needed to ensure my freedom.

"Life, not inheritance, made Susannah bitter," she said. "I feel she is a fork. Two paths. One event. Everything turned on a few seconds for her. He tried to save her, mend her, love her. But she refused, tragically."

I handed the journal to Dave, and as he paged through it, I looked at the sofa and stared into the brilliant, black, dead eyes of the stuffed monkey we presumed was Marzipan. His presence made me uncomfortable, but I said nothing. What could I say? *Please remove that disturbing primate held in the clutch of the dying man who overlooked sexual abuse perpetrated on my might-have-been mother-in-law who abandoned Jane?*

"So, on to Horace's parents then," I said, shaking off the dizzying thoughts.

"In a manner of speaking," Mariah said. "I believe Charles' story has parallels to Jane's."

Dave and I settled in. We watched for a transformation to fall over Mariah's face as she held the journal in her lap. Her introduction of Susannah into this genealogical mix was so enthralling, I felt a bit guilty for being entertained, so I was relieved when Mariah began to speak at last. She held the leather diary in her hands, opened it to the first page and closed her eyes.

"The journals of Charles Langley. Husband of Susannah. Father to Horace and Hannah. Grandfather of Victoria. Great grandfather of Jane. May these words continue to give us insight and guide us to understanding."

And so, with a heavy rain beating down outside, our great genealogical experiment continued into a stormy morning.

CHAPTER ELEVEN

Chicago — 1895

October 5

Here I continue to document my progress, following journal number 43. Continue citations on the experiments with helper monkeys. My curiosities in the divide between science and faith. Other notes that may prove useful to securing knowledge for future experiments. Lila is ready after six months of concentrated training. Specialty is grooming and fetching.

To-day smells are shifting in the laboratory. It is a strange alchemy—gases, chemicals, the dank odor of stale air, monkey cages. I wish to learn more about the olfactory nature of the chimps. Mother says these scents will always be familiar, that they were part of my pre-natal existence as I was born in a laboratory. I am amazed at the ways my nose can stand this olfactory assault and yet, if they have been part of my life always, why is this so? And, other experiments with perfumes, hair dyes, shoe polishes, snake oils, fresh cut lumber and the occasional small rodent. All the various experiments being carried out here now by our handful of new thinkers from the East.

October 7

Received word of interest from a New England science journal yester-day. They intend to consider two of my articles on monkey research and development. A new career?

October 10

About to turn twenty. Mother's promise to tell me more about her life before, my father and his fate. Her illness grows with each day and I have caught her preparing little notes about what she wants to tell me. Here's what I can deduce thus far from a few stolen glimpses:

Born in London

Father dead at my birth

Named after friend of mother's

Her family left behind in England: origins unknown

She suggests my profile regal. Looked in the mirror sideways and performed a self-portrait. Straight line of nose, dark hair, ample lip. A royal birthright of a father who didn't know I existed? Perhaps because of her illness, she is convinced there was a great romance between her and my father. A woman's hysteria? What I am to do with this, I do not know. From experiments in primate breeding, I understand male and female, if, of strong disposition, breed the most successful offspring.

I have only ever known her, and our monkey, Marzipan. With the increase in articles I have generated, publishers request a full author biography. Possible solution: with no family that I know of, may I compose one to my liking, one that does not depend on mother's fantastical suggestions?

October 12

As I now have the benefit of making presentations to potential prospects, I am thankfully free to spend time outside the laboratory. Made sketches yester-day of the new buildings. Rough sketch of the newly completed Reliant Building on Washington Street. To my thinking, it is by far the most elaborate decoration of the city. The papers say it will be a beacon to Chicago.

Mother continues her talk about my having a family. Laboratory is not conducive to these plans. Sufficient for me and mother, but when I acquire a wife, she says, I must think out the possibilities of where else to live. A regular house that does not sit over one's labor. Move from the city?

October 15

To-day, a successful campaign with Marzipan the third. Like his predecessor, this creature knows much I cannot understand about sensing the needs of others. His performance for the prospects was flawless. He can put a straw between one's lips, wipe a drooling mouth, brush a gentleman's hair as gently as a mother strokes an infant's cheek. And though I have grown up with these animals, they do not cease to impress. Note: include this demonstration in next article submission.

October 31

It would not be rash to suggest that events of to-day may have changed my life. I had a prospective suitor for a two-year-old chimp named Lila. Our increase in genuine interest has risen since showing at the World's Fair. Previous prospects have included a great many of the curious, people who seek to find out if the rumors were true, and if so, how they can find what has been dubbed in many city circles as "the monkey myth."

The introductions are the same as last year. Introduce the would-be owners to a trained chimp. The chimp helps demonstrate the myriad uses and benefits of the companion monkey. Here is where I have found a quality as a natural salesman. I have practiced in front of a long mirror at home, polishing phrasing and gestures, promoting the practical virtues of beast-servant over man-servant.

Note: This speech has the best effect.

"Primates can never quit on you and do not expect to be rewarded on holidays. With no family to tend in the evenings, they will never be a bother with asking for time away from your loved one. Tell them your secrets and they will be locked forever in a vault. The able primate asks only for your respect and companionship in return. A bargain, at any price."

With this speech in mind, I walked into the city streets with the chimp, Lila, in tow, confident that I would soon part with her.

Passed through streets filled with vendors and newspaper hawkers, Lila concealed under a cloth. My destination was Saint John Castius, the great beer-colored Catholic Church with its many steps leading into a narrow opening and door at its top. It has always appeared to me like a funnel, and equal in beauty to the modern structures. Note: make sketch.

The church rises in the Polish part of town, a very lively place. As I completed the walk to the top step, something made me turn and look back. There I saw a different view of the city, one that captured the senses, making the mounting of the steps the reward. To my left, the great buildings rose out of noise and steam and smoke. To the right, I saw the Chicago River with whiffs of white watery peaks lifted by the chilly wind. I am lucky to own more than one coat.

The great oak door opened and a couple bundled against the weather emerged. Inside the interior fanned out, bathed in reds and blues and hints of other colors desperate to be noticed. I have been told that the current priest is in charge of decorating, gathering paintings and so forth. All in all, a departure from the structured world being erected just outside.

Down the center aisle, my vision was drawn to a stained-glass arrow, pointing heavenward. At the sides of the church I noted the confessionals. I had no idea I would soon be eavesdropping on the city's sinners. Who can foretell what any day holds?

I carried Lila, who was thankfully silent, toward the front of the church, where a priest directed me to a side door, opened it and asked me to wait. The small room appeared to be a simple office. A desk, a lamp, a tattered black leather chair. More stained glass dotted the exterior walls.

Lila began to stir and, thinking it best to let her release some energy before the presentation, I let her into the room, only to have her skillfully open a narrow door down in the corner which led to a closet filled with what I believed were the vestments. A changing room? That was when I heard the sound of weeping and whispered words, noting that the closet's proximity to the confessional was an indiscreet choice as it allowed me to pause and listen.

"Father," a woman's voice said. "I have tried. No one wants me."

"Perhaps a relative you could go to, my child."

"No money to make the trip, Father. No one cares. If I were to disappear inside the convent, they would no longer be burdened."

"I will continue to pray for you ..." His voice faded, but I could hear the woman plainly.

"And I for you, Father."

Soon after, I presented Lila to the self-same priest who, in turn, accepted her and paid me a fair sum of twenty dollars. I inquired as to who would be receiving Lila, and he told me discreetly that she was to go to an aged priest with no family or care-takers. Within minutes, I was back outside.

Do I believe in fate? Certainly there is an order to even the greatest chaos. Fate or no, a gust of river wind blew up at an angle and I saw a woman lose the things she carried as she hurried into the crowd. Papers soared into the air and tumbled to her feet. I was there in a moment, not knowing how my feet had rushed me to the spot, gathering the papers and handing them to the woman. Her face was half covered, all I could see were her blue eyes, which beamed out brilliantly and reminded me of crystal.

"Thank you, sir," she said to me, and I instantly recognized her voice as the one I had heard speaking to the priest. Her gaze lingered on mine a moment and something passed between us. What, I cannot name.

As I watched her blend into the crowd, I experienced a lightness new to me. And though I had acquired the feeling through an ill-gotten piece of information, I was satisfied in a way I had never been before, feeling as I did that the voice I had just heard belonged to the woman who would become dear to me.

November 1

I walked past the church again to-day. Mother sent me out, saying she was feeling tired and needed a rest, suggesting I entertain her later by making more sketches of the city she will never see. I found a bench that offered a great view of the church from which to sketch and spent the day hoping to sight the young woman again. I did not. Mother enjoyed the sketches.

November 5

Went to my usual spot outside the church to-day with a Bible I borrowed from our housekeeper. I used the book more for a reason to loiter there in case someone has found me out. However, growing bored, I did begin to read it. I wondered if there exists an absolution for committing the sin of eavesdropping on a confession when it is unintentional.

November 6

Believing I spotted the young woman going up the steps, I entered the church once more, under the ruse of following up on Lila. The priest spotted me immediately. He assured me Lila was a success as a companion.

When he left his office, I feigned a headache and asked if I might rest for a moment before heading out into the cold. He obliged me and left to do his work. In seconds, I found myself back in the vestment closet, where its musty smell gave way to the familiar sound of her voice.

"Why can you not pray through it, my child?" I heard the priest ask.

"You know my affliction," she said. "It will not go away. Please. Can you help me with the convent?"

"How you feel about your affliction could change. Think of what Christ did for you. His suffering will ease your mind and give you peace."

"That seems impossible, Father, when every day the burn stares back at me from the mirror."

All this aroused in me the need to know more about the burn. Could my knowledge of science help in some way?

Still thinking on these things and hoping to catch another glimpse of the young woman, I stopped at a pew and pretended to pray. As in all experiments, I tossed in something measurable by asking for mother to recover.

November 9

Because of the woman, I could not sleep last night. I cannot determine her need. A list of things I know about her:

A burn

Desire for convent
A woman of faith
Muffled speech: foreign born?
Eyes that defy description

November 10

Returned to the church in hopes of seeing her again. I have decided the priest thinks I am interested in his theology as he invited me to Sunday mass.

Believe I may have achieved success. Lurking in a pew, I heard the woman's voice in conversation with another. Looking up, I saw that a veil concealed the lower half of her face, thus accounting for her muffled voice. Only her blue eyes were showing and they were as true as I had remembered. I wanted to sketch her right then, knowing I would lack the artistry to do it well.

Followed her through town where I noted she entered Janski's Bake Shoppe. Patronize tomorrow?

November 11

Visited the bakery to-day at the same hour she went yesterday. So as not to give my ruse away, I ordered a dozen pastries. Coaxed a few words from her and guessed at a smile beneath the cloth covering her mouth.

Upon my return home, I found an opened letter of rejection from a New England Journal. They called our experiments "lacking."

Dined with Mother. My ideas on a possible courtship proved to be a pleasing subject to her. She recommends I be forthright with the woman's parents and win their favor first. She further indicated gaining knowledge of the woman's family is essential.

November 12

Atlantic Reports has requested a two-hundred-word sample and sketches of our chimps, which I am happy to oblige. Marzipan to be my subject as his recent advances include anticipation of need and gestures of affection.

Returned to the bakery to-day, having determined to waste no time putting Mother's advice to the test. A man appeared behind the counter, whom I presumed to be the woman's father. He waved me to one side and said, "Sir, I appreciate your patronage, but I urge you not to try and speak with Susannah."

At last, I had acquired her name. Susannah.

The man continued, telling me she was fragile.

I said to him, "With due respect, how can you surmise about a man like me? I merely found her appealing and kind, and wished to make her acquaintance."

"She is damaged, sir, beyond repair," he told me. "I have tried hard to set her expectations in life. She expects no suitors. Do you understand my meaning?"

He must have seen the confusion in my eyes because he invited me to sit down on the bench outside and asked me to wait there to join him. In no time, he was there with me, offering me coffee and pastry, telling me her story so I could better understand why I should take my leave. This is what I best recall he said to me.

At birth, she had a lovely, heart-shaped face. By the age of ten, she looked like she could have been plucked from the bridges of Amsterdam with her Delft-blue eyes and milky skin (a keen description of her). By age fourteen, all that had changed. Her skin was as rough as leather, making her face look misshapen. And then he went on to tell me about flour and water and a tragic slip on the bakery floor where she struck the vat of boiling oil for frying pastries, tipping it toward her.

Since then, her father said, she had learned to hide herself behind her veil, to speak little and only venture out to church. We parted amicably.

November 15

For days I have thought of nothing but how I might help Susannah. It puzzles me. Why her? Her eyes, yes, capture my thoughts in ways no others have, for I have always known beauty is not a virtue I hold too dear. Very beautiful women with whom I have made some introductions often fail to amuse me beyond the first acquaintance. Is it, perhaps, that she knows something of the kind of people for whom I work hard to provide primate companions? To help those who seem damaged? So I have added to my list about her:

Compassionate

I went to Mother this morning to ask her advice and found her more ill than I have seen before, slumped over as she was in her fainting chair by the bedroom window. It was very cold outside, yet she had the window as wide as if to receive the warmth of a summer's day. I summoned the doctor.

November 18

I write now as I sit with mother. She has had weak tea and has finally fallen asleep. I have tried to work on my articles, but my mind lacks its focus. I have sent for another doctor, a specialist, to give his opinion. I am warned not to get my hopes too high. When I hear this, I wonder what the priest in the confessional would say to me. Perhaps I should have prayed inside the church?

December 1

They came for mother's body to-day and carried it away in the cold, biting rain. Shut down the laboratory. Mr. Dunlevy requests an audience with me, presumably to settle mother's accounts. His coldness in doing business matches the temperature of the season. But I remember that mother liked this about him, often telling me to be impersonal in business. It has occurred to me that he might have some of the information mother was to impart to me on my birthday. Have searched her room for the notes she was compiling and found none.

December 5

Walked the city streets after the burial. Mr. Dunlevy requests I stay on with the laboratory, the business and so forth, citing my talents as a salesman. And he is eager to switch the company name to Dunlevy Langley, adding his surname at the front. I may take the funds in whole that made up mother's share. A good investment? I told Mr. Dunlevy I would continue to work in his employ with a desire to pursue more articles about our successes. He is agreeable. Note: Dunlevy has no knowledge of the information mother was to share with me. Says she arrived in Chicago from Boston with me as an infant nineteen years previous.

December 10

Mother loved this time of year, with its merry décor and bright smells. I find I miss her company more than I thought I would. I continue to find subjects for sketches and, as I raise my charcoal to paper, am reminded of her absence.

On an errand for Mr. Dunlevy, I found myself in front of Janski's Bakery. The outside window was dressed in garland. Smells of cinnamon and nutmeg poured out from within, so I stepped inside to breathe more of them and forget my loss. Susannah was there. She caught notice of me, and I handed her the letter I had worked over last night. She read it, and I noted her ability to blush had not been damaged by her accident.

CHAPTER TWELVE

5:40 a.m.

"She read it and I noted her ability to blush had not been damaged by her accident," Mariah broke off, closing the journal.

"Ah ha," Dave said, looking at me. "You have been hooked by the story."

"I am a literature professor, Dave," I reminded him. "It is my job to study other people's words."

As Mariah began to flip through the journal once again, a brittle picture, splotched and bent with age, slipped from the pages. I caught it in my hand before it hit the floor and saw that the names Charles and Susannah Langley were penciled on the back along with the words "Our wedding day." The image had begun to fade, but it was still evident that the bride wore a beaded necklace. Though the photo was grayed, I was convinced that had the colors appeared, I would see the same pink and gold one Jane inherited from her mother. And as if Mariah read my mind, she nodded to me.

"Yes," Mariah said. "It's the same one."

"It's amazing that somewhere along the line Victoria did not lose it," I said. "It's strange to think of objects having lives before and after us." It seemed our endeavor was in fact painting a larger canvas of one family's personal archaeology, and for this I was intrigued further.

"Possessions are the true indifferent witnesses," Mariah said solemnly. "Everything you own has the potential to acquire qualities that survive ownership. The previous owners of a house continue to inhabit its walls. A man who was murdered lives on in the watch he wore. This is one of the reasons I am consulted in criminal cases, Tom."

It wasn't the first time during our odd threesome that I had the thought that perhaps Mariah needed only go back to Jane's crime scene, to objects around her that day, to tell me what exactly had happened. Not that I wanted to know each precise cruel detail or watch Mariah morph into Jane in her mad state. But still, it seemed a direct route to the truth.

For the moment, I shut these morbid thoughts out and turned my attention back to the photo of Charles and Susannah. Now that I knew something about these two, I searched for any visible resemblance to Jane. Charles appeared tall and broad, handsome and neat in a Cary Grant kind of way. Susannah had an attractive figure but wore that veil, which concealed her face. It made me wonder, what Charles thought the first time he viewed the whole of her scarred face. Did he see what he had expected? Did he press her to allow him to help her as he had intimated? And if so, was this one of the reasons she appeared to turn cold and hard as a wife and mother in later years? Inasmuch as her father had prepared her for a life of spinsterhood by setting her expectations low, she appears to have resented being made a wife and mother in the end. This struck me as a possible explanation for her chilling indifference to Hannah, but surely not an excusable one.

"Wait," Mariah said. "Listen to this. Here, in these last paragraphs, Charles writes that after he told her that he had seen worse malformations than hers, resentment began to grow in her and with it, an indifference which he thought would pass when she became a mother and turned her attention outside herself."

"And just as Horace intimated, that indifference remained," I said. "What a legacy."

I studied the wedding photo and listened to the rain coming down hard outside.

Early mornings like these, I used to love walking on the beach just after the rain passed. It was like being alone on an island where all sensations were clean and untouched. I wondered if I would ever have that sensation of newness again.

When the twins were only one month old, I remember whispering into their cribs that I couldn't wait to see them experience nature for the first time. That we would gather sea shells, watch the water melt our sandy footprints away and try and catch raindrops in our palms. Recalling this, I had another pang of longing for Sarah and decided I would make sharing the next rainstorm with her a priority.

When Mariah put a fresh steaming cup of tea in front of me, I detected a spiking of something alcoholic and looked at Dave, as if for permission. He was busy making notes so I helped myself to a welcome drink.

"This is good," Dave said, reaching for his own mug. I watched him take a sip, note the same mystery ingredient and give me a look which I summarily dismissed. "Horace and Charles' story is solid, but may not help us much."

"They were two generations of oblivious fathers, that's for sure," I said. "But unfortunately for our society, that kind of selfishness is not really a crime."

"Unless it makes you drown your children in a car because they are getting in the way of your romantic pursuits," Dave said. "You know, the Susan Smith case about the young mother who let her boys sink to a lake bottom so she could be with a new boyfriend?"

"Geez, I'd forgotten that case."

"Do you remember what you thought of her then?"

"Well, just from the news, I remember thinking it was pure selfishness to do something like that."

"So imagine you are a member of the jury, trying to wrap your mind around that act as well. It's tough. You want to find a greater motive than a fizzling romance behind the crime. In light of murder, that's cold-blooded selfishness. Mothers are supposed to put their children before their own needs, or that's what people want to believe. That's the challenge we face when we defend the Zoloft question, Tom. That Jane's act appears on the surface to have been selfishly motivated."

Dave is just doing his job, I told myself. An attorney's manner of categorizing events turns one simple day in the life of Tom and Jane into: *The Zoloft Question.*

It followed me, like a dark shadow of my conscience. Like the clarion call summoning me to face my "what if" dilemma. What if I hadn't arrived home early that day? What if I had graded essays at my office? What if she *had* given it to them? Sometimes now, from the perspective of life's rearview mirror, I think that might have been the turning point.

I remember how my tires had splashed through rising water that day as I drove out of the campus parking lot. There had been a water main break, so the school shut down. It was summer and I thought I would whisk my family to the beach and help Simon and Sarah build sandcastles. Or maybe put them down for a nap and spend time alone with Jane.

I had opened the back door wearing the big dumb smile of a husband with sex on his mind, only to see Jane standing at the kitchen counter with her Zoloft prescription bottle open beside the mortar and pestle she used for crushing herbs. There were the two Sippy-Cups full of juice.

"Jane?"

She looked up at me, her eyes brimming with tears.

"Jane, honey, what are you doing?"

"They won't settle down. I can't get them to settle down. And they've been potty training and making messes everywhere," she had said tearfully. "I thought maybe if I gave them a little of my pills they'd settle down. Tom, I don't know what to do. I can't think straight."

I remember how tightly I had hugged her then and how she had buried her wet face in my shoulder and we stood like this for half an hour with the twins pulling on our legs, trying to get our attention. I remember how I had to testify about this event at her trial and how, sitting in the witness box, I had gripped my knees until my knuckles were white as I recounted the story with forced indifference.

"Yes, the Zoloft question," I said wryly. "Makes you wonder how Susannah might have fared if antidepressants were available in the early 1900s."

"Interesting perspective, Tom," Dave shot back. "Still, I think I need to explore the similarities in preferring one twin over the other. If I don't develop a theory around this, we could be caught off guard."

"I guess I was afraid you might hit on that, Dave," I observed, "but I can tell you with one hundred percent certainty, that isn't the case. The twins were individuals and Jane relished their differences." At least I wanted it to be the case. I wanted to be one hundred percent certain.

Mariah added, "If you want to know my opinion, I think mothers were less isolated then. They had more family support around them and didn't feel the loneliness some mothers experience today. Drugs are often the substitute for multiple generations of parenting support."

"But I was supposed to be that support," I said without thinking.

The rain seemed to lighten then. Sun was starting to peak through the sky. I envied the people for whom this would be a brand new, happy day. A day when their wives were not in a mental institution. When their families were whole.

"I loved Jane, you know," I said to Dave, and he looked away as I did. "I still do in a way. That shouldn't get lost here." The words just kept pouring out like a confession of a secret sin from which I wished to be absolved. "I can't just throw away all the good memories. They were real. And I damn sure can't approach the duality of her crime. Isn't that what you called it, Dave?"

"I understand," Dave said finally.

"You understand that I'm confused or that I can still love a murderess?"

"Compassion is the highest form of love," Mariah said, touching my hand. "I'm sure I don't know how you feel. The confusion. It's okay to feel for someone who is in a fog."

"You believe in redemption?"

"We should get to the end of our journey before we start on another path, Tom. I sense you have many more questions for me."

"You know, we're just dancing around all this. Why don't you go back to the day, the hour, Jane did all this, Mariah? Settle the question once and for all."

"That would not settle it, Tom. I think you know that."

"Maybe not. But someday, Sarah will read the court transcripts and she's going to ask me more questions. She already collects articles about her mother. And if I could somehow know everything about that day, everything she witnessed, well, I suppose I wouldn't feel like I was lying to her every time I guess at what happened. So why not show me that day?" I broke off, unable to say more.

I took a deep breath, closed my eyes and tried to steady myself against the fresh wave of loss about to tumble over me. It always happened like that, coming wave over wave, unexpected and unwanted. Most of the time it was triggered by something small like finding an old ticket stub from the last concert Jane and I had attended or hearing our song on the radio. But tonight, the web of ancestors' questionable actions gave me no peace, threatening to pull me into the undercurrent of Jane's unthinkable actions.

Mariah said, "It will be a long time before you have peace. You have to desire peace. Allow yourself the freedom to stop questioning and have faith."

I opened my eyes and looked at her, a woman I wasn't afraid to appear completely unmoored around. "For me, faith is like stepping on a tightrope without a net."

She smiled at me in a kind way. "Some people believe the net appears after you step on the rope, not before," she replied. I thought this was something along the lines of what Pastor Jeff would tell me, and suddenly I wondered what he would think of our little retrocoging party and the biblical warning of passing family curses to future generations.

Now Mariah held the pink and gold necklace that Jane's mother had given her. It had been given to her grandmother before her. It was more beautiful than I had remembered, only having seen Jane wear it once to a holiday party.

I shored up for a new subject and said finally, "I wonder who knows the origins of this necklace. It looks almost foreign made."

"Charles' mother would know. Eliza Anne Langley," Mariah said in a whisper. And with that, Mariah held the necklace against her chest, rose and walked to the open window.

CHAPTER THIRTEEN

Chicago - 1885

I can see her there, sitting alone by a window, despair on her face as she looks down onto the street below where her son, Charles, plays with a neighbor boy. They kick a ball to and fro. She has observed Charles' keen physical abilities throughout his short life. Was his father adept too?

Today, her mood is somber. She had always hoped that, as Charles matured, she would recognize something in him that would remind her of the man who had fathered him. Now her eyes fill with tears, realizing her memories even of London are only as of a story she once read.

She moves from the window to her bed. She closes her eyes and replays her life, or what she knows of it, in her restless dreams. We can follow her there. Follow her to London, a decade earlier when she was just with child ...

Be silent and do not call attention to her. She will be out of this building in a few moments where you may gaze at her in full. For now, she creeps along the corridors of the hospital, careful not to make a sound. She catches herself before stepping into any of the puddles under the leaky hospital roof. Outside, she is quick in her escape and still as a painting if she thinks someone has spotted her.

The London streets seem narrow and the shadows make it easy for her to join all the others who do not want their faces shown. There is a light drizzle against which she lowers her head. She walks with a certain assurance that belies the fact that she is without direction, home or bed.

She does not know why she is hurrying as if she were expected somewhere, blending in with other night walkers as if she has a place to go. She only knows what the nurses at the hospital had told her and she has jotted these on a piece of paper.

London

1875

Name: Eliza Anne W?

Diagnosis: acute amnesia

Fleeing the hospital must have been an easy task. Her ward held various degrees of the simpleminded and insane. It was not unusual for patients to try to escape, and this night was no different. She only had to take advantage of a screaming man across her hallway to slip from her bed without notice.

When her disappearance is discovered in the morning, it will likely be a relief to those who tended her. She had no obvious sickness, and because she wasn't threatening or given to outbursts, she was thought by many to be feigning illness in return for a warm bed. In truth, she wasn't sure if she was ill. She lost her memory and along with it any notion of what to do or where to go.

So who is this creature?

There is the dress they found her in when she lay unconscious on a bridge, the one that has been washed clean, the one that she wears now. And there was the note they had found inside her clenched fist, handwritten to someone named Eliza Anne. The words were faded and blurred except for "Good-bye" followed by the letter W.

So the clues to her past life are few. Her possessions and appearance give away less information: the dress, cut closely to fit her figure, appears of fine cloth; a yellowing bruise on her right temple, indicates a potential blow days before. A farewell note. There is also a necklace that would have been stolen from her had she not awakened and snapped a clean bone break on the two cold fingers of a greedy night nurse. She does not know who she is, but she knows what is hers.

And then there was the man who deposited her at the hospital, claiming he had discovered her in a fevered state crossing Westminster Bridge. However the hospital attendants on duty that night provided only a rough description of the man, who had been anxious to be on his way.

But none of this had helped her remember who she was. She had stared at herself in the ward's only mirror. All that she saw staring back at her was the faded beauty of a thin and sallow face, making even her own age a mystery to her. Something in her look belies the youthful curves of her body. Her skin is pale and clear. Her hair, the best feature of all, is a chestnut brown, long, thick and full when unbound. Her figure is lean and compact, her stature, tall and poised. But her demeanor is forlorn and vacant.

The doctor at the hospital confirmed a diagnosis of amnesia, or what they knew of it. He had watched over her for five days, as she lay in a bed, staring at the dim ceiling above. She spoke little and when she did it was in an English accent that denoted a working class, or so she heard a nurse comment. Where she had lived, who her parents were, how she came to be on a bridge—she could answer none of these questions to the doctor's satisfaction.

So why she now hurries along London's streets with such confidence only you can guess. Is it instinct that keeps her going?

She can invent a history. Who of us would not like to do this? A way to escape the judgments we have already formed about ourselves. A way toward a future better than what might have been. A way to escape whatever cruel circumstance had given her a blow to her head and rendered her memory worthless? Right now she wonders only where her feet are taking her and how she will eat.

At this thought, she draws her hand to her neck, remembering her only possession, the gold and pink beaded necklace. The only thing she has in trade, unless she also considers her body, an idea that surfaces with such surprising speed that it stops her on the cobblestones and forces her hand to her neck. But then, continuing on, she is almost certain she has, in fact, used her body in this vulgar way before. Her stomach tightens at the thought, but really it is a child tumbling into creation. Yes, it will be a short while before she realizes what has taken root there. But planted by whom?

Even as these thoughts conflict her mind, her hunger begins to overpower her reason, turning her feet toward the section of London where the street names are known only to men who purchase pleasure and the women who provide it.

A blizzard of thoughts threaten her and she looks to the cobblestones with worry. When she looks up, she is near a tenement that somehow seems familiar. A man wearing a top hat, dressed in gray, blocks her way with his cane. One look passes between them and he jangles coins in his pockets. She nods "yes."

She signals him to follow. They enter through a door and up the creaking stairs, a door that seems familiar. And there it all is. The tall mirror in the corner. The basin for washing. The musty smells of sweat, candle wax and stale, spilled seed of man. There is the bed with the mussed, cold sheets, the empty hearth with a mound of ashes and no wood in sight. It is a blighted place that calls up only a vague sense of shame. But shame about being there in the present or the past, she cannot discern.

The man unbuttons his coat and walks toward the bed.

"Undress." His voice is direct and unquestioning.

She looks at him and he continues to disrobe. She flees before he can say or do more.

And later, when she takes cover inside a warm and musty tavern to get out of the cold, she will have time to consider her options, although you might wonder what choices she now has. She could return to the hospital and adopt a mad scream like the others in the ward. She could return to the dark part of town from which she fled and wait until she was too hungry to care if she were a whore. Or she could sell her necklace, though some unknown attachment casts this out as the last resort.

But never fear as fate will soon intervene.

At this sodden tavern, she will meet the man who will furnish a name for her unborn child. He is Vincent Langley. A man from Bromley, he is at least twice her age and wears a single glass monocle that is forever at risk of falling from his shallow eye. He isn't the sort of man who would corrupt a young thing just for the sport of it. He, with his own limitations, is just as incomplete in certain ways. An inventor living off a modest inheritance, he has never been able to show off his wares and experiments. Never married, he has taken comfort in this area of town many times, and each time, guilt becomes his unwelcome companion. But it is the only way he has with women. He is too eccentric for most and in possession of a nervous stutter.

Now, the tavern's owner has been eyeing Eliza Anne with a raised brow as she sits staring out the foggy window, wondering how her presence might benefit him. And strangely enough, she feels she knows this place, knows the stares she receives. Could she sit here long enough for someone to recognize her and restore her to her former self? Quite possibly. But that test will never come to pass because of the man coming through the door now.

Vincent bumbles into the tavern with his greatcoat and cane and she, about to take her leave, brushes against him, dislodging his eye-glass. She kneels, helping him to find it quickly on the sawdust-covered floor, just as it was at risk of being crushed by the foot of a drunken man.

He thanks her, stammering as he does, but she is gone before he can complete his little speech, leaving him to follow, calling after her.

"P–please, Miss," he says, "C–come inside again and have a spot of t–tea." She steps toward the stuttering man and feels the chill of night run down her back. He is quite possibly another demanding man with a cane. But then, she could just have the tea and deceive him later, and besides there might be a slice of bread as well as tea. With that decided, she touches her neck, nods to him and re-enters the tavern by his side.

From that evening on, Eliza Anne took up with Vincent Charles Langley, but not in the fashion you first thought. He needed an assistant with flash-quick reflexes. And she needed everything. Their first encounter over tea had led to the purchase of a meal, which enabled Eliza Anne to confess her plight and it ended with him feeling he could be redeemed of his past sins if he lifted her from the streets.

Yes, it was the start of her new family, for none before would ever be known, and the lengthening of Vincent's own significant work. She decided it was a temporary place to harbor, but in a few months' time, when evidence of her condition appeared, meeting Vincent Langley seemed like salvation's grace.

Langley had an elaborate laboratory in Bromley where he trained animals, monkeys mostly, to do the things helpless others could not. Some of them were in cages, while others roamed about the house, and all were at various levels of performance. Birds, especially parrots, were housed in large gold cages, some hanging from once grand chandeliers. Their chatter, mixed with that of the monkeys' calls, filled the house with sounds that seemed to brighten Vincent's mood.

Eliza Anne quickly realized that Vincent had no sense of time. He might continue working until well into the night, forgetting to eat or care for himself. In any case, there were no servants to establish a routine of meals and such. Just a big old house filled with an odd menagerie of animals, volumes of dusty books and scores of neglected clocks, all chiming randomly.

As for Vincent, he worked behind closed doors, keeping his experiments a secret from all but a few, and those mainly offered only criticism. Who, they said, would want a monkey in their home? How unsavory, they might say.

"But I did have a man, who, when he saw that my monkey would carry a cup to his mouth as well as stay by his side and listen to his ramblings, he felt reborn," Vincent told her.

So this was the sum of Vincent's current success. Eliza Anne seemed to be his next project.

"We shall tell others that you are my niece," he said, "come for a visit." He added that he would expect her help to care for the monkeys, to keep the records as he set about training them to perform new tasks.

It was a very tidy and convenient arrangement until her belly swelled. Afraid to tell him her condition, she tried to hide it. Once, for the briefest moment, she thought she might destroy it. But then the baby's little kicks and bumps reminded her that this being was her only link to the past, a place peopled with family who, she continued to imagine, still missed her each day.

Quick came the day when there was no more hiding to be done.

"It will be all right," Vincent told her. "I suspected as much and I will care for you both and arrange for a new member of our family."

"I do not know who the father is," she told him, "or even how …"

But she couldn't finish her thought. Despite her sense of having lived a life on the streets, despite the way it fit as no other explanation could in her mind when she looked in the mirror, she could not say it outright. Though she felt streetwise in every way, the distaste of it caused her to doubt that it had truly been her life. That she owned such a valuable possession as the necklace, too, convinced her that her world might have been clean if not dignified.

"Dear girl," Vincent encouraged. "Why do we so often think the worst when the possibilities of the best are endless? What you suspect may be true, but not likely, given how you carry yourself. I picked you out because of it. You have a straight, proud walk. Your diction is not perfect, but I have heard it more often in the countryside. And your necklace, I have only seen decoration like this when I traveled to Greece. Certainly, it was a gift brought to you by someone who loved you."

She welcomed Vincent's spinning of a story about how she must have been loved, possibly married. About the terrible accident that took the life of her husband, possibly a prince from Crete.

"Yes, this prince brought back this lustrous gift," he told her as a father spins a fairy tale. "He bought it from a vendor selling incense and saffron and colorful semi-precious jewels. See how perfectly the necklace sits around your neck? And how its colors compliment your skin? It could only be the gift of a loved one. And the note? It was, perhaps, just a tender goodbye, a farewell for now, from the prince off to another journey."

Eliza Anne turned to Vincent and looked at him fondly. He made her feel as protected as a child. And then her practical nature swiftly shifted her mind. If she was much prized and loved as Vincent suggested, someone would be looking for her by now, wouldn't they? But the fable might make a good salve for her child one day, perhaps even becoming one of those life-long entertainments that she imagines is embellished and handed down through generations.

But with no other options except for Vincent's kindness, she stayed on and soon gave birth to a big, dark-haired boy who forever ruined her body for any work as a whore on the streets.

What should he be named, she asked in a whisper to Marzipan? She knew no one to name him for, no relatives she could point to. So she decided upon Charles, the second name of her current savior. Her benefactor. Baby Charles at least, she thought, would always have a great uncle he could recall if she could give him no knowledge of his father.

It wouldn't be long after when an American contemporary of Vincent wrote him about his experiments. He spoke of combining their efforts at his laboratories in a far-off place called Chicago. The letter was signed David Dunlevy. Eliza Anne had never seen her protector so excited. So within a fortnight, they had set sail for America, docking in Boston two weeks and three days later. Her infant son, crates of journals and of course, Vincent's prized monkey, Marzipan.

She remembered the day they docked in Boston's harbor, she hugging her newborn to her bosom, Vincent struggling with the monkey cage. For a moment she lost sight of him in the crowd.

And then it happened.

She did not see who did it. Who stabbed him for the money in his vest-coat pocket. She remembers only finding his deflated, bleeding body on the ground. The baby squirmed in her arms as she bent to him.

"Vincent." He laced his fingers with hers and tried to give her a weak smile.

She steeled herself against tears as she watched him die. With no time for mourning, she slipped her hand inside Vincent's coat and retrieved the letter from the American inventor. Thankfully, Vincent's pocket-watch was there as well. As she stepped over the body, she had the distinct sensation that her hands had searched men's pockets before.

Now, years later, she opens her bureau drawer and pulls out the box containing the gold pocket watch, the same box that still holds her pink and gold necklace. She places it on her neck, clasping it at the back, and closes her eyes, still hoping this might be the day she remembers its origins.

CHAPTER FOURTEEN

7:00 a.m.

Mariah removed the necklace from where it had been resting along her collarbone. She spread it gently across the top of the trunk and looked on it, as we all did, with respectful awe, begging it for more information as Eliza Anne once had.

Her face ashen and gray, it took Mariah the better part of an hour to shake off the spirit of Eliza Anne. This trip back in time had been stronger, more intense for her than the others. When Dave replenished the wood on the fire, she moved her chair closer to it and stared into the flames.

So this is how it was, I thought. A woman with few ideas of her past catches a break with an English inventor and then chillingly leaves him dead on the Boston streets. *Film at eleven.* Or, more accurately, just change the location from Boston to St. Petersburg and you have the plotline of an undiscovered Tolstoy manuscript.

One thing was clear. Hearing about Eliza Anne added a new dimension to our quest. If I had been starting to draw conclusions, which I was, her concern for her own self-interest was as real as any modern-day single mother. She had done what any mother does. Press on. Keep going. Push aside hardship in favor of protecting your child.

I glanced at Dave and wondered: was he thinking the same thing? If such persevering stock had launched the maternal family tree, how had it grown a violent branch? Could we now boldly hang our hats on nurture?

Perhaps to break the tension that hung over the room, Dave switched on the radio and the real world rushed into the room— the cheery music, the pushy commercials, the holiday jingles urging shoppers to rush in and merrily make purchases.

The holidays are for some the intersection of dysfunction and obligation, but for Jane and me, it had never been that way. In fact, I didn't like the holidays until I met her. She brought something completely unaffected to the party, new and childlike. She even made my mother's soldier-like determination to create the perfect family holiday bearable.

Ever since Jane and I married, we had gone to my parents' house for an elaborate holiday feast every year. No detail was unattended by my mother's touch. My parents' black-shuttered colonial, three-fireplace, much-wreathed home was photographed by the local paper each year. Inside, it could have been a Hallmark store—staircases wrapped in magnolia leaves, chandeliers dripping with red roses, a manger scene on every corner table, two or three real Christmas trees, holly and ivy laced through curtains and bedposts. The overpowering pine scent left by the tens of bowls of potpourri never failed to give me an annual holiday headache. I recall that one year I felt lucky I had the flu because I couldn't smell the heavy scent of Mother's Christmas.

From our first visit, Jane slipped into our family in a way that astonished me. She had joked that she was produce-challenged, unable to tell "a good melon from a manhole cover." She made meals from boxes. She was the girl, she joked, who showed up at parties with a box of Betty Crocker Potatoes, still in the box, and begged the milk, butter and pan from the host. Once when we were dating, she showed up at a party with a half-empty bottle of wine.

So taking her to Mother's for the first time had made me more than a little anxious. Of course, I was attracted to Jane because she was the opposite of my mother. This didn't keep me from wanting her approval of Jane. I knew that Jane might commit a faux pas, but at the same time, part of me looked forward to seeing the two women in my life in the same kitchen. As with a chemistry class experiment in which you are fairly certain two ingredients will produce an explosion, I wanted to see it happen for myself and witness the combination.

Not that I was a total bastard about that first visit. I prepared Jane, told her all about the Nelson family protocol, although protocol was the last thing she cared about. It simply didn't exist in her world. Her only guidelines seemed to be the ones she created for herself, a kind of if-it-works-for-me mentality, she often told me. Still, I genuinely wanted my family to love Jane.

I drift back into memory and I am whole again and Jane is my wife and it is the first Christmas we are together with my family. I am sitting in my dad's black recliner, preparing to watch my mother's facial muscles go into hyper-contortion mode as Jane gives her the holiday bag containing high-quality screw-top wine. My mother takes a deep breath, tenses her shoulder blades and wrings her hands around many cluster rings in one fluid motion. It is something to behold.

My brother-in-law leans down and makes a bet about how long it will be before Mother will excuse herself and call me into the kitchen for one of her "special talks" about the right woman.

Instead, Jane endears herself to my mother by identifying her Kryptonite— the flattery that begs instruction.

"How did you select such beautiful garland, Mrs. Nelson?"

"You'll have to show me how you set such an elegant table, Mrs. Nelson."

"I've always wanted to learn how to make a fruit bowl like this, Mrs. Nelson."

"Oh, call me Lorraine, dear. I can show you how to make many things Tommy likes."

My mother's hand runs across her pearl choker, her signature move that she is happier than when she discovered wrinkle cream. When she led the way into the kitchen, Jane turns to wink at me, and my brother-in-law punches my arm. Neither of us had ever seen my mother react like this before. I knew that he was envious and with good reason. My sister was a mini-version of mother. He was in Hell and I had won the lottery. Jane had brought out the best in everyone.

And then we had our family, our twins, and holidays at Mother's had been nothing short of picture perfect for the next three years. The twins were dressed in one-of-a-kind matching outfits. Jane brought out her own pearl choker, a gift from Mother, just for the occasion. We men, thankful for the great meal, would push away from the table and go smoke pipes in the front room. The women, wearing hand-stitched aprons Mother had made just for this purpose, cleaned up while they discussed where they'd drag us to look at Christmas lights. Later, Jane told me about how she begged Mother for her recipes and how my mother lectured her on the virtues of a well fitted-out guest room. "It is the mark of a great woman," my mother had told her. "You should have your finest things there for them and invite people often."

It was an annual scene I thought I could count on for the next twenty years. With Jane by my side, the pressure for me to be perfect was off. I loved her more, watching her meld with my family, watching my mother wink at me with the approval I never thought I would gain.

The spectacular thing about these events was how quickly Jane's Junior-League/Martha Stewart-wannabe veneer vanished as soon as we packed up the car to leave. Within minutes of leaving, the twins had Cheerios scattered throughout our minivan, and Jane would have taken off her shoes and told me she craved a beer. We went from Cleaver to Griswald in 2.6 seconds. It was better than good. It was our life.

The song on the radio was Nat King Cole's "I'll Be Home for Christmas" and I was certain I couldn't bring myself to sing along and mean it this year.

I went to the bathroom and splashed cold water on my face. The face that stared back was grayer and more deeply lined that it had been last year when my biggest concern was what to get Sarah as a gift. She had asked for a dog, and I was too chicken to get her anything animate.

Trying to re-imagine the next holiday dinner was depressing at best. The year after Simon's death, the family had been focused on Jane's trial. Now, there was my trial to think over as everyone passed the honey-baked ham and Jell-O salad. Or possibly this year they would gossip about me and give me gifts in absentia, were I to spend the holiday with a new roommate, both of us wearing our holiday orange jumpsuits. If that was the case, I could almost hear Mother's voice. "Now, let's remember that the one good thing about this is that Tommy will stay sobered up while he is away."

Away. That is most certainly how she would characterize it until my dad corrected her with a blunt, "For Heaven's sakes, Lorraine, he's not at a country club."

I'll Be In Prison For Christmas.

I was humming the tune to myself when Dave swatted me with a newspaper.

"Perk up, Buttercup," he said loudly. "Time to march onward."

"Just tell me this," I snapped back. "Are we making any progress? From a purely legalistic point of view?"

He thought on this a moment. "I'd wager this Vincent Langley character knew Eliza Anne before the accident. It's too clean, him coming into the tavern, picking her out. There's a history there."

"Interesting theory," I said. "What do you think, Mariah? You have any theories?"

"You know, when I started trying to reach her, I got a very black feeling," she said, standing by the fire now, her silver rings sparkling in the light. "There was definitely something in her psyche she was trying to block. I've encountered this before."

"In what kinds of circumstances," Dave asked.

"I met a man years ago," Mariah said, "who admitted he was a hired killer. He told me this after I gave him a reading that was black. People who kill block out a part of their psyche so that it doesn't affect their normal lives."

"Like a sociopath," I guessed.

"Yes, I suppose that might be so."

"Did you ever find out more about that man?"

"He was never able to unblock. That is when I asked him for an object that he owned and he refused," Mariah said. "There are so many levels to the human mind. What we accept. What we access. What we deny."

"You know what I think," Dave announced. "I think people like to be fooled, plain and simple. As hard as the legal profession works, you can't work against a jury set on wanting something to be true. Unfortunately for you, Tom, that truth may turn out to be that this jury feels they will have done a service to the world by making you an example."

"Gee, is this part of the pep talk? Because I'm feeling much better," I said.

"You asked if we were making progress and my answer is a firm yes. The family tree on Jane's maternal side gives examples aplenty of selfishness, which if I'm not mistaken, can both be nurtured and inherited," Dave said proudly, like a candidate making a promise.

With fresh cups of coffee, we gathered again to look at a newspaper clipping that Mariah had selected as our next passport to the past.

The yellowed paper showed two men. The elder had a handkerchief in his hand, the younger his hand on the man's shoulder. Beside the grainy image ran the announcement.

Boston Fire Hero Nathaniel Scollay Weds Winthrop Beach Hotel Heiress

"Father and son," I said. "They are smart looking men. Able men."

"We'll see," Mariah said. "Mathew Scollay, the older man, was Jane's paternal great grandfather. This time, we shall begin with a man who entered the world in the 1800s and go forward into the future." She held the thin news clipping up to the firelight. "I would say he is in his fifties here, middle-aged, but his thoughts were on his childhood. I believe we are going to a wedding, gentlemen."

A new thread on Jane's father's side of her family was about to be woven and I braced myself for the yarn, welcoming the stories now with an open mind and a greater enthusiasm for the journey the three of us were taking.

CHAPTER FIFTEEN

1905 – Winthrop Beach, Massachusetts

Mathew Scollay sits alone at a linen-covered table.

"For my dear father, thank you for your generosity," says his son Nathaniel, toasting him at his reception. "Your example as an honorable man has brought me to this day where I hope to follow in your footsteps, with Abigail by my side."

The wedding guests turn and smile approvingly at Mathew while Nathaniel leads the room in applause for his father.

It is uncanny how many features they share, how much Nathaniel mirrors his father. Both father and son have a drawn-down look to their faces, sharp chins pulling their features south and deep grey eyes that are prone to a primal, cold stare. Each has a thick shock of dark hair, though Malcolm's is dusted with silver now. They have ramrod-straight backs that wear a suit well, though Mathew's slightly less so.

By the time he reaches the privacy of the parlor, he is coughing into a handkerchief that is soon stained with blood. Leaning against the mantelpiece, he looks at a framed picture of Abigail at the age of thirteen. She looks happy, and Mathew is proud that Nathaniel has chosen such a fine woman, a woman his departed Becky would have loved as well.

Before he can have a moment to miss his wife, a man's voice startles him and he turns on his heel.

"So, Mr. Scollay, is it?"

"Yes," Mathew answers, searching the man for recognition among the party guests. "I'm sorry, were we introduced before?"

"Not today, no," the man replies, then, lighting a cigar, takes a heavy puff and lets the smoke fall between them. "You don't remember me?"

"I'm terribly sorry, but I was never a great one at remembering faces," Mathew says, batting the smoke from his face.

"But you do remember names, no doubt. Mine is Jacob Lively."

Mathew searches his mind, but finding no recognition, nods to the man.

"Perhaps you recall the name Cinnamon House then," Jacob Lively says, and with this Mathew takes one step back and ballasts himself against the mantel. "I see there, you have remembered me after all."

"Jacob Lively and your two brothers, David and Cole," Mathew says quietly, almost to himself. "I thought you three had gone off to the war and not come back."

"Well, I am back now, old friend."

"I don't recall that we were ever friends."

"I can see you are still sharp with your words. That's good, Malcolm."

"That is not my name."

"Oh no? Seems I used to call you that."

"What do you want?"

"What do you think I want? The advantages you stole from me, but since that is not possible, I'll take your money instead."

"I never stole a thing from you, Lively."

"I have to disagree. Let us say you can repay me."

"Money," Mathew almost laughs, "You want money? Our lives are almost done and we have each done what we could. Gotten through the world, and such."

"Yes, but you rose up on the Scollay name, did you not. But me and my brothers, did not the nurses call us 'lively' and send us off with that surname? And how many of the boys were so named Mr. Charles for the Charles River? It's funny to think on that now. Where did that name get us?"

Mathew looks at him sharply, a hint of fear behind his eyes.

"A name that was," Jacob continues, "how might you put it, Malcolm, *borrowed?* So just so your new daughter-in-law doesn't have to learn her name as a missus, so gracefully written up in the society pages, is a fiction, let us say you are finally making payment on use of that fine surname you have just passed on to her, yes?"

Jacob Lively puffs again, this time filling the parlor with a cloud of tension. "Let's be gentlemen about this, Malcolm. I presume you still know where Faneuil Tavern is located. Let us say you meet me there later this evening. Agreed?"

"You have no proof of anything."

"We could let your family decide. Aren't they making toasts now? I could add something, perhaps."

"Go on, then. I will meet you at the tavern." And with that, Jacob Lively exits the parlor, leaving behind his smoky stench and a pang in Mathew's gut.

He feels a cold shiver wash over him even though he is sweating beneath his wool jacket. It is a natural reminder that his days are few and there is much he has not told his son. Or more accurately, there is much he has not confessed.

He looks up as Nathaniel enters the parlor.

"Father, are you all right?" he asks. "You're ashen."

Mathew acknowledges him with a nod. "The wedding was lovely."

"Abigail seems pleased, though I think your uncle went to too great an expense on her account," Nathaniel answers. "The photographer is setting up now. Abigail wants us to have our picture made too. Are you up to it?"

"Sit down, son," Mathew says. "I need to talk to you."

When Mathew goes into a coughing fit, Nathaniel takes a step toward him, but is brushed away.

"This is my house. It has many rooms, Father. It is near enough to the sea to walk. The air is good for your condition. Please reconsider and come and live with us."

"A newly married man does not need his ailing father in the way," he says, coughing into his handkerchief once more.

"Father?"

"Nathaniel, listen. The feeling strikes me that I should tell you a few things straightaway."

"There will be many days for that."

"The toast you gave," Mathew says, ignoring him, "The things you said about me left me uneasy. I do not want you mourning over my grave, recounting the life of a man I would not recognize in the mirror. I do not want that hypocrisy."

"Father ..."

"Nathaniel!" he shouts with as much breath as he can muster. "Please. You must understand. So much of what I have told you— my parents, my life ... There are things you don't know."

Nathaniel recognizes his own eyes in those that look back at him. Their desperation stirs him, frightens him even.

"Go on then, Father. What is so upsetting that you must tell me now?"

How can he explain this to Nathaniel, Mathew wonders. From the beginning? That he is not who he says he is? But then, is that really true? For so many years, working side by side with his uncle, had he not worked doubly hard and earned a good life, a life that brought him happiness and with it, opportunities to be generous with his earnings? Opportunities, too, for Nathaniel, so fine a young man, educated and smart. And now, Jacob Lively was going to change this? No, a man's life can only be proven, he thinks, through the years of his accomplishments.

Would they even listen to Lively in any case? That he, like Mathew, had been born as a result of a moment's indiscretion and entered the world alone in 1838 Boston with not so much as a glass of milk, much less a wealthy uncle.

"Nathaniel, what I am going to tell you, I can only trust that you will hear me out until the end," he says rapidly. "Delay your judgments until you have heard it all."

"Father, you sound rash," Nathaniel says. "Allow me to take you home and we can talk later."

"It has to be now, Nathaniel."

"All right, father. If it's so important to you."

"It is, son. It is."

How do I tell Nathaniel all that I am not, he wonders before taking a deep breath, as deep as is possible for him, and begins.

"To begin, I have to tell you I didn't know my father. I still don't. I suppose I was lucky to have a place to call home at all. Boston was exploding with hungry immigrants and ambitious men of all shades at the time. And many left to a worse fate than the walls of a decaying orphanage could provide.

"For a long time I thought that if only I had known the man who begat me—my father, your grandfather—I might have had some real knowledge. Any fact is better than a scandalous rumor, Nathaniel. Early on, I learned that a name with a past is a dual gift. And where a man is from is weighty and names him too, for better or worse. Think of it. William of Orange. Eleanor of Aquitaine. Joan of Arc. Jesus of Nazareth. And then there would have been me. Malcolm of Cinnamon House. And this was not going to be my legacy, Nathaniel. I knew it from birth.

"Why, none of us had names. All we had in common was Cinnamon House, a distinction that marked us as not only orphans of bastards and whores, but then as thieves and no-accounts too. When we were small, we did not know better. All the children were born stained, so we were alike. It was rumored among the housemaids that we were all that remained behind of felons carried in bondage in transatlantic vessels, the offspring of those transported from England or Ireland, and met our mothers in the alleyways of South Boston. Sometimes the birth took place at the house. Many times I heard an infant being born. Hearing the screaming mother cry out for her child as it was taken, I would wonder if my own mother had done so too.

"And so Cinnamon House raised us to be rough-hewn children, all suspect, all born of sin to be taught the meaning of God, for if so much as an apple went missing, it could not be because of our hunger, no, but the earliest sign that a sin-born child needed God and penance through a cruel beating.

"The name Malcolm, well, it was only given to me because a boy of the same name had just died. And then fifteen years later, that dim orphanage that had housed me like one stick on a hearth, spat me out to make a weak and wobbly start on my own.

"I did not know enough then. I thought I was about to have a great adventure, out from under the sharp whippings I had endured from housemaids, deprived of affection. But yes, they did teach us some, mostly from the Bible. Do-gooders would sometimes gift us and from that I had my one and only possession, Nathaniel Hawthorne's *The House of the Seven Gables.*

"Whole sentences strung out, Nathaniel, sentences that expanded the world and opened my mind. The house in Hawthorne's book, Pyncheon House, took shape to me. The generations of people who had lived there became real, and it was enough to escape to when I needed it. I know your mother and I were hard on you to read, but it is the best thing a man can know. It improves a life beyond its station.

"I see you nodding your head now, scoffing at my way of

description. You have always chided me for that. Maybe you have been embarrassed. But I have always loved words. Words set people free. They lock people away. They mark people. They invite others inside a heart. Words are powerful, Nathaniel, and as such, should be respected.

"But I stray off too much. Forgive an old man. There were cruelties there, yes. Many. Little food, as I said. I was severely beaten once for giving a scrap of bread I snuck from the kitchen to a mother cat and her younglings. I still remember them, nestled together as snuggly as I had seen the younger children of the house huddle together in fives and sixes on one warm mattress. And I thought that all God's creatures must know to sleep that way instinctively.

"My good deed, well, it was caught by a young boy and his brothers who saw the cats and ratted me out so loudly that the headmistress had to make an example of my theft and call the entirety of the house together to witness my beating. But what I want you to know is that then, as now, I thought my action was justified. With each lash, my mind grew strong with imaginings of my future life. And I did not feel sorry for what I had done. I felt sorry that I was caught, and I vowed it would not ever come to be again.

"I had to take you down that little road, Nathaniel, because it was what led to a wider country. From that time, I began to volunteer for any chore away from the house, no matter how far or difficult. I thought I might find clever ways to earn pennies along the way. I made deliveries and carried packages. I rode in buggies to bring back other children from faraway towns. I asked town men for any kind of work. And in doing so, I began to notice the ways of other men, well-dressed townsmen with flawless hats, clean nails, straight backs and look-you-square-in-the-eye smiles. Happy men who lived in proper houses and ate hot meals. It was not long after I had been on my own that I took our family name from one of them. Among all the things I stole in my life, none compared with the worth of a good name.

"I took the name Scollay, the name of a mercantile. It was known by everyone in town, including me, for I had taken more than an apple or two from its storefronts. How did I do this? Well, it came to be that it was the surname of a dead man and he was no longer in need of it. Yes, I see the flash in your eyes, Nathaniel. But no, I did not commit any violence upon him. It happened simply, really. Looking back, it was too easy. No one witnessed my thievery. But then, perhaps that was not true, since I seem now to be caught.

"I and two other young boys set out from Cinnamon House on our fifteenth year."

Mathew pauses a moment, feeling that prickly sensation in his chest that precedes a cough. But then, it is only the salty taste of blood in his mouth, and his mind returns to the dirty little threesome who had left the orphanage that summer, among them the wicked Jacob Lively.

"We had little, Nathaniel, less than that, I suppose. An apple and bread. A winter coat in a box if we were lucky and a paper acknowledging we were students from Cinnamon House, as if this unsavory detail might help us gain entry into the world. As it was the custom during the summer months to let the eldest go first, we set out for the south docks or the Long Wharf where we heard able-bodied men could find work with the ships. Soon we discovered from others like us that there was a great demand, and that there was no place to bed down but an abandoned wooden crate.

"Each day, we appeared alongside a boat, hoping to be picked for labor. And so it was that every third or fourth day, we worked next to Irish and Blacks for a few pennies. Sometimes not even that. Stealing became the only way we could survive, and we became clever at emptying pockets when feigning to help a new arrival. We knew there were people at the markets who would make a purchase of our stolen goods, and we could exchange the money for food. Food was always the quest, food for another day.

"Not that I wanted any part of what that life had to offer. I still had my dreams of being one of those clean men in white shirts, and to come back to Cinnamon House and spit in the maid's eye while I delivered goods and passed out free apples. But after months near the wharf with nothing to eat and winter on her way, my dreams dimmed. What could I do but what I must? Hunger can change your morality, Nathaniel. When your empty stomach cries, you must eventually answer it. Food becomes the very focus of an entire day, leaving room for nothing else.

"So when it happened, the best and worst day of my life, I had gone without for three days and I felt like a sick dog, vicious and ready to attack. I trolled the dockside, if you will, looking for any newcomers that I could relieve of their coins. There, at that moment, my life went in another direction.

"What I have to tell you next is difficult. I came across a man with a violent cough. Strange to think that I will die the same way now, as he did there when he fell into me, clutching my chest, unable to breathe and looking at me with stricken, watery eyes. I am ashamed to say that I instinctively thieved his pockets. But he continued to fall until he was at my feet. I remember seeing him lie there with his face slack against the dust. The other boys I guess had the noses of vultures because they were soon there, attempting to pick over what remained. He is sick, I told them, and they laughed at me, sensing my weakness, I suppose. They started for him again, so I threw the coins at them, telling them that was all there was. They left and I stayed with the man until I was sure he was dead. I took his watch. It had a tin-type photo of the woman who, it turned out, was his mother. And there were papers, including a letter saying he could be given a wage and a room at Scollay Mercantile. There was no other option. I exchanged his clothes for mine and let Malcolm of Cinnamon House slip into the harbor. I walked away Mathew Scollay.

"I took myself to the mercantile, a place I already knew well, and introduced myself as the young Mathew, just arrived by boat. The man you know as my uncle, well, he surveyed me wisely, and I was fearful he would recognize me from having relieved him of his goods. Fortunately for me, Uncle did not say anything except to question that my accent did not sound too English. He looked at me in a way I was accustomed to being looked at, with suspicion and blame. But then Fate, God love her, stepped in and gave him a shove when he asked if I had liked the book he had sent me.

"'The book?' I asked.

"'Yes,' he answered, 'the Hawthorne.'"

"I began nervously to quote verses from *The House of the Seven Gables*, and his eyes shaded with guarded hope. Which, you know, my son, is the reason you are named Nathaniel, for that book saved my life.

"Oh, I had to be clever. I did my best to adopt a new speech, which became a mix of how I thought proper people talked and the vague Irish tone I heard at the docks. Eventually, this would not matter as I was accepted as having been young and mindful to blend into my new home. Quickly I came to understand that my mother had died in London, leaving me in the charge of her Bostonian brother who had never laid eyes on his true nephew. I set her tin-type photo on my night-table and assumed a doleful expression anytime someone mentioned her name. It was assumed I was too full of grief, and the family set about ceasing any reference to my former life.

"Before the season took cold again, I was living in my own room, can you imagine? I had an uncle, aunt and cousins. I was given responsibility in the store, which as you know, grew into more.

"And then I met your mother and we had you. She made me want to tell her everything, but I would not for fear of losing her. A good woman will do that. She will steady you in the places a man cannot steady himself, and she will make you want to be better in all ways. You will find that in Abigail, I hope."

"So," Nathaniel says finally, "I am sure I don't know what to say."

"Since the boy had died, I convinced myself I had done no real harm to anyone."

"Until today, that is," Nathaniel says, rebuffing his father's tone. "On my wedding day."

"Son, please know, I am not proud of all I have done. I have stolen to feed my starving belly. And our name I took without asking. Your mother said I stole her heart, which I tell you, I needed more than food to survive. And now you know the rest. At least you know. Of all I have done in my life, I am most proud of you. Most proud. You are a fine man, Nathaniel."

Mathew cannot read his son's countenance, except that he still sees the dark flash in his eyes. It is, he thinks, anger and confusion.

"I had to tell you now because the truth was at risk of being exposed by a sour friend from my past. I intend to convince him to stay silent, but in any case …"

"You wanted to die peacefully after unburdening yourself of your private lie," Nathaniel angrily interrupts.

"Nathaniel! Please. I thought you would understand," Mathew says, reaching out for Nathaniel. "I wanted good things for you. Think of how damned a life I would have had if not for this chance opportunity to better myself."

Mathew lays a comforting hand on his son's back, but his son knocks it away and in doing so, almost sends him onto his back.

"This is not like you, son."

"What do you know of what I am like?" Nathaniel responds

caustically. "I now know I have lived up to a phantom standard for the family's sake. Acquired an occupation because I thought it was doing right by you, when in fact, you had me doing it for your own pride, didn't you?"

"You've made a good life for yourself, Nathaniel. An honest life."

"What do you know of honesty? What you know is that you feel relief from confessing this to me. And perhaps if you had granted that freedom to yourself before today, allowed me to speak freely as well, then I would not also have something to confess."

"What are you talking about, Nathaniel?"

The photographer enters the room and begins setting up his camera.

"Ah, here we are. Groom and father. This will take just a minute," he says. "If you will stand before the mantelpiece. There. That is perfect."

As he hears the camera's aperture open and snap shut, Mathew considers what is to become of his relationship with Nathaniel and what possible secret he needs to make known. Further still, he wonders what is to become of Jacob Lively this night and if it may be his last.

CHAPTER SIXTEEN

8:30 a.m.

I had closed my eyes while listening to Mathew Scollay and I suddenly opened them when I heard the quick-fire snapping of a camera lens, a sound that should be infrequent in the life of a professor. I whipped my head up to witness it and found with relief that it was Dave, speedily typing away at his laptop. His focus was strong and certain, so I focused my gaze on Mariah, whose eyes were closed, her mouth still pursed in the position of the last words she had spoken. I thought I would use this spare moment to step outside and breathe the full, cool air, but as I did, Dave raised his arm.

"What is it?" I asked.

"She isn't done."

"How can you tell?" I looked at Mariah to see if there was something I had overlooked in her countenance.

"See how tightly she is gripping that wedding photo," Dave answered.

So I looked and I could barely make it out there, squeezed between her fingers, only the faint edges of Mathew's newly wed son visible to me. Upon seeing the photograph for the first time, I had thought his face looked tense and nervous, as any new groom might appear. But Mathew's story called that into doubt, and I suddenly read his son's expression. I knew it intimately. It was one of controlled hostility.

CHAPTER SEVENTEEN

1905 – Winthrop Beach, Massachusetts

It is awkward at best, as most conversations with my father have always been. The room is stifling from the heat of the fire. A light snow is coming down outside and I want to be there, with the flakes falling and melting on my face. The cool weather always makes me feel freer. My whole life, I have felt some constraint or another pin me down. But today weighs heavier than most because I am now a married man.

Mind you, I have taken on that mantle by choice, although mostly out of the pressure to do what is right. Abigail? Yes, I have an affection for her. But she regards me as a hero, waiting to do another heroic deed. She is consumed with her philosophy that it is action that defines people. So I have done what is right. Or rather, what is right in the eyes of those around me who find it unacceptable that I should not have a wife and family at thirty. And I have made all the excuses I could summon—the need to travel, to gain more education and larger sums of money on which to rely.

Father stands by the fireplace, wheezing into his cloth. The warmth must have loosened his chest to a degree of discomfort, and more blood spots his white handkerchief as he pulls it away from his mouth. But he has been steadfast in keeping me in the room. This despite my protestations of getting a drink of punch, mixing with the other guests, even showing him the new dog tied in the yard out back. He is determined to tell me something more although I have already heard enough. And I am certain Abigail must be disturbed over my prolonged absence, a misstep a new husband should not be making.

"Sit down, son," Father says.

I am certain he is going to hedge around the subject of a man's husbandly duties toward his wife. Perhaps he thinks this because he had no father of his own to pass on that kind of knowledge. But as it is, I have never made him privy to the fact that I am experienced with women, and have been for more than fifteen years now. Whatever he has done himself, whatever deeds of which I would not have chosen to know, he has, like all the others, always thought of me as honorable. I cannot disabuse him now that he is so clearly on the brink of death.

A piece of wood spits and crackles in the fire. A larger log has split and a burst of smoke gently rises from its middle. Since that blazing day, fire has always transfixed me in a way difficult to describe. I smell it as I believe only a dog can, its scent something akin to butter and hot iron ore. And the appearance of flames, well, when I am near them, everyone smiles at me with those doleful looks that are meant to express admiration. It is an uneasy relationship that fire and I have. It brought me out from my father's shadow, but it cast a new one onto me.

I was a short time away from freedom then. Or so I believed. My preparations were already underway for me to escape by train and start another life out West. Actually, the preparations had only included learning the price of a ticket, but that was enough to form a plan to save or steal the money for it. But my father and mother were insistent upon my learning the family trade, which was working at the mercantile. Father had injured his back and, though we were not completely without means, our cups were not running over either. As a gift to father, and to help with the family expenses, I reluctantly agreed to take a position at the mercantile, though I wished to work anywhere but there. Mine was the very same job Father had held when he was my age. Despite my loathing of the store, Mother's push was stronger. Her love for my father, I have no doubt, pushed her on. A love I have never completely understood or recognized in any others. Its mystery was a secret in a box I wanted very much to open.

Mother described for me in great detail what the day would be like when she could take Father into the store and have him see me working "a clean job in a clean shirt." This oft-repeated phrase had been a chorus in our house from as early as I can remember. Three times she sent me downtown before I actually arrived at the mercantile. Other times I wandered by the bay, watching people, listening to scraps of conversation or trying to identify accents unfamiliar to me.

Something in me finally yielded, though I cannot say what. I do not understand the continent of my heart now that I am a man, and I knew it even less as a twelve-year-old boy. Through all my life, I have been told that everything will become clear as pure water when I become a father myself. Somehow the idea of my having a child escapes me. And Abigail with a child? Well, she has insisted the dog be tied in the back and not let to run free. Not that I should look on her treatment of animals for signs of maternal tenderness, but still, it raises some degree of curiosity.

So I arrived at the mercantile on Pearl Street on an October day, ready to do whatever was asked of me so that I would have a good report for Mother.

A Mr. Cardwell was the shopkeeper then, my uncle and father having turned it over to him. He was, I believe, a distant family relation. In any case, I silently detailed everything he said to me. My father had taught me this. I counted the number of planks stacked on the hardware floor, learned the way all nails must be displayed with the head toward the customer, that the reams of fabric and threads must be set in the most appealing fashion for the ladies, and the delivery dates of the candy manufacturer. After learning the facts,

I intended to use mimicry to impress my employer, and mostly, to amuse myself. I ran my thumb and forefinger between my shirt and suspenders as he did. I arched my back and puffed out my chest to speak with a vendor. I nodded my head only slightly to acknowledge a young woman and immediately put my eyes back to stocking or sweeping.

"Tis a fair price," says Mr. Cardwell, rubbing his left suspender. "Go to any other place in town and compare. I will not sell it to you until you do."

The customer, a house builder, tipped his hat and puffed blue smoke from his cigar. As he left, Mr. Cardwell turned his attention to me.

"See there, Nathaniel. There is the way to do an honest piece of work. Learn fast and you will one day run this shop as your father did. Perhaps better." And with a wink, Mr. Cardwell disappeared out the front door to check the produce shipment on his steps.

But I had great plans that all these Boston men, even Father, knew nothing about. I would move west where there were fewer people and more land. I had read about progress in the papers or heard about it from men who discussed these things in the shop. Out west, I could be a stranger to all men, and for reasons mysterious even to me, my heart has always longed to be someplace where I was unknown to anyone, where I could silently observe others, perhaps even write about them. When one day I stumbled upon the word *wanderlust* in a book, I felt a kinship with those who had created the definition and felt it spoke to my soul's desire: *an irresistible impulse to travel.*

But all this changed with the fire. The one they call the Great Boston Fire now.

Mr. Cardwell grew pleased with my work and entrusted me to come in at five in the morning two days a week to count the cans and goods on delivery day, marking them off on a piece of yellow paper.

The wintry, early-morning walks had begun making a mess of my head and lungs, and this early hour gave me less time to rest. So I implored Mr. Cardwell to let me sleep in the storeroom overnight, sparing me a return home in such bad weather. Seeing my condition, he agreed, with a smiling reminder that I was a lucky boy to have so much to look forward to in the running of the place one day.

That night, I lay on cold flour sacks as my bed, munching a piece of stale bread. At the end of this particular day, I had barely a whisper of a voice left as I lay down to rest. But it did not stop me from amusing myself by making characters out of two bits of bread.

Hello, Miss Peterson. Afternoon, Mr. Cardwell. Is the calico print in? Indeed it is. Allow me to get my assistant, Mr. Scollay to help you. Why thank you. You are the one about to travel to California, did I hear? How very exciting. And by train, too. Do write to us with detailed reports of the creatures and landscapes you witness!

In time, I fell asleep and dreamed of a train ride across the whole of the country that separated me from my future. By the time I had reached the great plains of Nebraska, I was startled awake to what sounded like a sharp axe on wood. Although my head and nose were clogged, I could detect the odor of something burning.

Through the storefront glass, I spied a fire sweeping across the street, its reflection a glittery orange glow. I remember thinking that, like all dangerous things, it had a beautiful quality I longed to name. Quickly, I ran out the door, only to find myself in the midst of fiery chaos. Firefighters and their wagons rolled by. Men shouted. Glass split and shattered. Embers rained down. Further down the street, a clutch of people were breaking into stores.

Seeing this, I felt energy fill my body like a suit from inside, and I looked for something more to do than stand and watch. And Fate, God love her, stepped in and gave me a task.

I spotted an elderly man and woman caught at the top floor of a jewelry shop, flames leaping out beneath them. A fire truck stopped about fifty feet from me. I raced to it and tore away a side ladder before anyone could stop me.

For some reason, I remember that I was not afraid as I placed the ladder against the building and began to climb. I got within a few feet of the trapped couple and observed their necks and hands dripping with jewelry. The man pushed the woman out first, thrusting a bag into her dress.

"You'll have to climb to my shoulders," I shouted hoarsely.

She finally allowed herself to dangle from her window, pressing her feet onto my shoulders. She was wobbly, but I steadied her with my hands. We did not notice immediately, but flames licked at both of our clothes. The woman had to let loose a few necklaces as I pulled her along, hurrying down the ladder. On the ground I blanketed her body with mine, smothering the flames.

The man jumped from the window, landing on his side, and crawled toward us. He held his leg and winced in pain. I heard a fireman tell us to move from the street.

"He is injured," I said.

"They are setting up a post at the Common for any injuries. Go there."

We three were still in danger of further injury as carts and loose horses were making havoc of the streets, so I swung the man about my back, carrying him the way I had learned to unload goods into the mercantile. I grasped the woman by the elbow and hastily made for the Common.

When we arrived there, we saw scores already gathered, some in worse shape than we, some better. But all were silent with terror as we sat and watched the city burn.

The old man turned to me and pressed his hand to my chest, muttering his thanks.

"Rest now," I whispered, my throat burning.

"For you," he said then, thrusting a small box into my hand. "For you, good boy."

Later, I would open it and find a brilliant gift, a miner's cut diamond ring. The stone I would one day give to Abigail.

I made my way back through the street to spy anyone else who needed assistance, and in all, I helped a half dozen more to the safety of the Common, feeling my body was growing in size with each trip down Pearl Street. Eventually, I made my way back to our shop, Mrs. Cardwell tended to my burns and cuts and Mr. Cardwell sent a letter home, informing my family and our neighbors of the tragedy that had occurred, a letter I still have in my possession today.

Mr. Mathew Scollay:

As you surmised, we were among the burned out, but think ourselves lucky in having saved all our books and papers down to the bill-heads, which plenty of poor fellows were not able to do.

I noticed the fire from the R.R. Bridge near our house about ten o'clock Saturday night and thought they were having a pretty stout fire in the city, but I believed the Boston Fire Department able. I have since lost some confidence in them since I do not yet know how the fire got such a start, but imagine it came from the decision to substitute men to draw the steamers to save the sick horses. I imagine if that was the case, the chief has by this time made up his mind it would have been as well to have killed a few horses rather than to have had as brilliant an illumination.

When I first got to the city and saw the desperate fire, I at once remembered our young Nathaniel holding down the place. By then, some of the other clerks and Mr. Chaffee's men were also on foot toward Pearl Street. We later learned Nathaniel had made it safely out to the Common, bravely rescuing the jeweler Mr. Hazel and his wife.

We worked for a while to rescue a few of our goods. We packed our books and papers. We set about packing in trunks the pocket knives, razors and any cutlery, plated ware and a few articles not too heavy. By this time, the fire was getting uncomfortably near. The Pearl Street house was a sheet of flame from the cellar to some twenty feet above the roof. Buildings were blowing up all around us and it was getting pretty hot so we concluded to retreat.

We are keeping a stiff upper lip, finding we have a pair of hands left and will go in again to try our luck once more with what we saved. Your Nathaniel risked himself to save the jeweler and his wife and several others owe their lives to his swift action. I must surely share in your pride at his courage. We regard young Nathaniel fondly and wish him well enough soon that he can rejoin us.

Truly yours,
John Cardwell

Following the fire, there were many stories told of kindness throughout the town. But Mr. Cardwell, being the talkative man he was, liked to boast that it was his employee who must have done as much as a fireman twice his age. And this story was repeated and bloated until I found I was shy to be in his presence when the subject came up. I was more interested in how the city would rebuild herself and the wild fate that had spared some structures like the Old North Church, but had destroyed others.

My father, of course, took the greatest pride in these stories, and for that I suppose I was glad that I had pleased him. But for years, even until today, his esteem of me became exaggerated far beyond that which I had earned. Because I had been bold in a time of need, he and Mr. Cardwell and all others mistook this as an ability to be bold at will, assuming that at any moment I could perform another feat of courage, assuming, too, that I should naturally go into a profession that demanded such bold leadership. I must have recognized, even at that age, that my westward dreams had been extinguished by the fire, and it had thrust me into a spotlight I did not want.

Even so, I longed to speak with Father about the rush of energy that I had felt that day, to tell him that, even though I knew I was not endowed with special gifts, my body wanted that feeling of invincibility to return. I thought quite possibly of going into the firemen's service or police work. But he wanted me to be an educated man and said as much, dismissing the questions I tried to ask of him as boyish fantasies. I grew angry and more resigned at once, a strange combination. This provided the fuel for the other part of my life, I guess, the part I long to confess to him here today. Or confess to my beloved Abigail. For, to put it frankly, I am afraid of how I might handle her as a wife.

Three years after the fire had seemed to prove my bravery, I found myself committing an act of violence against a woman, someone strange to me, and all because of an upsurge of that energy that once had made me a hero. The girl did not make a sound as I pressed her backward into the brittle grass of the Common, and I despised her for it, since I had hoped, I think, that with her screams she would give me away.

I remember vividly when her body opened to me, her eyes had streamed with tears. And when it was over, the sky above me unfolded its own watery weight, and all my power drained away with the rain that fell on us. She rose and vanished in the mist, leaving me to tremble with my own sadness.

I knew I would never do it again. It had released me from feeling I needed to live up to my heroic reputation. Knowing I had the power to overtake someone enabled me to silence the compliments I knew to be but hollow words. Forever after, I could go back to this moment and remember my black side, and dare people to see it lurking there in my eyes. In my dreams, I held onto the hope that the girl might accuse me in the future, and the world would find me guilty and lock me up, thus setting me free.

And now, here comes the merry photographer to capture Father and Son. We stand so near to the fire, the natural witness to my life's biggest turn, is it not? So it is perhaps no accident that it has eavesdropped on this revelation from Father. For the benefit of giving me a material life, he denied me the knowledge of my own nature.

As the photographer makes adjustments to his instrument, my mind wrestles with laying blame on my father. My whole life, I hid my own sins not just from myself, but for fear of disappointing him. He had done as much with me. And as much as I hate the deception, it is somehow a release to know that I have not come from a line of mild-mannered men. There now exists the possibility that dirt and sweat are just as much a part of my true nature as a clean shirt. Not that this excuses my fits of carnal energy or bursts of compulsion to flee the confinement of walls, but it leaves me feeling somehow less alone in the world.

My suit collar feels tight against my neck as I consider my current placid state. I have been sentenced to an educated life, a life of running a shop, a job I despise, a good little wife. I know what that dog feels like, tied up against its will in the backyard now, yelping all day, wanting to run wild, to feel different earth beneath its paws. I feel that all too familiar upsurge in my blood rising, filling me with a sense of entrapment, and it takes the whole of my control to tamp it down and still myself for this ill-timed photograph. The power of the few words spoken here next to the fireplace has forever altered my future.

CHAPTER EIGHTEEN

10:00 a.m.

"The power of the few words spoken here next to the fireplace has forever altered my future," Mariah said firmly as she stood before my own little hearth. And though it was a bright morning outside, I would swear shadows crossed her face as Nathanial departed.

"Amen," said Dave. "All it takes is a few words to change any relationship. Take 'I do' for example. That's a biggie."

"Or 'I love you.'" I chimed in.

"How about, 'we need to talk'"?

"I can trump that. How about '9-1-1, what's your emergency?'"

I don't know why I said that. The words unfurled without my control. So I hadn't really lightened the mood in my living room, trying as I was to play along. Except, I was right. Those words irrevocably changed my world. And I remember everything that followed them, too, because the second time I listened to that damn tape, I held out hope that I could crawl back to before the call was placed at 8:45 a.m., June 21, 2001. When life was still safe enough for sleep to come, a place where I could take cover from the fury of what had happened and what was happening. I tried to silence the noise in my head but it shouted its way through and I'm suddenly three years younger and gasping for breath as if a giant concrete block has been placed on my chest.

"911. What's your emergency?"

"This is Martin Oliver with UPS. Uh, I … I need some help here. Two children are dead. I think they are dead. I just … They are under a sheet."

"You think they are dead?"

"Yes."

"Is anyone else with you?"

"Yes. A Mrs. Nelson. I think. I don't know. I'm just here to deliver a package. Are you sending someone?"

"Yes. I have already dispatched someone. Where are the children?"

(Background noise of steps, rustling fabric …)

"Sir, are you there?"

"Hello. Uh, there might be a pulse on one of them. Please hurry. I don't know. I don't know what to do. They are wet or something. Maybe drowned."

"It's okay, sir. Help is on the way. Where is the mother?"

"She's in the kitchen."

"Okay."

"Should I go in there too? She's crying."

I've heard that your mind runs its own tapes, tapes you play over and over again until you banish them through therapy, drugs or religion, or all of those things at once, until you replace them with new thoughts that you can live with. As it is, I find myself constantly returning to the fog of the 911 tape. I have it memorized. I know what is going to happen with each new sentence, each syllable Martin Oliver utters. I even know where he lives and how long he has worked for UPS. I know the 911 operator's name is Yvette and that she is the single mother of two high school-age children. I know all of these verified facts, yet every time I hear the tape, I hold out hope for Simon each time Martin Oliver says "Please hurry."

I remember when the Dean raced into my class, interrupting my lecture on *A Farewell To Arms* and Hemingway's stormy relationship with the journalist who inspired the work. I used to love this story. I used it to show students that all things in life inform their writing. That even the smallest detail worms its way between the skin and nail until it inhabits the world of a character. Of course, now I hate the tale because of the memories of that day that are forever associated with it. There is an eerie irony about this fact too, in that it was disclosed by one of my students to a *National Enquirer* journalist who later used poetic license to change the Hemingway text I had taught so he could sub-head a paragraph of his diatribe with "The Bell Tolls for Thee, Tom Nelson."

I remember the officer saying, "We believe your wife harmed the children. She has been taken into custody. You need to come with me, sir. To your residence."

He held his cruiser door open for me and I stood there expressionless, numb inside, replaying his words. *Harmed the children.* How delicate and formal, I remember thinking, words that led the mind to wander in a thousand directions. This, I recall Jane telling me when she worked in the hospital, is why you must say the words "dead" or "died" to family members.

She had said, "Saying passed or gone ahead leaves too much room for hope."

But the officer had not received this training, so I had not lost my capacity for hope. I sat in the back of his cruiser wondering how my children had been harmed and by whom. I thought that perhaps they had touched an outdoor air conditioning unit and received a shock, or that a speeding car had come onto our front yard while they were playing. That Jane could be responsible was unimaginable.

One would think I would have peppered the officer with all my questions, but I remained silent. This, I would later find out, would be a crucial piece of the prosecution's case against me. Presumably, I had shown no surprise because something like this had been expected, they surmised. Perhaps such behavior is listed in the police procedural manual under the characteristics to look for in "potential persons of interest."

Potential persons of interest often display little or no emotion when given grave news.

Said persons will not ask questions about what happened because, being guilty, they already know.

Said persons will ask officers for a glass of water, their thirst a sure sign of guilt.

And so it went for those would-be jurors in the press.

First we went to the house. It was surrounded. Media. Police. The curious and nosy. Though it was a crime scene, the officer told me to pack an overnight bag, change of clothes if I wished, and any items I might want my daughter to have at the hospital. He also told me to get their birth certificates.

Next, we arrived at the police station and I was asked to give a statement to the detective.

"Sorry for your loss, Mr. Nelson," he said with all the emotion of a table leg. "Anything she tells you would be helpful for our case."

"Okay, but what has she told you already?" I asked.

"Not much more than a basic statement. Most of the details have come from the officer at the scene. But she has asked what the UPS guy was there to deliver," he said.

"Deliver," I said loudly, standing up over the man, "What has that to do with it?"

"Calm down. It was the UPS man. A Martin Oliver. He found her and your children. He was the one who called 911 and fast. He may have saved your daughter's life."

"Find out what's on the property now," Dave was saying, holding the phone close to his ear while Mariah unpacked more relics from the old trunk. "It used to be called Cinnamon House. Take a picture of it if it's still standing. Look up any and all records of other children at the orphanage. Link to any databases in the criminal records division as well. Yeah. I need it yesterday."

The zeal with which he dispatched these requests revealed the inner longing pulsing inside every media-savvy lawyer—the prized book deal. I stared at the floor, wondering what he would title this saga.

"Tom, you okay?" Dave asked, hanging up the phone. "What's the movie playing in there?"

"Not one I want to see again," I said, quickly adjusting my thoughts. "So, what do we make of Nathaniel and Malcolm?"

"He was urgent to set the record straight with his son. Confess before he died that he might have been the offspring of a ship of criminals. More importantly, have his son hear the truth from him before it could be exposed by Lively. That's the Hollywood ending, isn't it? Redemption on the heels of death."

"What we don't know about our mothers and fathers may be all for the better," I said. "But truly, would it change a person to learn in the middle of life that his bloodline is something altogether different than he thought?"

"If you suddenly found out you were the illegitimate child of Prince Charles, I'll bet your life would turn on a nickel," Dave observed, his faraway gaze making me wonder if he was picturing himself as Prince Dave. If you learn you are royal, perhaps you want to act royal. Would it really be an act?

"Of course," Dave said, "if you found out at age twenty that you were John Gotti's bastard, wouldn't you feel like this was the reason you shoplifted as a child or bullied someone in playground? Wouldn't it let your conscience off the hook? I think that's what Nathaniel was reckoning. That his impulses finally had a root."

Dave raced to his legal pad and excitedly began making notes.

"Tom we are getting to the heart of it. Nathaniel's violence and poor impulse control. Jane was genetically susceptible. That's what we are arguing for. Her dark genetic susceptibility overpowered her reasoning, making you innocent on every level. So they must acquit."

"Thank you, Johnny Cochran."

"You know I'm right, or you would not have drawn that scholarly conclusion," Dave said, smiling. "I'll have to write what you said down before I forget it."

"Might I add something here?" Mariah said. "If I were on the jury and bought that argument in favor of Tom's complete innocence, I would have to believe Tom had never heard all these stories we are unearthing."

Dave looked at me.

"Are you kidding me?" I said. "Like I said before, if I had even an inkling that a dead monkey lived in the attic above me, it would have come up in conversation. And besides, my work traffics in interesting fiction. These stories are fascinating on some levels, and I sure as hell would rather have learned them, say, with Jane over a cup of coffee, than this way."

"You're sure? There's all this stuff, all these pictures, the diary. Right under your nose. You can unequivocally say you never knew about this trunk and its contents?"

"I would swear it under oath, counselor."

My head still ached and I longed for deep sleep. I got up and peeled the curtains back for a look at the confident universe that lay out of my grasp. Even in the daylight, a camera flash went off. A lens stole my image. Later it would appear in a paper with the headline, *Weary Husband Holes Up With Attorney.*

My phone rang and Dave answered for me. It was the school, wondering if I was planning to show up today. Was it only yesterday morning that I was teaching classes? It now felt like months since I had opened a manila folder with notes for enlightening young minds. Yet overnight, my life has been sent into a heightened state of drama connected to Jane.

We all agreed a break was needed and I could see Mariah was exhausted by the path of personalities traveling through her. She had not complained once, but her eyes looked red and dazed, and all of her bangles and adornments now made her look like someone trying too hard to appear young. Still, any questions I might have had about her extraordinary powers were gone. She got up and said she was going outside for a quick walk.

As for me, I was eager to continue, but needed to refresh, so I excused myself and went upstairs while Dave made more phone calls, which I presumed were interrupting the lives of those he phoned.

Only when I was alone, having showered, could I confront the new grief I felt, the grief from which, throughout the night, I had been distracted. Because there was something Nathaniel had said about his private agony that resonated with me in a way I myself could never put into words.

In my dreams, I held onto the hope that the girl might accuse me in the future, and the world would find me guilty and lock me up, thus setting me free.

After dressing in fresh clothes, I found Dave and Mariah sipping tea in the kitchen while she made toast. There seemed to be no end to the string of beverages and food to accompany our research. Still, a silent calm had settled over my house. It occurred to me that this was the first time my roof had held so many people under it for such an extended period. Not since Jane and I had been a family had there been meals and companionship and conversation throughout a night. Mariah pushed a plate of toast lathered in butter toward me, and I ate it greedily. The last time I could remember having such decadent bread was on a trip to Savannah, Georgia. Just looking at it pulled the plug on my tear ducts, and I could not hold back. I felt foolish for crying over bread, but somewhere on this archeological road trip, there had to be some pleasant rest stops.

So I told Mariah and Dave how I had surprised Jane on our first wedding anniversary by planning and packing and jetting her away. I had been the hero husband, then. Everything about the trip was perfect. Except for the deviled-egg tray.

We had searched for one from morning till night, skipping the usual tourist attractions. There were walking ghost tours, the Bonaventure cemetery, the John Mercer House. But we missed them all. We had to find the tray. Jane was obsessed.

"Your mother says that all respectable Southern women must own one," she had told me.

"My mother also says casseroles are a sign of friendship," I had reminded her. I thought it might make her laugh, see things in perspective. But instead she answered angrily, "Is this trip a present for me or not? Because if it is, I'm not leaving without a tray. To say it is from Savannah will be the crowning touch."

So we spent two days, darting in and out of tiny antique shops throughout the town, searching with detective-like ferocity through shelves, trunks, cob-webbed corners for the item on which to display a dozen eggs. We found a couple of them, but they weren't the exact ones Jane had in mind. "Too simple," she said. "Not right." One complaint followed another until both of us had forgotten our wedding anniversary.

If only then I had known that among her childhood preoccupations were dumpster diving and shoplifting, I would have understood what acquiring something prized by all "respectable Southern women" meant to her.

Alas, more pieces of Jane were falling into place, and I eagerly awaited any mention of her father, who, up until two days ago, I would not have thought mattered to my life, much less my legal case.

This time, our weary trio regrouped on the living room floor. Mariah had already sorted through the trunk and showed us a picture frame encrusted with sea shells, the backing made of gray wood, brittle and dry. It framed our wedding photo.

"Uh, I'm going to have a problem with that piece of evidence, as you can surely see."

"Nice dress," Dave remarked, looking at the wedding photo of Jane and me inside the frame.

Jane was wearing a lace dress, cut at the ankle. I was in a suit. The picture shows me facing the camera, beaming with confidence. Jane's face is turned and she is looking at me with a half smile. It always looked to me like an old-fashioned 1940s photo. Mariah stared at it, running her hands over the shells.

"This," she whispered, "Clementine, Nathaniel's daughter, made this frame. One of many she created, I suspect."

With that, Mariah pealed away our wedding picture. Behind it was another, this one of a tall, thin man standing next to a younger girl whose eyes were bright and full of the kind of merriment one sees in young lovers and expectant mothers, and I paused to wonder if this young girl was both of those things. I made out a parked car in the background, but couldn't place the model. Behind the couple was a roadside sign bearing the greeting *Welcome to Texas*.

"Clementine Scollay," Mariah said. "Daughter of Nathaniel and Abigail."

"I thought Nathaniel would have left *tout de suite* after the wedding," Dave said. "He didn't sound like a man who would be tied up any longer."

"Oh, he did leave eventually," Mariah said, her voice low and confidential. "Not before one long wedding night, however. Poor Abigail was the recipient of the anger he felt toward his father. I have an intuition it was taken out on her. Which might explain some of the desperate images I am receiving from Clementine now."

"Desperate?" I asked. "In what way?"

"Well, she wants us to meet her at age fifteen. The images are growing closer," she said, closing her eyes tightly, her fingertips running over the sea shells on the frame. "Someone is running. Water. I see a great deal of water. Sea shells. In the house where your father's wedding took place, yes. Her mother is shouting. Do tell us your story."

CHAPTER NINETEEN

1920 – Winthrop Beach, Massachusetts

I like to collect shells in the early morning, when the sun barely gives out the light of a candle and the night is still deciding if it will yield to the day. I think I read that description of a sunrise somewhere. In any case, when the sun is up at this angle, I can walk alone and feel the breeze blow away all the dust and dirt my clothes have collected from cleaning the house. Or so I imagine. I would like to think that is what the wind does.

I carry a small basket, but I prefer to put the shells in the pockets of my apron. I like to feel them there and hear their sounds as they *clack clack* against one another. Mother used to think this was a foolish hobby, but I suppose now that it earns her a little money, it is acceptable. Or at least now she does not scold me for getting the hem of my dress dirty with sand. Now she allows me to buy plenty of glue and wire to build the frames on the back porch of our house.

Across the broad planks of the porch, I will sort the shells by size, which is another of my favorite things to do. You might think this a boring task, but really, it is something that calms me. It is as if I have the power over some small thing in the world, deciding what I can choose and in which box they go.

If you want to know, I choose the shells to make picture frames. I put a circle of glue no bigger than a woman's ring against the back of each one and place it against dark pieces of wood or old planks from shipping crates. Anything will do as long as it provides a straight, smooth surface. I have managed to use a jigsaw, too, to cut the ends of the wood and make them fit properly.

Maybe this isn't the kind of work a young girl should do, but it is something just for me. Mother sells them, but I create something out of nothing. Well, not nothing, actually. God did provide the shells and all their translucent, peach and ivory beauty. But I put them together so that they can surround pictures, mementoes and such, and it gives me a feeling of completion I get from nothing else.

The travelers at our guesthouse seem to enjoy them as well, purchasing them as souvenirs of their visits. Which is odd to me because many of them never even set foot on the sand, and still I hear them say, "Oh, what a nice reminder of my trip here to Winthrop Beach."

I like to imagine all the faces and scenes that might be framed inside my creations. If a man buys one that is rimmed with tiny, delicate ivory shells that are no bigger than a pea, I imagine that it is to frame the wedding photo of his bride. Or if an older couple chooses a frame made of the gray-green shells, I see them standing before their Christmas tree, their children all around them.

But mostly, I picture the person who bought the frame, staring back at me from the blank square, alone. In my mind, I only change the scene behind them. Sometimes, it is the ocean. Most often, it is the hearth and mantelpiece at our house. We have many pictures of our family members there. I wish I could dream up other backgrounds for these made-up pictures in my silly little homemade shell frames. But there is only so much a girl like me can do.

I guess this is why I started talking to Joseph Downing. He wore a fine suit, paid in cash and had a camera, and he seemed like someone who had seen photographs of a lot of people in different places. Joseph is one of our guests. We get a lot like him, travelers who are quiet about where they just came from and quieter about where they are headed next. Mother says our business will always give us a living since people are traveling all over the country these days, looking for jobs. I have to take her word for it. I have rarely been more than two miles from our house, so it is the world that comes to me instead of me going into it. Sometimes I wish it were the other way around.

Joseph seemed like one of the quiet ones at first, but then he talked to me and showed me his camera and told me about all the various pieces and attachments that went with it to create just the right vision of our great country. That's what he called it. A vision.

"Yes," Joseph Downing said to me, "You would not believe how different the country looks in places. There are flat spaces, green spaces, mountains cropping up suddenly, deserts filled with so many cacti that at dawn they look like an army of men surrendering."

"Why do you travel around so much?" I asked him.

"You cannot, Miss Clementine, take another man's word for it that the world is round," he said. "You must go and see for yourself."

I want to be the kind of person who writes things like that down. *Deserts with so many cacti they look like an army of men surrendering.* I wish I were the kind of person who collects sentences in a little notebook like that one, but I am not. I collect seashells, make frames and let Mother sell them to others. That is the kind of person I am.

Joseph catches me now as I eavesdrop on my mother and father from the landing at the top of the staircase, and instead of yanking me up by my arm as most people older than me do, he sits down next to me cross-legged and asks, "Who are we spying on?" I give him my best indignant look, but his handsome grin makes me waver and I spill my answer. "My mother and father," I say in a whisper. "They are arguing about the wedding ring. The one he wants back that she has hidden amongst my sea shells, of all things."

"Your father?" he asks, raising his ginger-colored eyebrows so that they form an almost perfect point above his green eyes. "I thought you said your father was dead."

He is a dapper man really, a gentlemen in some kind of sales profession that requires photos, but he has asked me so very many questions since he arrived as a guest in our house. Mother says I am tiring with my questions, but if she talked to him, she would think me a mouse.

"As my mother would say, someone being dead depends on one's perspective. Now shush!"

I turn my ear back toward the banister, trying to make out their conversation. You can hear my mother in the background. Her voice is high and shrill when she is angry. And she is angry now. I would know that tone a town away, and it is not just reserved for absent husbands who show up after being away for years. The tone can be used when I look at someone I am not supposed to, or when I ladle too little or too much sauce on her noodles. It can be directed toward the housekeepers when they do not fold a towel just so or to a delivery man when he is shy one bottle of milk. And most often, a lower octave of this tone is used anytime someone in the house mentions any connection to the Scollay Mercantile on Pearl Street. Or for that matter, any mention of the name Scollay at all. When this happens, her tone is clipped and sharp. Her mouth looks like she has just tasted a sour apple, and her eyes look at you as if you were cruel for offering her a bite.

I am not as familiar with the tone of my father's voice, as he has been absent most of my life. Still, I imagine that he saves his harshest inflections for the gravest of subjects. I suppose I think that because of his dark eyes. To me, they never quite look like they are at peace. And I am not presuming this. He looked that way in his wedding photos too, so it is not just now that I am laying eyes on him and reading him thus.

Of course, I don't know if I am right. As I said, he has been absent from me since I was an infant, and being only fifteen, I cannot say I have any memories of him. You could say I know a lot of facts about him that I learned from my mother. But they are all crude references like "a dirty louse," and "good for nothing" and "The Scollay name is never, ever to be spoken under this roof. Do you understand, dear girl?"

My body jerks back when I hear the parlor's pocket doors slide wide apart, and Joseph puts his hand ever so lightly on my shoulder to still me. I see my father standing in the doorway, looking back inside the room. His profile, I think, is handsome and mysterious in a way. His thick, dark hair is slicked back with some glossy pomade that smells of almonds. It is, I have learned to my great delight, the exact same color as my own hair.

"Abigail," I hear him say sternly, looking back into the parlor, "if it is not too much to ask, have I not always taken care of you materially? I have at least been fair in that regard."

"Is it fair that you ruined me and left me with child?" she replies coldly. I feel goose bumps rise on my skin even though I am a far distance from her. And when my father does not move, I see the shadow of something reflected in the parlor mirror, and I realize she has thrown an object toward the mantel wall. From what I know of the parlor, which is a good deal since it is my job to ensure not so much as a mote of dust lands on any of its many decorations, I suspect the broken object was the blue and white Chinese vase.

"Damn you, Nathaniel," I hear her say tearfully. "Why did you do this to us?"

"I have explained the best I know how," he says.

"But now, when you could make things right to us, you still will not stay?"

"You know I cannot, Abigail."

I want to call out to him, but I see him turn. I see him remove his hat from the bench in the foyer and put it on. I see his bright white shirt collar rising up against his much tanned neck and I stare into his back, willing him as if by telepathy to turn and see me there. I want him to feel my eyes burning across the space of the house.

Please, Father. Turn and see me. Just once.

My hands tightly grip the spindles of the staircase, so tightly my knuckles go white. I must see his face one more time because I fear I will never see it again. And as if he can finally read my thoughts, he turns and looks at the room and then up the stairs. I smile at him, or try too. I am excited and fearful at once. If Mother catches me, it will mean a night in the attic for sure.

But there we stay, our eyes locked on each other's, each of us ignoring Mother's wrath in our own way. And he smiles at me now, and waves gently. I cannot make it out completely, but he mouths something, a whisper really. So I stand to see better. He is out the door before I can ask him to repeat it.

And then I hear Mother shouting for me. "Clementine! Clementine! Get your pretty little self down here and clean up the parlor."

I turn to look at Joseph, who is impossibly relaxed and cross-legged where he first sat. "What did he say? Could you make it out?" I ask him. "What did he say?"

"I believe he said 'I'm sorry,'" he answers.

"Do you really think so?"

"I do."

And she screams my name again, and I slip down the steps, but this time he catches my arm, almost tripping over his feet as he does so.

"Can we talk again tonight? On the beach? I will take your picture so I can remember you. Not that I could forget you if I wanted to. Where did you get such rich, dark hair and that angel face?"

"Shush," I say, trying my best to sound annoyed even though I am starting to love these little flirtations.

"You'll get me in trouble," I whisper. But he does not move. He just stands there, smiling that smile of his.

"I will if I am able. Now go."

The day Joseph arrived, which was just two days ago, was my birthday. My fifteenth birthday. I will probably always remember this year's celebrations as one of the best because of him. Not that it was really a celebration, but because he was kind to me.

He had ordered a piece of cake from the kitchen and gave it to me as I had none. Or perhaps because I had expected none. Mother had told me I could have a piece if there was any left after the guests dined. Knowing there would not be, I allowed myself a piece of hard candy that I stole from Mother's bureau when I dusted her room. Ha! I told myself. You have given me a present, and you don't even know it!

So Joseph offered me his slice of chocolate cake when he heard the housekeeper wish me a happy birthday. Then before you know it, after Mother had left the room, we were talking in low voices. The next night, we listened to records on the Victrola, our ears pressed to the mahogany box as we could not open the swing doors lest we wake her. And the evening after that, we dared to take a walk on the beach, which is a stone's throw from our guesthouse. The Winthrop Beach Guesthouse to be precise.

But that was the day *he* showed up, too, the man who turned out to be my father. I did not know it then, of course, as she turned him away at the door. But the next day, I knew something had passed between them. Mother had changed, wearing her hair in a tighter braid against her head, wearing her newer dress with the elaborate brocade pattern around the waist, walking with a freer gait and speaking her wishes with less sharpness.

On the day my father arrived and left, I had to cling to any scraps of gossip I could get from the house staff about what had transpired between them. I did so at my own peril, but simply being aware that he was a relative of hers made me want to know more.

The housekeeper told me that Mother requested lemon tea be brought to her, and that afterward she was to be left alone. So I insisted I be the one to take it to her. This, however, turned out to be a very bad idea. Mother and I never talked like mothers and daughters do. We talked even less about my father. I had seen families stay at our guesthouse long enough to glean the kinds of conversations that transpired, which usually consisted of a mother's urging a daughter to write her correspondence, wear a certain color or fashion her hair in the style of a Gibson Girl.

Mother and I exchanged words about dusting and what I was to buy at the market and couldn't I stop asking her stupid questions. Oh, this is not to say life with her was always dour. There were times when someone told her what a good student I was at school, and she would repeat the compliment to me and nod. Occasionally she would like a frame I had made and tell me she was going to keep it for herself. That is when I knew that she was not a hateful being. And I do not hate Mother, but she has never made me feel like I belong to her. For this reason, a part of me is always prepared to leave Winthrop Beach.

So on the day she retired to her room alone, something pushed me on, some part of me having an instinct that my life was about to, or could soon, change, and that we might share a moment of conversation, if not kindness.

"Mother, I have your tea," I said as gently as I could, entering her room. "Some toast as well."

"After all I have done, you would think people would be more grateful," she said bitterly.

"I don't know what you mean."

"Don't look at me, girl. Must I have his constant reminder around me all the time?"

And with this, Mother picked up her teacup and hurled it at me. As I ducked, the cup smashed against the flowered wallpaper that covered her room, and I remember thinking how the tea stain made it look better.

"Are you upset about that man?" I asked.

Even as the words slipped from my mouth, I had the feeling it was not me asking the question. Mother sat upright, trembling, and then got out of bed. Though I was taller, she still had the power to banish me to the attic for a day. Of course, I could never let her see that this was not a punishment to me. It was the one time I could look at old photo albums or simply rest without fear.

"He was your father, you will be glad to know, you idiot girl," she said. "And since I presume you are going to press me further about him, I will tell you this. He was audacious enough to ask for the diamond ring he gave me. And since I know he will likely be back again to try and persuade me further, I have hidden it among your shells in a place he will never know to look."

"Did he ask about me?" I asked, knowing Mother was at the outer edge of her patience with me.

"You? Why would he ask about you? Do you not understand these are hard times that we live in now? No, of course you would not. Clementine, people care for themselves and not about a woman whose husband left her with a bad name and unborn child. But he will never get that ring. It is the only thing he wants from me so it will be the one thing I deny him. Remember this, young girl. Men are gentle until they get what they want from you. Then you are easily discarded, treated worse than a dog."

She wiped the back of her hand against her eyes and I could see she was weeping.

"Clementine," she said. "I know you think me hard on you, but there is so much you do not know. In my own way, I want to spare you a world where only love and beauty are prized. Now, you know what to do. Go about your work."

And she said it with such sadness and regret that it made me certain of the one thing I had guessed about. She had loved my father deeply once. His absence had cut her, I had always known that. But I had not known until then that she wished me to inherit that hurt as well.

So my father did return and they fought in the parlor and he mouthed "I'm sorry" to me, which surprisingly caused me to say the same to him.

I repeated all this to Joseph as we walked along the beach, having crept out well after midnight. Certainly, this was improper in so many ways, I knew, but he had promised to take my picture, although I could not see how in the darkness.

"Do you think he is sorry he could not talk to you?" Joseph asked.

"I could not guess why. We have never talked."

"You are his daughter, though. That is something."

"Yes, that is something. Or, it should be something. But it is all in the past. Maybe we could change the subject and you could tell me more about you."

"What do you want to know?"

"Well, for instance, you know when my birthday is. And I don't know yours or even your age."

Joseph is shy about telling me that he is ten years my senior, but I smile and he continues. He says his birthday is in January and that he hopes to be in Texas by then because there are still many opportunities for a man to earn a good living and settle down in that state.

"Clementine, may I kiss you?"

He does not touch my shoulder or elbow to make me stop walking in the sand. My heart does that on its own. I wish I could help but smile and blush. It reveals too much, more than I want him to know about my feelings for him.

"Is it because you are leaving tomorrow that you want to kiss me?" I say this with too much giddiness, I know. I sound nothing like I want to, like the young women who men write poetry about.

He almost laughs at this, but I can see he is measuring his words and actions now as he reads the disappointment that must surely be written on my face.

"It is because you are very dear to me, Clementine. And yes, because I am leaving tomorrow."

So I decide right then that he can kiss me and I prepare to do so, though I have never kissed any man or boy. I assume the pose of how I believe a girl is to be kissed—eyes closed, mouth pursed and tilted up, feet rocking slightly off the ground.

A moment passes and still there is no kiss, so I open my eyes and, as I do, he draws me closer to him, but not close enough to kiss.

"And because I think I love you, too," he says, smiling that smile of his that bewitches me.

"Oh."

And finally, Joseph Downing kisses me. And when it is done I ask him, "Are you going to take my picture now? So you can be reminded of me in your travels?"

"Well, I was kind of hoping I wouldn't need a picture to remind me. I was hoping I could look next to me on the train to Texas and say, 'Good morning, Mrs. Joseph Downing. My, your dark hair and ginger eyes have always seemed to me to be the most beautiful I have ever seen.'"

At that moment, I decide it is possible to become three things: Mrs. Joseph Downing, the kind of person who goes into the world instead of it coming to her, and the kind of person with a notebook who writes down sentences like the ones he says to me.

"How will this work?" I ask him.

"Are you saying yes or are you saying you have to think it through?"

"I am saying yes. And I am saying it is a bit overwhelming, too." He takes my hands in his and brings them to his lips, kissing them lightly. Suddenly I feel I have little to worry about, and my mind alights on a very practical, unromantic matter. What to pack in my suitcase when I slip away from Mother's house tomorrow.

CHAPTER TWENTY

11:45 a.m.

The room was cricket-singing silent as Clementine left us. You could almost see the black and white movie title come up on the pair of them, standing on the beach in the moonlight as the words "The End" rolled up. I had to silently admit to myself that this story breathed new hope into the line of Jane's family, an optimistic, forward-looking branch we had seen little of on our climb up Jane's family tree. I recognized this trait at once in my Jane, and I had to keep myself from shouting to Dave, "See there! A positive strand of DNA. Her grandmother was evidence in favor of what I have been telling you. Jane was a romantic, too."

I was also left with a biting curiosity about what it would have been like if Mariah had conjured Joseph Downing and his impressions of young Clementine and her mother as well.

While I waited for Mariah to reorient herself, I stared at the shell frame sitting in her lap. Her palms were sweaty and I could see they had wet the shells, giving them a shiny glimmer. Then I noticed her hands started to shake.

"Mariah? What is it?" I looked to Dave. "Is she gone?"

"I don't know," Dave said. "You're not supposed to wake a sleepwalker are you?" Dave took a step closer to her. "Clementine," he whispered, bending down on one knee. Mariah's eyes sprang open and she and Dave stared at one another until I saw her own spirit return to her eyes.

"It's all right," she said. "I was just getting another spirit as Clementine left. They crossed."

"Who crossed?" Dave asked.

"Clementine and Abigail," she said. And then her hands twisted on the corner of the frame and I saw a shell cut into her hand. It created a tiny ribbon of blood that bent its way from her palm to the frame itself, and when I stepped forward to help, she whispered for me to wait.

Then she looked at her lap and twisted one of the shells away from its wooden frame. It looked like a glob of glue had come loose. Something shone and sparkled in the daylight.

"Holy shit!" Dave said, and it was, appropriately enough, the exact same expression that ran across my own mind. "Is that what I think it is?"

And there, in my living room, Mariah handed the diamond ring to Dave.

Dave removed a pen from his shirt pocket and slowly worked the aged glue from the stone. He extended it to me, carrying it across my living room as if it were the Holy Grail itself.

"That's definitely a miner's cut diamond, at least one carat," Dave said. "They don't make those anymore. It would be interesting to hear what Antiques Road Show would price this puppy at."

"Abigail glued it to the frame," I said. "That's where she had hidden it among Clementine's shells. Unbelievable."

"The very same stone the jeweler had given Nathaniel during the Boston fire, I suspect," Dave answered. "There you are, ladies and gentlemen, the *objet d'art* that has survived them all. If that doesn't make you feel like you are just passing through this world, leaving everything behind, I don't know what would."

"It's as if Abigail wanted us to know it was there," Mariah offered. "Hidden well enough from her husband, but not hidden forever."

I held the jewel between my thumb and forefinger, replaying in my mind all the events this rock had been witness too.

"I'm in debt up to my eyeballs," I said. "Does anyone here still think I might have known about Jane's family?"

But the value in terms of dollars meant nothing to me. All I could think of now was that it proved I knew nothing of Jane's background, and I would be vindicated, by virtue of being ignorant and ill-informed. This small item would help Dave prove that, since I had been unaware of her family history, I was certainly unaware of the genetic danger that she posed.

On the other hand, had I known these details of her past and the theoretical luggage that came with them, wouldn't things have been different? Wouldn't I have approached Jane differently?

Feeling the magnanimity of Nathaniel's diamond—or was it Abigail's really?—I gave it to Dave and turned my attention back to the frame. I replaced my wedding photo within its borders and stared at Jane's face. What a happy time that had been in my life. How I thought marriage would be. How blissful the wedding had been. But then, I mused, isn't the difference between a wedding and a marriage as wide a chasm as between being pregnant and actually caring for a child? Don't we deceive ourselves that everything will be champagne and baby booties?

I let the memory unfurl. Why not think of that now, I told myself. Jane wasn't always a murderer. She was once a bride.

Our wedding day was bright and fresh. My whole being tingled with anticipation. I still couldn't believe this woman had agreed to marry me. Looking back, she was still very much the nurturing woman I met in the hospital that day with Roger and all the other burned kids. I remember that she attended to all my needs when the idea of a wedding ceremony arose. Looking back, I see that it was the only time I remember us talking in detail about her family. Discussing it seemed to bring out a certain edge in her, an uneasy disposition that I took for embarrassment. Who isn't embarrassed by a couple of relatives? I thought I'd asked a normal set of questions pertaining to a guest list. What I couldn't know then was that it was a painful territory.

"So how many people should we invite? Will your father give you away?"

She laughed. "No, my mother already did that. Ha ha."

"I don't get it," I had said. "What do you mean?"

"It's nothing."

"Well, your father is still living, right? I thought you said so."

"Tom, no family on my side, okay? If it's all the same to you, we can just have a small ceremony. Outside maybe. My love is big and that's all I care about. Small group. Big love."

It was one of the many ways she charmed me, saying something like that and following it up with a lush, long kiss. Getting to the bottom line and getting on with the show was her formidable talent. And I enjoyed it for its contrast to my family, accustomed as I was to parents who talked in cryptic slights, innuendos and not so subtle sarcasm.

So we married outside in the spring with no family on her side. The setting was a brilliant green park. A willow tree served as our arbor. She wore a long lace dress with a ribbon headband in her hair, carrying white baby's breath. I wore a dark blue suit, no tie and a huge smile.

Only a few friends gathered at the ceremony—my parents and sister, of course. A poet I knew recited original verse on what inspires love. What was it he called it? "The Night of the Day." We drank fruity champagne and ate cheese and red grapes. A nurse friend of Jane's played the violin. And Jane glided down a rose-petaled path toward me. She smiled and winked at me, putting my nerves at ease as we faced one another and pledged our love for better or for worse. Then the pastor said a few words and suddenly we were married. I was surprised that I felt no different after that pronouncement because I had expected my life to change dramatically.

"She looks happy there," Mariah observed, placing a hand on my shoulder, ushering me back into reality. "It must have been a beautiful day."

"I think she was happy then. We were a good match, and I remember thinking it was us against the world," I said. "Pretty sappy, huh?"

"Everyone deserves love," she responded.

By now, the sun was up in full, spraying its light through the windows, and there was no denying we were into another day, tired and wan as we were. I had tried to ignore the cheerful morning noises wafting through the front window. Birds. Holiday music. Car doors slamming. A delivery man shouting something. All the evidence that life churned on beyond the confines of my walls, now haunted by so many members of the same family tree.

"That's what you will tell Sarah," Mariah said. "You will one day tell her about your happy wedding day. A child needs to know that her parents created her in love."

"It's good of you to say that, and I will try and remember it," I said as I turned to face her. "It's funny. I think she would like you. You have a very kind spirit, if you don't mind the pun."

We both laughed.

"I can't help but think of all the questions this new information raises," I told her. "I don't know where to start. That Jane's mother Victoria wasn't just dead, but murdered? Just think of how that would affect a ten-year-old."

"The more you know, the more you don't know," Dave said, looking up from his laptop. "It's one of those tricky things that makes my job so complicated, trying to tie this web of people together."

"Is that what you've been drawing over there on your legal pad?" I asked.

"In a manner of speaking, yes," he answered. "But not to put too fine a point on it, there are still blanks. Gaps really that give me, too, a whole new set of questions beginning with 'why?' Those answers usually come to me when I'm in the shower."

Why? The smallest question with often the largest answer.

I had once learned in college, in a public relations class, of all places, about the 'Principle of Why.' On the first day of class, the professor wrote it in bold chalk on his board and then wrote the number five beneath it.

"You can drill to the bottom, get the answer by mining the why of the previous question," he had said. "Each time you hit upon an answer, ask why of the next question five times until you get to the bedrock. If you are ever forced to talk to the media, this is imperative."

After all the many media nightmares I had had in the past several months, why did I not remember The Principle of Why?

Why did you drown the children, Jane?

Tom, I had too much. I was done being a mother.

Why were you done being a mother?

It was too hard.

Why was it too hard?

Because you didn't help me.

Why didn't you ask me for help?

You should have seen it.

Why wasn't there another solution?

Don't you know me by now, Tom? Big burden. Big solution.

Mariah spoke up then. "Dave. Tom. Please sit down."

"Okay, let's get things rolling. Last one, right?" asked Dave as he swigged down another coffee. "Jane's father. Samuel Downing. Child of Clementine and Joseph. Husband to Victoria."

"That makes him grandfather to Simon and Sarah," I said, feeling a lump form at the base of my throat. For this retrocognition, I wanted to learn enough positives to tell Sarah, to tell her about her mother's father. He had cared for her after Victoria's death, after all, so I was certain we would find something redemptive in his character.

For the first time, Mariah seemed uncharacteristically shy.

"I have to tell you, I am not looking forward to this one. It is too close," she said. "I have to get clear."

"You have to get clear?"

"I told you I was related to her family. I made you think that perhaps I was a cousin," she said. "That is what I told Dave if I remember correctly."

"Yes," Dave said. "That's precisely what you said."

"Although that's what my family always told me, that Jane and I were cousins, I knew differently. It was a small town. People talked, looked. It was one of the first ways I knew I had the gift to see what others could not," she said. "But that isn't the point I am making, Tom. You see, Jane is my half-sister. She and I have the same father. Samuel Downing."

CHAPTER TWENTY-ONE

Texas – 1976

Samuel Downing hardly knows what to do with the daughter, Jane, he has seen little of in her ten years on earth. A tall, sandy-headed man with broad shoulders and a confident grin, he looks to be the kind of man who can bear much. Like his father. But this is his daughter on his doorstep, here in Del Rio, a mere two days since they put her mother in a pauper's grave up in Dallas.

Was it just a week ago that he was called?

"Is this Samuel Downing? Sir, we are holding your daughter Jane Anne Downing in local custody … picked up for shoplifting at a convenience store … Mother allegedly fled the scene … several stab wounds believed to have been perpetrated by … has been identified in the morgue … listed you as next of kin … Jane is being counseled by family services … come immediately … burial is imminent."

And he had gone. Drove past the speed limit the whole way, imagining the cold anger he would show any officer who tried to stop him. He remembered his father's words, to take it moment by moment. Resist the desire to be angry at your dead wife. Don't stoke the fire. Be slow to anger.

He stares out the windshield at the gray-green road in front of him. It won't get under his truck fast enough. He pulls over to fill up for gas occasionally, and on impulse, buys a truck-stop teddy bear for the daughter he might not recognize.

And then, the weary ride home, with Jane sleeping most of the way, which he was glad for. His eyes constantly look at her, take her in, note how she has grown.

Jane seems shocked and sad, or so he thinks. What does he know of her catalogue of expressions except from a photo he has of her at

JANEOLOGY ■ **209**

age three?

She has nothing, except a few things she took from her mother's apartment: a necklace he remembers seeing once, some paperbacks, a pillowcase full of clothes that look too small, nails painted a shocking pink. And, impossibly, an old trunk from Victoria's side of the family. How the hell did she get that when he was sure as salt that Vicky had kept nothing from her father? And then, when he empties the pillowcase to wash her clothes, there's a stack of magazines.

The magazines.

Was there ever a time he didn't see Vicky reading those things, quoting from them until he had to leave the room? He wonders how ten years of living with magazine advice has already affected Jane.

And then there is the fact that she is dead, his ex-wife Victoria. Murdered, no less. How to deal with this? Family Services said they would check in on her, on him as well. A woman named Rose Davis has called three times, saying she can advise him how to talk about Jane's mother. Still, he is unsure about what to do with her, so he does the only thing that comes to mind and makes her a peanut butter and jelly sandwich. He cuts off the crusts for her because that is how he thinks she might like it. Not that he ever had a sandwich that way. His mother was firm on eating the whole thing.

Jane eats silently, and he tries not to stare at her. He jumps up, leaps really, from the table because he feels like a poor parent already, with her sitting there eating peanut butter and jelly with no glass of milk to go with it.

"Thank you," she says softly, accepting the glass of milk he hands her, then continues eating. "For the teddy bear, too."

"Welcome." Samuel steps back into the kitchen, pours himself a cup of hours-old coffee and carries it back to the table.

"What are we going to do now?" She asks the question with such adult assuredness he is taken aback, flattened by her blunt attitude.

"Well, I'm not sure. You are going to stay with me, though. I hope that is okay."

"I won't be any trouble."

"No, I expect you won't. You don't need to worry about that. When you finish your sandwich, we'll go see your grandfather, okay?"

"Have I met him before?"

"In a manner of speaking, yes. When you were just an infant."

"I don't want to ask too much, but how come I haven't seen him since then? I mean, with us all being in Texas and all."

She takes a sip of milk, leaving her eyes trained on him as she drinks. Something about this gesture reminds him of Vicky. She could perform a simple act with such poise and charm that you could not turn away. His mother would have called it "beguiling," but can that word be appropriately used for a girl of ten? No, but she is so much her mother. She was beguiling. The way she had moved with such grace and refinement when he first met her at, where was it, Mrs. Parsley's Boarding house? That was so many years ago.

So his mind goes back to the question at hand. How come Jane hasn't seen her grandfather since she was a baby? And for that matter, why hasn't he seen his own daughter in what, seven years? Shouldn't Jane be asking that question first? Or has Vicky already answered it for her? There are so many divergent paths each of his answers can travel, and he can't be sure which of those paths will lead him through a minefield. He takes his head into both hands and runs his fingers through his hair. He lets out a heavy sigh.

"Jane, I'm not quite sure what to tell you. You've been through a lot."

"You can tell me anything. I know a lot more than most ten-year-olds."

"Yes, I expect you do."

"I read a lot."

"Magazines?" He takes a step out, daring to see if his instinct is true.

"Romance novels, if you want to know."

And with that, he almost spits out the coffee in his mouth. "Romance novels?"

"Yes."

And he thinks, how far we have come since his family handed down a love of stories by Nathaniel Hawthorne, the writer his own grandfather was named for. And here she is, his own flesh and blood, and he doesn't have to venture a guess that she may never have heard his name before.

"Jane," he says, taking another sip of coffee to calm himself, "I hardly know what to tell you, what you already know, what you may think of me, even. But we are family, and I have been raised to leave no presumptions on the table."

"Presumptions?"

"Uh, things you might assume to be true in advance."

Her screwed up expression tells him to try again. "Like when you pre-decide you don't like a certain flavor of ice cream although you have never tried it."

"What do you do?"

"What do you mean?"

"For a living. How do you get money?"

"I repair things, build things. And I own two laundromats and a café with your grandfather."

He sees her eyes sparkle at this, and he cannot understand why.

"That sounds cool. I like to do laundry."

He wants to hug her now. There is some force pulling him to do so, to love her, to embrace the child she still is and protect her from what he is not sure.

For so many years, Vicky would not let him come within a twenty-mile radius of her or talk to Jane on the phone. She would not accept his Christmas gifts. She returned his letters unopened. And now, she is here, just a few feet away. How could he fill in all the spaces that had opened up over the years? How could he explain that, after being so beaten down by his attempts to see her and the constant fighting with Vicky, he had to let it go and go on in life without them, forgetting he had a girl out there being raised under who knew what circumstances?

It was his mother who had urged him to leave it be. When he had complained to her that it wasn't fair, she had told him not to try and make his own justice. *Life does that all on its own, Samuel. Life does that. God does that. Fairness is meted out in ways we cannot begin to understand. In the world's own time, Jane will come back to you and you can explain everything.*

How ironic that his mother's words had proven so true. Prophetic even. Jane has come back. Here she is, sitting there with grape jelly on the corners of her mouth, not looking the least bit sad or lost.

"Jane, I'm going to tell you several things. A long, long story, in fact. If I say too much, or you want me to stop, you tell me so, okay? But you might as well know the truth up front. You should know I will never lie to you. I will always be honest. And there are no questions you can ask of me that are off limits. Okay?"

She nods and looks at him with undivided attention, as if she is fully prepared to take in a sermon from the pope. And he hopes, at least, that he can be kind and speak the truth, as well. He wishes he had a seat belt in which to buckle her. It was, he knew, going to be something like a verbal roller coaster.

"Jane, you know your mother and I met a few years before you were born. We lived in Fort Worth. I had moved up there to get away from my own father. Which now, looking back, feels like a whole other story. But I was young and wanted to be on my own. Father never interfered with that. In any case, I met your mother while I was brash and out of sorts. Without direction. Not for any specific reason other than the rebellious fuel of youth that wants to burn through anything and everything that tries to tamp it down. So we fell in love like that."

And, as he looks across the room, Samuel snaps his fingers, thinking of how beautiful Victoria was then. He notices that Jane has taken his mug of coffee and is now, in fact, drinking it herself.

"We both wanted a family. And we both wanted to get away from our own folk. For me, at least, I wanted to run, I knew that. So it seemed we had enough in common to make a marriage. When you get older, you will see that for yourself. There must be something more there than the common desire to run away. In any event, you should know we were thrilled when you came along. Know that you were the most wanted little child on the face of the earth. My father, your grandfather, he must have taken fifty pictures of you if he took one. When you were born, did you know you had red hair? Just like my father. Of course, that has been replaced by your beautiful dark hair, like your mother's, huh?"

"Like it was, yes," Jane says as she wipes the corner of her eye, signaling to Samuel that the weight of her mother's death is soaking in now.

"She was a striking woman, your mother. In so many ways. But then, I wanted to really, really settle down. I had been listless in my work in Fort Worth and having you, well, it seemed right that we should be around family. My family, that is. So I packed us up and we moved down here to Del Rio.

"And it was okay with your mother for a while. It really seemed that way. She adored you, and she and I got along very well. We started talking about buying a house. Well, around this time, she got a letter from her father. It talked about some very bad things that happened to her a long time ago. Things that your mother had tried hard to forget. That letter stirred up so much anger it made us fight." He is unsure of how much to tell Jane. How far he can go into the unkind territory of those fights, how he had tried unsuccessfully to ease Vicky's pain. How she had somehow confused her memories so much that she became convinced Samuel was the one who had not protected her. "It made us fight," he says firmly. "Have you met your Grandfather Langley?"

"Horace?"

"Yes, I believe that's his name."

"No. She hated him. And the monkey too. And her uptight grandmother, who, if you ask me, seemed like a nut-job."

"Wow."

"She would ramble a lot when she drank."

"Victoria! Your mother drank?" Samuel is overwhelmed. The woman who wouldn't let him have a beer, who hated the smell of alcohol of any kind.

"Yes. She drank. When she and Carol went out, you know. Not sitting around the house drinking, but going out drinking."

"I just never thought she had the taste for it."

"It really made her chatty. That's when she told me about you. And about Horace and her family."

"Well, you know that much. You know she hated him. She called it a clean hate, didn't she? She might have told you that she had decided to break it off and never look back, so that the pain he caused her couldn't touch her again. That's what she told me when we first met and were sharing our stories. But then came that letter, and the pain was still there. She had traveled from Cape Cod to Texas, and it was still in her heart.

"Now, I don't want to be indelicate here, but I have to tell you, after that our marriage was over in the …" Samuel stumbles for the right word and, finding none, reaches for Jane's half-full glass of milk and downs it whole.

"In the biblical sense," Jane offers matter-of-factly. "Yes, she told me that. She said it was one of her better mistakes. Although I'm not sure how you can have a better mistake. Wouldn't all mistakes be equally bad?"

Samuel looks in Jane's incredible face, so filled with light and youth, yet the words coming from her mouth are of a person twice her age.

"I didn't know that."

"She loved you. She said so. Big love. Big mistake. That's what she used to say."

"Well, Jane, it comforts me to know that. I have never since loved anyone like your mother. So, as you might expect, since we were no longer married in the biblical sense, I, too, made one of my biggest mistakes. And by the look on your face, I see you must already know this too. I was unfaithful to your mother. Mind you, that is not how I was raised to be, and it was the most damning thing I ever did to myself. It cost me much, but mostly it cost me knowing you, Jane. All these years, I have wondered about you, cared about you, prayed about you. You see, that's the good/bad thing about life. It can turn on one thing. One thing can alter everything, for better or worse. Having an affair, that was it for me.

"But it can be good too, you know, I don't want to sadden you more. There are a million great examples of lightning striking for better. Why, the chance meeting of my mother and father in Massachusetts is one great story I will tell you one day. And it all turned on a dime, too."

"I don't hate you, you know," she says evenly. "I tried it once and said it out loud to her, and she slapped me good. She said I could go outside and say it, but never in her presence. So you can imagine it made me wonder, when she got to hate her father so much, why couldn't I hate mine?"

"So why don't you then?"

"I don't know. Besides you just not being there, there wasn't much of a person left to hate. I don't know you enough to hate you. I would think you would have to live with a person every day to have them let you down enough. Then you could hate them, maybe."

Samuel thinks a beer would be the perfect thing right now. Something to steady himself against this formidable child. He should have known, he thinks. So like her mother. The best of her mother, really.

"I intend to change all that, Jane. I do. We're a family now." And God, he thinks, how will this all work? With his "other" family still in the wings. The woman. The child. It is all so messy. All his bad choices come back to haunt him at his kitchen table. He hasn't even told his girlfriend Bianca about Jane being here or about Victoria's death.

Sure, Bianca knows all about Vicky and Jane, but they don't talk about it. It was she who, in point of fact, had broken up the marriage, the one he had turned to when his marriage had gone from "biblical" to hell. And now, what had started as a relationship with a come-hither woman and a warm bed had evolved into an on-again, off-again romance. Mostly off when her family came into the mix. The family despised him for making her with child and not marrying her. But how could he have? He still hoped Vicky would come around.

Hell, he thought. Two daughters, one ex-wife, a mistress, and he'd been raised mostly by his mother. Surrounded by women his whole life and no clue how to handle the fairer sex any better. All he could think to do with the one in his kitchen now was to ask his father's own fail-safe question.

"Do you want something else to eat?"

"Sure."

He carries her empty plate to the counter and stares out the window. He scans his countertop and decides on an apple, cutting two of them into quartered chunks.

"Do you have any more coffee?"

"Yes," he says, carrying the plate and the coffee pot to the kitchen table. "Where did you pick up a liking for coffee? It's an acquired taste."

"Actually, this is my first time. It just smells good."

"Yes, it does, doesn't it? Maybe I'll put some milk and sugar in yours."

"No. Black is fine."

He has to smile at her. He hides his desire to laugh. She is so self-possessed yet so young. What must be lurking beneath, he wonders?

"I have to tell you more. I have—sort of have—a family here too. Besides your grandfather. I have a girlfriend. And this girlfriend and I, we have a daughter together. I want to be up-front with you, Jane. No secrets. I would have told you all this, you know, if we had … been in touch."

"Is she my age?" Jane asks soberly. "Your other daughter?"

"A couple years younger, actually. But you will like her. She doesn't live here, as you can see. It's complicated in that way, but still, these two ladies are important to me just like you are. And I just wanted you to know they will be part of our lives.

"I want you to stay here with me, I truly do. I hope you will eventually feel comfortable, like this is your home."

"Okay."

"So if there's anything you need, you let me know."

He drinks his coffee and she drinks hers. She nibbles on an apple slice. Both of them stare out into the small living room. He feels as if he is sitting next to a stranger. Yet, she is his. Half his, anyway. Half of him is in her make-up and being. Hell, he could be the one, after all, to introduce her to *The House of the Seven Gables*. She is ten. Not all of her slate has been written on. With all her knowledge of the world, her mother's world, he could still have a chance of slowing it down within the small confines of Del Rio. He could teach her to fish, build a fire, and take photographs. After all, his mother married at fifteen and created a whole new life, a whole new family when she was young. And then, later, with all the u-turns he'd made, didn't he turn out okay? Sure, it will be okay, Samuel told himself in his most convincing self-voice, the one he turned to when he was blue and out of sorts. Jane will be okay with me, his mind repeats. Jane will be okay.

He looks at her now, her hands tightly cupped around her coffee. Her eyes stare into it as if tea leaves are at the bottom, divining her future.

"What are you thinking about?" he asks.

"Do you think we might get a cat?"

And he smiles at her. Grins really. The little corners of his mouth turn up slightly, and for the first time since he's laid eyes on her, she smiles back and he sees it, that smile of his, shining back at him. He sees the hope there, the sparkle that he sees in himself sometimes. And he has the feeling the future is going to be just fine.

PART THREE

CHAPTER TWENTY-TWO

2:00 p.m.

"So you see, I knew her father—our father—very well," Mariah said finally. "Possibly better than Jane since he had been around since my birth."

"What happened," Dave asked. "Why didn't they marry?"

"My mother got pregnant as a result of their affair," Mariah answered, her gaze looking across the room as if the embarrassment of the infidelity had haunted her too. "By the time his life was sorted out, it was too late. Her family, my family, shamed her, saying he was not good enough, that she was wrong to have been with him and should do no further harm. So, they did have, as Samuel said, an on-again, off-again, romance, if you could call it that. And then, when Jane returned to his life, everything halted, I believe. My mother had her pride and couldn't see how Jane was his first responsibility. I think they tried to make things work. There were a few occasions when the four of us did spend time together, but it was always very tense. And then it just stopped altogether. I lost track of Jane after she graduated from high school and went away to college. That is, until I read about her in the papers and saw her on the news."

"And Samuel? Where is he now?" Dave chimed in.

"No one knows," Mariah said. "My mother said he moved from Del Rio after Jane went to school and after his own father died. She received a call from a Greyhound station once and though he never spoke, she said she knew it had to be him."

"Yes, but you know," Dave said, looking her square in the eyes. "You have a sense of it, don't you?"

Mariah was silent. She looked like an uneasy witness taking the stand. "Yes, I do. But his whereabouts are not important to Tom's case, are they?"

"I hope you don't mind, then, if I do a search in the nationwide criminal database," Dave retorted. I looked at both of them, staring each other down, each holding firm ground.

"I would prefer if you did not, Dave."

"Very well. I'm going to go sit in the kitchen," Dave said, as he gathered his laptop and notes. "I need to put all this together on one pedigree chart."

"Have any grand conclusion yet?" I asked, posing the question with a forced hope.

"The same one I had going in. You are not guilty. Go get some fresh air. Both of you."

"I think I'll lie down in the bedroom, if you don't mind, Tom," Mariah said.

"No, go right ahead."

I grabbed a bottle of water and did as Dave asked. Sitting alone on my porch in the light of day I felt fearless of any hidden photographers, or at least I had come to the position that I just didn't care anymore.

I wondered if I was coming any closer to believing that ancestral time travel would help my case, or, in a larger sense, my life. Would it relieve my deep sense of doubt? There were so many outcomes to consider. Dave had told me that if I went to prison at all, it would only be for five years. *Only five years.* Five years for bearing partial responsibility. And that, he had emphasized, was if the prosecutor could make enough valid connections about my knowledge of Jane's approaching breakdown.

After hearing all the stories in these many hours, what did I really know? Both sides of her family had shown the plucky, pull-yourself-up-by-the-bootstraps attitudes of Eliza Anne, a possible English prostitute, and Mathew, an orphan likely of dubious paternity. The bloodline that had started so optimistically bent on survival hit snags in the next generation once the basic hierarchy of needs had been met by their parents.

This was certainly the case with Eliza Anne's son, Charles Langley, who ignored the cruel treatment his wife meted out to her twins, Hannah and Horace and then gave abominable advice to his son about how to deal with Victoria's molestation.

She is young and will forget. Why ruin a good man's reputation?

And of course, I conjectured, it was perhaps Horace's chilling denial, not the abuse itself, which forever wounded the motherless Victoria. Victoria, who would turn out to have even poorer parental skills than her own father, leaving Jane to grow into adolescence without a positive feminine influence.

And what about the Scollays, or whatever their rightful surname should have been? Nathaniel certainly had a dark side, capable of rape and possibly more.

In my dreams, I held onto the hope that the girl might accuse me in the future, and the world would find me guilty and lock me up, thus setting me free.

And who knows whatever became of Jacob Lively, the man who intended to expose Mathew Scollay for stealing a man's identity? An equally grave end could have befallen him. These men, then, grandfather and father, created in part the gentle Clementine, handing her off to the bitter Abigail. Of all of them, Clementine appeared most likely to pay the biblical bill—generations shall inherit the sins of the fathers. But she struck out when chance offered her an escape in the form of Joseph Downing. That was something, wasn't it? Which brought about Samuel, Jane's father, a seemingly compassionate young man who made several bad choices. A man who could be, as Mariah's eyes suggested, currently exploring his own wanderlust among us. What kind of parent had he been those eight years he had Jane?

My water bottle was empty now, and I tore the label off in bits, letting them collect at my feet. Jane hated me doing that, saying it was a bad way to idle my time away and made an extra mess for her.

"All I want is for you not to make more work for me around here. Is that too much to ask?"

"I'll clean it up. Relax, Jane."

"You just come home and do stuff like that."

"It's just paper."

"So I guess I can come to your office and sprinkle Cheerios everywhere and that would be all right with you?"

She said that all the time. I guess there was some truth to it. Not that I made more work intentionally, mind you, I just forgot her rules, telling myself it was because there were too many of them now that the children had come.

"Don't forget to put a bib on them when you feed them, Tom. The food stains their clothes."

"Tom, I asked you to rinse out their bottles."

"Tom, I asked you not to leave your shoes there. I almost tripped while carrying the babies."

"Tom, I can't believe you just blew off that doctor's appointment. I needed you there. Do you know how hard it is to pee in a cup while watching your children?"

She had really been furious about that one. And of course, I understood. There was no excuse for my not having been there. I had merely let time slip away, talking to a student in my office.

I went back inside and found Dave typing away at his computer. I sat down at the table next to him, eager, for the first time in two days, to hear what he had to say.

"You didn't kill your son," he said, annoying me with his habit of reading my expression, making me wonder at how transparent I was. "That is the focus of your case. You want to do penance, you do it after the trial. Call up your preacher friend or something."

"Overwhelmed. I feel utterly overwhelmed and I can't remember the last time I felt like myself. I don't know what to feel. I'm flying blind."

I spun the empty water bottle around and it nearly careened off the table before Dave caught it in his hand.

"Ever heard of the milk-bottle effect," Dave asked.

"No."

"It's a dangerous flying condition in which the sea and sky appear to meld together until the pilot is unable to see where horizon and water meet. He flies instead on instruments and instinct. But too often, it leads to tragedy. The pilot is unknowingly off course and plows into the water before he knows what hit him. If you are guilty of anything, it is that you were caught in the milk-bottle effect. I think when you were married to Jane it got hazy. You loved and trusted her and you couldn't see."

"Or didn't want to see. I don't know. I'm having all these thoughts now. Of things she said and did."

"You're not going to crash this time. I'm your co-pilot. I've got your back."

Dave went back to his notes and I went to the freezer, still thinking about that last bottle of vodka waiting there for me. I took it out, downing a single shot of it, daring Dave to say I didn't deserve at least a small dose of liquid courage.

All I could think about was Simon and my supposed responsibility for his death. The pain of it seemed larger now. The power of suggestion had always fallen hard onto my psyche. If I had been a medical student, I would have been one of those who believed they had every illness they studied. The legal charges of failure to protect had not only planted a seed, but had taken root despite Dave's attempts to hack it away. Perhaps I hadn't given my subconscious enough time to absorb Jane's family the same way I had sponged up my guilt. Shake it off, I told myself, taking another shot of Vodka. Focus on the facts, I repeated. Focus on the facts. *You loved her. You loved your children. Hell, you loved your little dog, Ricky, too.*

But then, there was a dark intruder, always there to blot the positive thoughts from my mind.

You had seen increased doctor's appointments. The little cards attached to the fridge with times and dates. You'd seen her overwhelmed by laundry one day, only to become Martha Stewart the next. You'd seen the increased purchases and odd visits to your office. You called it a phase. You called it hormones.

I took another drink. The truth was, she was my children's mother, and I had believed that was all the guarantee I'd ever need that they would be safe under her care. I thought motherhood was natural. Now, after having her ancestors appear before me, I saw that wasn't true. There was no gene that made one fit for parenting. One couldn't assume that the instinct to protect exists in every individual, not if they haven't been protected themselves. I need only look at Dave's pedigree chart to remember these lessons. And the realization came to me then, like a fist in my gut, that I was more guilty of making assumptions about Jane than anything else. And wasn't this largely what the Langleys, the Scollays, the Downings, and all of us do with the people in our lives? We assume the best. We don't look for markers of mental illness or violence. You can find anything you look for, can't you? Isn't that what I spend hours of lecture time telling my students? If you look for a certain kind of symbolism, you will find it.

And so, we three had begun this odyssey looking for traits foretelling danger and we had found them. We found evidence that supported how Jane could have been the inheritor of characteristics that perhaps predisposed her to a personality ill-suited for parenting, its mounting pressures and the daily treadmill of maternal monotony.

I was done being a mother, Tom.

And she had found a way. Her way.

I went back to my living room where Mariah was putting all the objects from Jane's trunk back in place.

"I wish I had known you under happier circumstances," she said with a kindly smile.

"Of course. Me too."

"Maybe when all of this is over, I could meet Sarah," she said, almost as a question.

"Yes, we should do that. You are her aunt after all." This acceptance earned me a wide smile from her, and I guessed she, too, might be reeling under the weight of what was to come.

"And if I am convicted," I said, "I would be counting on you to take that role in Sarah's life quite seriously. For better or worse, Jane was a spirited individual, something my family lacks in spades. If Sarah were to have only my family as an influence, well, I can't bear thinking how she might turn out."

"You're a good man, Tom," Mariah said. "I will be happy to do anything you ask."

It was then I knew I had to do one more thing before facing my jury. I lacked the courage to fall on my knees and go straight to God, but at least I could say I had the wisdom to call on God's man.

CHAPTER TWENTY-THREE

Somehow, Jeff's reaction was unexpectedly calm when I told him about our retrocognition party. It was no surprise to him that family history was a viable explanation for Jane's mental health.

"I have a lot of questions," I responded without reservation, feeling bone-tired from lack of sleep. "A lot."

"Don't we all," Jeff answered.

"Tell me what you think about family curses," I asked him, sitting in his sparse church office. "Do you believe that the sins of the fathers descend from generation to generation?"

He smiled at me and batted the question back to me the way a trained psychiatrist does. "What do you believe? That's what's important."

"I believe my mind is open wider to the acceptance of all things being possible. I never thought what Jane did to our family was possible, but it was. It is." It was true. My mind was irreversibly bent into the open position.

"Tom, you are an educated man and I'm a pastor," Jeff said, boldly laying his hand against mine. "You know the next thing I am going to suggest."

"I suppose I do."

This was the conversation I had been avoiding my entire life. For years, I had avoided evangelism and Bible beaters of any shape or form. I considered talking to God to be something good for my general health, like going for an overdue dental checkup or finally getting that mole removed. I have always assumed those items could wait on a to-do list of my own making until I had the inclination to move up their priority. Yet here I was, hearing Jeff step lightly around the issue of my own faith, and all I could think was that it meant I had to abandon my anger at God for taking Simon. He and I both knew I wasn't ready to lay that down completely. But then, it was a possibility now.

"I don't even know where to start," I said finally, my heart racing. "You know I want to have peace over this whole tragedy. In some ways, it seems fruitless to start having faith now."

"Tom, you didn't come here for yourself today. That was plain to see when you walked in. You came here for Sarah, and if you can't turn the page for yourself, you should for her."

"You sound like my attorney," I said.

"Then he's a smart man," Jeff said, rising and pouring me a glass of water. "You don't have to start all at once, you know. Just the fact that you are here, well, that is the biggest step, isn't it?"

"What do I do about Jane?"

He looked down and studied his hands. "I'm not sure there is anything you can do about her, Tom. I wish there were. We can pray for her. But you now have a great amount of information about Jane's family that you can share with Sarah at the appropriate time. You can lead her to an understanding of the good and the bad. And then there is a way of thinking in the faith that tells us we can break the family curses off."

"Yes, I remember Mariah saying something about that."

"Breaking them off essentially means praying over them fervently, asking for forgiveness for the past sinner while at the same time asking for protection so that specific iniquity doesn't fall on you."

"Protection," I mused. "That word keeps following me."

"You aren't alone. Someday you will see the full circle of these events that led you here today, Tom," he said so earnestly that I wanted to leach some of his peace from him and claim it as my own.

"Yes. You are right. Sarah. The next generation." I took my head into my hands and pictured Sarah's face. Hot tears formed at the back of my eyes as I felt the heaviness of missing her, mixed with ideas about how Jane's lineage might flow down to her.

"Will you go to see Jane with me," I asked. "For some reason, I just have to face her once more."

"Of course I will, Tom."

"I want to believe," I said in almost a whisper.

"First the action, then the motivation. Not the other way around," he said. "It will take time."

Of course it would take time. That's all anyone had said to me for the past two years.

So we went to see Jane. The pastor and his doubting Thomas.

At the chosen hour, it was as if the stage was being set for a Greek tragedy, as if God had called his prop masters and arranged a "dark and stormy night" as the backdrop for the drive. Winter winds cut sideways, and an unseasonably cold rain cut into me as I played the role of rain-soaked, grief-weary husband, not unlike the circumstances in which Jane Eyre's Mr. Rochester went to see his deranged wife after his own Jane left him for deceiving her. There was only one real problem with God's setup. He didn't give me the script or the lines or the conclusion. Perhaps He wasn't keen on being ignored through all this, so I couldn't blame Him.

Before we entered the hospital, I heard the familiar click of a Nikon behind me. I wondered what kind of skewed caption would accompany my image. I turned and faced the photographer head on. If he wanted a picture of misery, I would give it to him.

We signed in and a young orderly dressed in crisp white from shoulder to toe escorted us upstairs. The happy spring in his step told me he hadn't read the script either. He led us into the viewing room. One wall featured a framed opening with a two-way mirror.

Through it we could observe Jane conversing with her doctor.

While we waited, I looked about the room, which was decorated for the Christmas holidays. What had I expected? A movie version of a gray interrogation room with two plastic chairs and an exposed light bulb? This room resembled a teacher's lounge. There were comfortable chairs. A huge pot of coffee percolated next to all the necessary java accoutrements. The recessed lighting was low, and easy-listening holiday music played faintly. It was an inviting place where people could hang out for a while, presumably to watch what happened in the next room.

I knew my expectations of what I could accomplish here with Jane were too high, but I was faced with the lesser alternative of never having tried to make a connection with her using my newfound knowledge and compassion for her lack of motherly love. Then there was the competing logic that split me in half: that I must reach beyond the Jane I knew and see her as a jury might. See the stark facts of her life as plain as the black headlines. I was now prepared to give this a try, although I harbored the hope that my Jane would surface.

I took off my coat and poured a cup of black coffee. Jeff settled into an overstuffed chair to the right of the viewing window. The drapes on the other side of the window suddenly pulled back. Jane sat at a table in the plain room on the other side. She was dressed in a gray hospital shirt and pants. A measure of the length of her incarceration showed in the roots of her hair. Her store-bought blonde had given way to three inches of natural mousy brown.

Her eyes looked sunken and dark. Dr. Hamilton sat across from her, wielding a clipboard. He looked to be in his fifties, and I don't know why but I judged his grayness as a sign of capability.

"Are we ready to begin, Jane?" he asked, his voice coming through speakers on my side of the window.

She was silent. "Okay, I'm turning on the tape recorder now. This is Doctor Hamilton. Subject is Jane Nelson. Is this all right with you, Jane?"

She nodded. The rest of her body remained still as a statue.

"Tom is here. He would like to talk to you."

But Jane was resolute and said nothing. Not a single muscle moved at the sound of my name.

"Do you have a cigarette?" she said after several minutes.

"You don't smoke, Jane," Dr. Hamilton said. "Tom said that if you won't talk to him, I should tell you he loves you and misses you and that Sarah is doing well."

She eased back into her chair and assumed what I could only describe as a rebellious posture. One leg hiked into the chair while she twisted strands of hair with one hand.

"Tom wasn't there so why is he here," she said *sotto voce*. I nearly knocked my head into the Plexiglas window at this comment.

"What do you mean, Jane?" the doctor probed. "What do you mean he wasn't there?"

"He was at first," she went on. "But you know, how come I can't wear nice clothes when I'm a mom? I'll tell you why. Because you can't get a shower until one o'clock a lot of days and then it's like, what's the point? Because you got a whole box full of beautiful jewelry, but who you gonna wear it for? Someone with applesauce on their chin?"

"How does this mean Tom was not there?"

"He didn't get it. With kids, I mean. I think he thought being a parent would be like in the bad movies. They don't know what they are talking about."

I recognized pieces of this opinion from our early years, before we were parents. She loathed movies that showed single moms, up against the world, getting their lives together and tucking a precocious five-year-old into bed. Films that made it look easy for the women to leave the abusive husband.

"Did you ask for more help from Tom?"

She thought about it a long time. Her shoulders stiffened and she brought both legs up to her chest, wrapping her arms around them. She began rocking and weeping.

"I couldn't make them develop right by myself. They weren't developing right. So I left them at the store. I knew someone would come and get them."

"You left who at the store?"

"The kids. I left them there so Tom could come get them. Didn't he get them?"

"No, you didn't leave them at the store, Jane. Remember, you told me once that your mother left you at the store? Do you remember that?"

"She did?"

"Yes. It was your mother. You told me you were very angry about that."

"Who wouldn't be?"

"That's true. And it's okay to be angry."

"Can I have something to drink?"

"Certainly. I'll have them bring you something. Do you want anything else?"

"I need a book. A book. A book. A book."

She put her head between her legs and never looked back up, even though the doctor continued to talk to her. An orderly brought her an Ensure. I felt like breaking through the window and embracing her. But that thought was fleeting. She was ill and I couldn't be Superman. She was unreachable to me now, and I suppose that was the litmus test I wanted to conduct: would a mention of my name or my love awaken anything in her? Answer: no.

Later, the doctor told me that in his opinion the reality of her actions touched off her mental illness more than anything, so I "shouldn't take it personally."

"She sometimes sinks so far into her past that she cannot move easily from period to period. What you just witnessed was her inability to distinguish between herself as a grown woman and as a child," he said succinctly.

"Do you think she will ever recover to the point where we can talk about what happened? Or even have a normal conversation?"

"Normal is relative in the mental health sense. But for Jane, I would have to say her mind has retreated significantly into a dimension that is unreachable by our therapies unless she consistently takes her medication," he said. "And she will not take them consistently. Best of luck."

Best of luck, ha! I looked to Jeff. He was looking at Jane as she was led out of the room by the orderly. She was less than twelve feet from me then, but miles beyond my reach.

"Let's get out of here," I said to Jeff, and he nodded.

"You did a good thing coming here, Tom," he said. "You showed her compassion, and I have to say, with all she has done, that would be a tall order for anyone."

Perhaps compassion, pity even, described how I felt about Jane that night. Being stuck in her childlike world had its benefits. I hated to imagine what it would be like if the real Jane ever woke up to find her son dead and quite possibly, her husband in prison.

CHAPTER TWENTY-FOUR

On the third day of my trial, Dave congratulated me for being able to look at a poster-sized picture of Jane across the courtroom in the manner he had fought for. He said I had achieved a defendant's crucial, believable "affidavit face." Her visage received an ambivalent gaze from the jury, especially when angelic images of Sarah and Simon popped up on a screen next to Jane's picture. That Sarah was permanently separated from her twin was difficult for them to hear, I could plainly tell. It made the female jurors cross and re-cross their legs several times.

Next, the 911 tape played and I had to keep myself from mouthing the words like a song I knew by heart. Martin Oliver testified. He didn't look as weary as he had at Jane's trial. The responding police officer told the courtroom that Jane was silent when he questioned her at the house. He told them about finding our dog Ricky. An expert witness testified this drowning was her practice attempt. Even though I had heard that language before, I swallowed hard on it.

The doctors spoke. These were new ones, men who ably defended their points of view in the face of cross-examination. They stated that Jane had an extreme personality disorder, that she was and is a pathological liar, a sociopath. They said she sought out control, and her ability to manage life disappeared when she became overwhelmed.

Dave surprised me by telling the jury the story of how we first met. And damned if I didn't look at him with gratitude, feeling a spontaneous, sentimental smile spread across my face as he deftly recounted Jane's tender care of Roger at the hospital. If he had wanted to remind the jurors that Jane was once nurturing, he did.

Next he skillfully inserted information about Jane's forbears, casually tossing a green Granny Smith from hand to hand as he declared the apple does not fall far from the tree. His words were enough to whet the appetite of the jury without sounding sensational. He emphasized her own relationship with her mother, which one expert witness shored up with "the same-sex parent is a child's biggest influence. This relationship will write on the permanent slate of a child's personality." And he added that depriving a young girl of her mother in such a grievous fashion would surely alter the course of her life for the worse.

Of course, I would be called to the stand, I knew that, but when the female prosecutor called me, I felt so removed that it sounded like she had announced someone else's name. I was sworn in on the Bible, which I admit gave me a slice of comfort. It reminded me that Pastor Jeff was in the room, going before God on my behalf.

Then there was the ramp-up of prosecutorial questions designed to rope-a-dope me. I was prepared.

"Mr. Nelson, you first described Jane as a beautiful woman."

"That's an amazing ring you bought her."

"Mr. Nelson, would you describe your marriage as peaceful?"

"And the birth of your twins was a joyous time?"

"She got on well with your family?"

"The day you came home and found her with the Zoloft, crushing it into the twins' juice, you just happened to be coming home early when you witnessed this?"

"Mr. Nelson, would you describe the morning of June 21 for us as you remember it?"

Then, summations by the prosecution and defense produced a tight denouement. Dave's closing was especially powerful.

"Jane Nelson suffers from the disorders the doctors have named. And they are part and parcel of her nature. No person, family member or spouse could have predicted her actions. That is, unless perhaps they had psychic abilities."

I shifted in my seat. Dave walked past the defense table and tapped the photo album again, directing my gaze to the branches of Jane's family tree. He fixed me with a look that said, *Where is your affidavit face now?*

"Just as I cannot predict what any of the twelve of you will do this evening, it is ridiculous to suggest my client, who loved his children, knowingly put them in harm's way. He left them in the care of their mother, who, up until this time, was a loving, caring parent. She struggled with depression, yes, brought on by the miscarriage of her child. She struggled with balancing the day-to-day activities of being a mother, which can overwhelm any woman. But nowhere in her actions did she portray herself as a threat.

"Jane Nelson could have kept going. She should have kept going. We all wish she had kept going. But she had a breakdown. Not because she had it any harder than anyone else, but because she was weaker. She had suffered the fractures caused by bad parenting and poor impulse control like her parents, grandparents, and great-grandparents before her. But this hardly absolves her from her crime. Her illnesses are an explanation, ladies and gentlemen, not an excuse.

"Jane had a breaking point only she could discern. No one else. Not even the doctors treating her before the incident, as you have heard, foretold in any of their records, interviews or examinations that she would be a risk to her own children. Ladies and gentlemen, do you blame the gun or the shooter? The shooter, of course. The person who made the decision. For this reason, you must acquit my client. For if Tom Nelson, upstanding citizen, professor and father is to blame, then you had better watch out. You will be the next person responsible for your neighbor's actions."

It entertained them as I now realized it had morbidly entertained me. He pulled it all together with the grace of a great mythic storyteller along with the hook of a good movie trailer. He spoke so fluidly, it sounded even to me as if he'd known her family history for a decade. And then he pulled the Houdini trick and ripped the sheet from beneath them, verging on insulting their intelligence. It was risky, but I could, I thought, read self-reflection in their faces as he forced them to consider that if I was guilty, so too was grandpa, and wasn't that ridiculous.

"The absurdity of this is our national attitude to assign blame to anyone except the perpetrator," he said boldly. "Is it so terrifying, ladies and gentlemen, to stare truth in its face today? Are we so frightened in this politically correct society to call a duck a duck? If you see a duck swimming, it's the duck doing the work. Not the water beneath it."

A part of me wanted to review Dave's eloquence and irony with my best friend. Jane. The loving side of me wished we could stride off to a coffee shop and discuss the events of the day, analyze them and comment on parts we thought were effective. That was the old us, though. The us I was still allowing myself to dream about when I was lonely. I supposed widows did this too. They see something they think the other would like and rush home with anticipation of telling their spouse, only to relive the pain and disappointment of loss all over again. I felt that crush as I recalled Jane's pathetic image through the two-way mirror.

The sleek-haired prosecutor made a solid attempt in her closing to remind them that I actually lived with this woman, thus, should have known every nuance of her thought. I should have recognized the "Zoloft in the orange juice incident" as a crucial turning point. I should have spent more time at home. And perhaps most powerfully, the prosecution read from a statement Jane had given to one of her doctors. The report quoted her as saying, "Tom was not there for me. I felt alone. I felt overwhelmed and bored at the same time. Tom, with all his intelligence, could not understand a person being overwhelmed and bored."

But Dave had successfully addressed each of her points throughout the trial. It was plain to see that there was a lack of true evidence. And even I could see that the other cases they had been using to establish precedent had evidence the spouse was actually present during a prior abuse. That was the deal breaker, Dave had said. They cannot cite that I was there. He passed me a sticky note.

They've just lost their case.

The jury departed to deliberate and had to be sequestered overnight. We got word early the next morning to appear in court at ten. I walked in, carrying the defense photo album under my arm and scanned the room for faces I wanted to see. Jeff. Mariah. My mother. They all sat in a row in the back, and I marveled at their odd combination, resisting the desire to create a bad joke.

A pastor, a clairvoyant and June Cleaver walk into a bar …

The judge read his instructions and addressed the jury.

"Have you reached a verdict?"

And here, I remember the room did stand still. I had the hope that the next words spoken would set me free, either way the verdict read. The words would answer the questions I had not been able to, despite the constant hammering of my brain for any missteps I had made in not seeing the real Jane. I knew the truth, didn't I? What did it come down to, really? Who bore the blame for Simon's death? Nature? Nurture? Biblical curses? Tom Nelson being an inattentive husband? Although Dave didn't want me to think this way, I realized there was no verdict that would ever satisfy the loss I felt of Simon, and by extension, of my marriage. Jane was ill, perhaps genetically so, but I had lived with her.

The forewoman stood. "Yes, we have reached a verdict, Your

Honor."

"What say you in the matter of the State of Texas versus Thomas Nelson?"

Dave bit his lip. The judge sat up tall and the court reporter held her hands flexed above her machine in expectation. I studied her long, pale fingers as they positioned to capture the final words of this long story. My life would be decided by the next words spoken. *Not Guilty. Guilty.* I pictured the two opposite fates spread out before me. And as the thick, stand-still air of the courtroom filled my lungs in deep breaths, I became acutely aware of one thing. Even if the verdict was not guilty, it would not mean innocent.

EPILOGUE

Galveston, Texas - 2020

They were supposed to be here a half hour ago. This part of Jamaica Beach is out of the way and uninhabited so maybe my father got lost. You only know about it if you are a local. Still, I'm trying not to arouse any suspicion, sitting here as I am, killing time by writing letters in the sand and trying not to think about that article I read earlier today about an East Texas woman who smothered her two boys while they slept in bed. Reports say she was ranting psychotic ramblings that God told her to do it. That was as far as I could read. Unfortunately, I still read about all cases like this one, hoping the last paragraph will finally contain a scientific explanation for the cause of the tragedy, like there is something polluting the water in Texas. Perhaps something has been leaching from the soil into the wells, and we can thump our collective heads and move north, away from the bad pipes that make bad mothers.

But I am vowing, tonight, to give that miserable habit up.

Of course, those stories still get to me in the worst way and because I scanned the paper tonight, I may have bad dreams about the water. I have the sensation of going under and I hear myself crying out that I want to save everyone, especially Simon. Sometimes when this happens, I write letters to her and journal all my feelings onto paper. I've even written the words "I forgive you" and more often than not, I mean it. Still other times, I write letters to the newspaper editor about their articles on infanticide. In them, I highlight all the things the so-called reporter got wrong when making his assumptions about the case. Some of them are quite inspired, but I never send them. The stories have the same basic facts anyway and who wants to keep the story alive longer than necessary? I know. I have an old box, dating back to her case so many years ago, filled with news clippings and pictures of mothers in handcuffs. And I have found that there's not a big difference in any of the cases. For example, here's the general breakdown leading up to the snap, Dave Frontella's nature/nurture arguments notwithstanding: insecure young child becomes overwhelmed young mother with a lack of extended family support, lives with a distracted husband, develops an increased reliance upon religion and/or substance abuse, and then Cheerios spill on the floor in all directions, triggering a chemical imbalance in the brain and everything goes to hell. Okay, so I should get a better hobby than analyzing this unpleasantness, but this is what I know for certain. They are the same story. They are the same woman. Only the dates change.

What I really can't get past is that even after all this time, I wonder if she thinks about me. If she thinks about our family, or what used to be our family. If she remembers what it felt like to hug me close or just sit down to breakfast together. Sometimes I think I might muster the courage to talk to her. I've gone to the institution, too, and watched her from a distance. They said years ago it was unlikely she would ever be released and that has proved correct. When I saw her there the last time, she was wearing solid blue clothes and looked peaceful enough. She has put on weight and her hair has grayed and now hangs loosely around her face like a sad curtain. Because of this, I can't recognize any familiar feature in her face. She looked in my direction once. I thought perhaps that she might wave, but there was no gesture at all. So I took a picture of her as the orderly walked with her back inside the building and vowed that would be the last time I visited. Her doctors say I could talk to her if I wanted too, but that, if she was having a particularly lucid day, the reality of seeing me and facing what she had done might make her plummet and they would have to increase her meds. You could argue that I might want to cause her that pain, and there have been times, I can tell you, when I needed someone to braid my hair or pick out a prom dress, that I really did want to make her cry. Ironically, her biggest legacy to me is her absence, not her crime. No matter how strange it sounds, you end up wanting the mother God gave you, however bent they are. However they hurt you. It makes me ask dark questions like, why am I the one who survived? Why isn't my brother here instead of me? The two people who might be able to answer that, she and my father, well, they don't know either. She can't talk and my father won't talk. Sure, there have been times he has indulged my questions, but then he morphs into an apologetic mess at risk of getting back on the booze wagon so I back off because I know he has already paid a high price for the whole incident. I don't want to upset him further, especially now that he has a new wife, who he waited until I was grown to marry. The lawyers and their experts, they had their palatable theories, buried within the court transcripts.

Over the years, there has also been the parade of Grandma-purchased shrinks who offered their child-friendly insanity explanations and heavy doses of "don't blame yourself for your mother's illness." As far as I was concerned, they never got to the question I wanted answered. How does someone just up and kill one day? Only recently, I enjoyed stumping my latest doctor with questions about causality. Inside his pale yellow office, I compared what she did to the "which came first, chicken or egg" dilemma, trying to get him to answer my question. I showed him my notepad where I had diagramed her life, borrowing heavily from facts produced at my father's trial. He rubbed his chin and asked me to continue.

I asked him which came first, motherhood or the insanity? Did having children so overwhelm her that it triggered her madness? If she had been childless, would her latent insanity have stayed a secret? And if that's true, are there thousands of childless women whose sanity stays in check only because they've never owned a Sippy Cup? Chicken/egg? Mother/killer? Where do you come down on this causality, doc?

He just told me it was unhealthy to continue playing the role of detective as it concerns my mother.

Two days ago, before I made the decision to come to Jamaica Beach and be done with the whole mess, my therapist phoned me at home and said he was firing me as a patient. He said he didn't think he could help me anymore because of my fixation on the question of "why?"

I ate too much pizza and drank too much wine and alternately thought about how unfair it was to be fired like that and how he was possibly right on the mark. Again, I cannot shake my mind's twin struggles with the causality of everything. It paralyzes me into doing nothing and makes me wonder if it is because my twin is gone that I am only half of something, that together we might have been able to answer each other's questions. And why did I not explore that theme with my therapist.

Tired of chasing my own mind, I drank more wine and called my Aunt Mariah, the only person besides my therapist who would still talk to me about my mother. I knew what advice she would give me.

"You should do what I've always told you we should do," she said

Yes, I know what she's always said I should do. That I should get rid of the articles. The objects. The pictures. The trunk. That I needed to burn it. Clear out my life the way a fire clears a forest so the sun can hit the earth and allow new trees to grow. It's all I've ever had of my mother. And what if she wants these things someday? And then I realized I had said all of this to Mariah.

We continued talking, or rather, she continued talking. And I half-way listened and flipped through the TV channels, stopping on a story about a missing girl under a blue "Breaking News" banner.

On the screen, a woman was shaking and trying not to sob while holding her young daughter, Madeleine, whose face was so hopeful and warm and wet from her mother's tears. And her mother said, *I just wanted her back home and I am so thankful to the police and everyone. I have my daughter back and she has me. Thank you. Thank God. And no, I don't think I'll ever stop hugging her.*

I said goodnight to Mariah and stared at the young girl's face, so full of love. After a while, I looked across the room at the old black trunk and pictured what kind of plant I would buy to put in its place.

And here they come and I uncross my legs, sliding off the trunk. My feet sink in the sand, then kick away the row of smooth shells I had gathered from the beach. From the way the wind blows, I can already smell the gasoline my father carries. We find a spot near the tide's edge and slide the trunk into a wet groove of beach. I grip the book of matches tighter and glance at my father and Mariah. She holds her Bible and prays with elegance, "Whatever is true, whatever is noble, whatever is right, whatever is pure, whatever is lovely, whatever is admirable, if anything is excellent or praiseworthy, think about such things, Tom and Sarah. Whatever was old is made new in Christ. And the God of peace will be with you."

My father kisses my cheek, says he loves me and I mouth the same back to him. He coats the trunk with fuel, and they nod at me, and I strike the match. The trunk, and all its contents, light up in an orange glowing mass, giving off the scent of butter and hot iron ore. The wind plays with the flames and I think, wind must be the one true thing, tonight as it was in the past.

We may all be hauled off by the Jamaica Beach police because of it, but it will be done. The heavy branches of the forest are burning down and God willing, sunlight will hit my face tomorrow.

About the Author

Karen Harrington is a Texas native who has been writing fiction for more than twenty years. Her writing has received honors from the Hemingway Short Story Festival, the Texas Film Institute Screenplay Contest and the Writers' Digest National Script Contest. A graduate of the University of Texas at Dallas, she has worked as a speechwriter and editor for major corporations and non-profit organizations.

She authored and published *There's a Dog in the Doorway*, a children's book created expressly for the Dr. Laura Schlessinger Foundation's "My Stuff Bags." My Stuff bags go to children in need who must leave their home due to abuse, neglect or abandonement.

She lives in Plano, Texas, with her husband and two children.

KÜNATI

MADicine
■ Derek Armstrong

What happens when an engineered virus, meant to virally lobotomize psychopathic patients, is let loose on the world? Only Bane and his new partner, Doctor Ada Kenner, can stop this virus of rage.

■ "In his follow-up to the excellent *The Game*.... Armstrong blends comedy, parody, and adventure in genuinely innovative ways." *The Last Troubadour* —*Booklist*

■ "Tongue-in-cheek thriller." *The Game* —*Library Journal*

US$ 24.95 | Pages 352, cloth hardcover
ISBN 978-1-60164-017-8 | EAN: 9781601640178

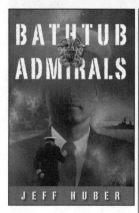

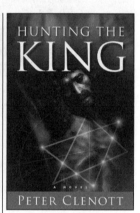

Bathtub Admirals
■ Jeff Huber

Are the armed forces of the world's only superpower really run by self-serving "Bathtub Admirals"? Based on a true story of military incompetence.

■ "Witty, wacky, wildly outrageous...A remarkably accomplished book, striking just the right balance between ridicule and insight." —*Booklist*

US$ 24.95
Pages 320, cloth hardcover
ISBN 978-1-60164-019-2
EAN 9781601640192

Belly of the Whale
■ Linda Merlino

Terrorized by a gunman, a woman with cancer vows to survive and regains her hope and the will to live.

■ "A riveting story, both powerful and poignant in its telling. Merlino's immense talent shines on every page." —Howard Roughan, Bestselling Author

US$ 19.95
Pages 208, cloth hardcover
ISBN 978-1-60164-018-5
EAN 9781601640185

Hunting the King
■ Peter Clenott

An intellectual thriller about the most coveted archeological find of all time: the tomb of Jesus.

■ "Fans of intellectual thrillers and historical fiction will find a worthy new voice in Clenott... Given such an auspicious start, the sequel can't come too soon." —ForeWord

US$ 24.95
Pages 384, cloth hardcover
ISBN 978-1-60164-148-9
EAN 9781601641489

Callous
■ T K Kenyon

A routine missing person call turns the town of New Canaan, Texas, inside out as claims of Satanism, child abuse and serial killers clash, and a radical church prepares for Armageddon and the Rapture. Part thriller, part crime novel, *Callous* is a dark and funny page-turner.

■ "Kenyon is definitely a keeper." *Rabid*, STARRED REVIEW, —*Booklist*
■ "Impressive." *Rabid*, —*Publishers Weekly*

US$ 24.95 | Pages 384, cloth hardcover
ISBN 978-1-60164-022-2 | EAN: 9781601640222

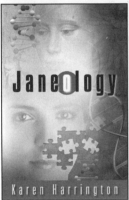

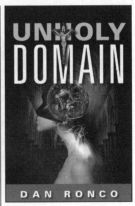

Janeology
■ Karen Harrington

Tom is certain he is living the American dream. Until one day in June, the police tell him the unthinkable—his wife has drowned their toddler son.

■ "Harrington begins with a fascinating premise and develops it fully. Tom and his wife emerge as compelling, complexly developed individuals."
—*Booklist*

US$ 24.95
Pages 256, cloth hardcover
ISBN 978-1-60164-020-8
EAN 9781601640208

Miracle MYX
■ Dave Diotalevi

For an unblinking forty-two hours, Myx's synesthetic brain probes a lot of dirty secrets in Miracle before arriving at the truth.

■ "What a treat to be in the mind of Myx Amens, the clever, capable, twice-dead protagonist who is full of surprises."
—*Robert Fate,*
Academy Award winner

US$ 24.95
Pages 288, cloth hardcover
ISBN 978-1-60164-155-7
EAN 9781601641557

Unholy Domain
■ Dan Ronco

A fast-paced techno-thriller depicts a world of violent extremes, where religious terrorists and visionaries of technology fight for supreme power.

■ "A solid futuristic thriller."
—*Booklist*
■ "Unholy Domain...top rate adventure, sparkling with ideas."
—*Piers Anthony*

US$ 24.95
Pages 352, cloth hardcover
ISBN 978-1-60164-021-5
EAN 9781601640215

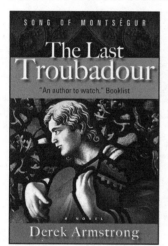

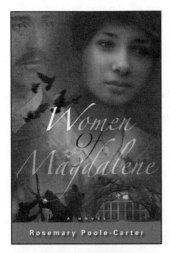

Women Of Magdalene
A hauntingly tragic tale of the old South by Rosemary Poole-Carter

An idealistic young doctor in the post-Civil War South exposes the greed and cruelty at the heart of the Magdalene Ladies' Asylum in this elegant, richly detailed and moving story of love and sacrifice.

■ "A fine mix of thriller, historical fiction, and Southern Gothic." *Booklist*

■ "A brilliant example of the best historical fiction can do." *ForeWord*

US$ 24.95 | Pages 288, cloth hardcover
ISBN-13: 978-1-60164-014-7
ISBN-10: 1-60164-014-5 | EAN: 9781601640147

On Ice
A road story like no other, by Red Evans

The sudden death of a sad old fiddle player brings new happiness and hope to those who loved him in this charming, earthy, hilarious coming-of-age tale.

■ "Evans' humor is broad but infectious ... Evans uses offbeat humor to both entertain and move his readers." *Booklist*

US$ 19.95 | Pages 208, cloth hardcover
ISBN-13: 978-1-60164-015-4
ISBN-10: 1-60164-015-3
EAN: 9781601640154

Truth Or Bare
Offbeat, stylish crime novel by Richard Cahill

The characters throb with vitality, the prose sizzles in this darkly comic page-turner set in the sleazy world of murderous sex workers, the justice system, and the rich who will stop at nothing to get what they want.

■ "Cahill has introduced an enticing character ... Let's hope this debut novel isn't the last we hear from him." *Booklist*

US$ 24.95 | Pages 304, cloth hardcover
ISBN-13: 978-1-60164-016-1
ISBN-10: 1-60164-016-1
EAN: 9781601640161

The Game
A thriller by Derek Armstrong

Reality television becomes too real when a killer stalks the cast on America's number one live-broadcast reality show.
■ "A series to watch ... Armstrong injects the trope with new vigor." *Booklist*
US$ 24.95 | Pages 352, cloth hardcover
ISBN 978-1-60164-001-7 | EAN: 9781601640017
LCCN 2006930183

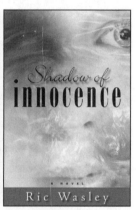

bang BANG
A novel by Lynn Hoffman

In Lynn Hoffman's wickedly funny *bang-BANG*, a waitress crime victim takes on America's obsession with guns and transforms herself in the process. Read along as Paula becomes national hero and villain, enforcer and outlaw, lover and leader. Don't miss Paula Sherman's one-woman quest to change America.
■ "Brilliant"
STARRED REVIEW, *Booklist*
US$ 19.95
Pages 176, cloth hardcover
ISBN 978-1-60164-000-0
EAN 9781601640000
LCCN 2006930182

Whale Song
A novel by Cheryl Kaye Tardif

Whale Song is a haunting tale of change and choice. Cheryl Kaye Tardif's beloved novel—a "wonderful novel that will make a wonderful movie" according to *Writer's Digest*—asks the difficult question, which is the higher morality, love or law?
■ "Crowd-pleasing ... a big hit." *Booklist*
US$ 12.95
Pages 208, UNA trade paper
ISBN 978-1-60164-007-9
EAN 9781601640079
LCCN 2006930188

Shadow of Innocence
A mystery by Ric Wasley

The Thin Man meets *Pulp Fiction* in a unique mystery set amid the drugs-and-music scene of the sixties that touches on all our societal taboos. *Shadow of Innocence* has it all: adventure, sleuthing, drugs, sex, music and a perverse shadowy secret that threatens to tear apart a posh New England town.
US$ 24.95
Pages 304, cloth hardcover
ISBN 978-1-60164-006-2
EAN 9781601640062
LCCN 2006930187

The Secret Ever Keeps
A novel by Art Tirrell

An aging Godfather-like billionaire tycoon regrets a decades-long life of "shady dealings" and seeks reconciliation with a granddaughter who doesn't even know he exists. A sweeping adventure across decades—from Prohibition to today—exploring themes of guilt, greed and forgiveness.

■ "Riveting ... Rhapsodic ... Accomplished." *ForeWord*
US$ 24.95
Pages 352, cloth hardcover
ISBN 978-1-60164-004-8
EAN 9781601640048
LCCN 2006930185

Toonamint of Champions
A wickedly allegorical comedy by Todd Sentell

Todd Sentell pulls out all the stops in his hilarious spoof of the manners and mores of America's most prestigious golf club. A cast of unforgettable characters, speaking a language only a true son of the South could pull off, reveal that behind the gates of fancy private golf clubs lurk some mighty influential freaks.

■ "Bubbly imagination and wacky humor." *ForeWord*
US$ 19.95
Pages 192, cloth hardcover
ISBN 978-1-60164-005-5
EAN 9781601640055
LCCN 2006930186

Mothering Mother
A daughter's humorous and heartbreaking memoir.
Carol D. O'Dell

Mothering Mother is an authentic, "in-the-room" view of a daughter's struggle to care for a dying parent. It will touch you and never leave you.

■ "Beautiful, told with humor... and much love." *Booklist*
■ "I not only loved it, I lived it. I laughed, I smiled and shuddered reading this book." Judith H. Wright, author of over 20 books.
US$ 19.95
Pages 208, cloth hardcover
ISBN 978-1-60164-003-1
EAN 9781601640031
LCCN 2006930184

Rabid
A novel by T K Kenyon

A sexy, savvy, darkly funny tale of ambition, scandal, forbidden love and murder. Nothing is sacred. The graduate student, her professor, his wife, her priest: four brilliantly realized characters spin out of control in a world where science and religion are in constant conflict.

■ "Kenyon is definitely a keeper." STARRED REVIEW, *Booklist*
US$ 26.95 | Pages 480, cloth hardcover
ISBN 978-1-60164-002-4 | EAN: 9781601640024
LCCN 2006930189